PATRICIA WEN

RED SHADOW

PATRICIA WENTWORTH was born Dora Amy Elles in India in 1877 (not 1878 as has sometimes been stated). She was first educated privately in India, and later at Blackheath School for Girls. Her first husband was George Dillon, with whom she had her only child, a daughter. She also had two stepsons from her first marriage, one of whom died in the Somme during World War I.

Her first novel was published in 1910, but it wasn't until the 1920's that she embarked on her long career as a writer of mysteries. Her most famous creation was Miss Maud Silver, who appeared in 32 novels, though there were a further 33 full-length mysteries not featuring Miss Silver—the entire run of these is now reissued by Dean Street Press.

Patricia Wentworth died in 1961. She is recognized today as one of the pre-eminent exponents of the classic British golden age mystery novel.

By Patricia Wentworth

PATRICIA WENTWORTH

RED SHADOW

With an introduction by
Curtis Evans

DEAN STREET PRESS

Published by Dean Street Press 2016

Copyright © 1932 Patricia Wentworth

Introduction copyright © 2016 Curtis Evans

Cover by DSP

First published in 1932 by Hodder & Stoughton

ISBN 978 1 911095 93 4

www.deanstreetpress.co.uk

Introduction

BRITISH AUTHOR Patricia Wentworth published her first novel, a gripping tale of desperate love during the French Revolution entitled *A Marriage under the Terror*, a little over a century ago, in 1910. The book won first prize in the Melrose Novel Competition and was a popular success in both the United States and the United Kingdom. Over the next five years Wentworth published five additional novels, the majority of them historical fiction, the best-known of which today is *The Devil's Wind* (1912), another sweeping period romance, this one set during the Sepoy Mutiny (1857-58) in India, a region with which the author, as we shall see, had extensive familiarity. Like *A Marriage under the Terror*, *The Devil's Wind* received much praise from reviewers for its sheer storytelling élan. One notice, for example, pronounced the novel "an achievement of some magnitude" on account of "the extraordinary vividness...the reality of the atmosphere...the scenes that shift and move with the swiftness of a moving picture...." (*The Bookman*, August 1912) With her knack for spinning a yarn, it perhaps should come as no surprise that Patricia Wentworth during the early years of the Golden Age of mystery fiction (roughly from 1920 into the 1940s) launched upon her own mystery-writing career, a course charted most successfully for nearly four decades by the prolific author, right up to the year of her death in 1961.

Considering that Patricia Wentworth belongs to the select company of Golden Age mystery writers with books which have remained in print in every decade for nearly a century now (the centenary of Agatha Christie's first mystery, *The Mysterious Affair at Styles*, is in 2020; the centenary of Wentworth's first mystery, *The Astonishing Adventure of Jane Smith*, follows merely three years later, in 2023), relatively little is known about the author herself. It appears, for example, that even the widely given year of Wentworth's birth, 1878, is incorrect. Yet it is sufficiently clear that Wentworth lived a varied and intriguing life that provided her ample inspiration for a writing career devoted to imaginative fiction.

It is usually stated that Patricia Wentworth was born Dora Amy Elles on 10 November 1878 in Mussoorie, India, during the heyday of the British Raj; however, her Indian birth and baptismal record states that she in fact was born on 15 October 1877 and was baptized on 26 November of that same year in Gwalior. Whatever doubts surround her actual birth year, however, unquestionably the future author came from a prominent Anglo-Indian military family. Her father, Edmond Roche Elles, a son of Malcolm Jamieson Elles, a Porto, Portugal wine merchant originally from Ardrossan, Scotland, entered the British Royal Artillery in 1867, a decade before Wentworth's birth, and first saw service in India during the Lushai Expedition of 1871-72. The next year Elles in India wed Clara Gertrude Rothney, daughter of Brigadier-General Octavius Edward Rothney, commander of the Gwalior District, and Maria (Dempster) Rothney, daughter of a surgeon in the Bengal Medical Service. Four children were born of the union of Edmond and Clara Elles, Wentworth being the only daughter.

Before his retirement from the army in 1908, Edmond Elles rose to the rank of lieutenant-general and was awarded the KCB (Knight Commander of the Order of Bath), as was the case with his elder brother, Wentworth's uncle, Lieutenant-General Sir William Kidston Elles, of the Bengal Command. Edmond Elles also served as Military Member to the Council of the Governor-General of India from 1901 to 1905. Two of Wentworth's brothers, Malcolm Rothney Elles and Edmond Claude Elles, served in the Indian Army as well, though both of them died young (Malcolm in 1906 drowned in the Ganges Canal while attempting to rescue his orderly, who had fallen into the water), while her youngest brother, Hugh Jamieson Elles, achieved great distinction in the British Army. During the First World War he catapulted, at the relatively youthful age of 37, to the rank of brigadier-general and the command of the British Tank Corps, at the Battle of Cambrai personally leading the advance of more than 350 tanks against the German line. Years later Hugh Elles also played a major role in British civil defense during the Second World War. In the event of a German invasion of Great Britain, something which seemed all too possible in 1940, he was tasked with leading the defense of southwestern England. Like Sir Edmond and Sir William, Hugh Elles attained the rank of lieutenant-general and was awarded the KCB.

Although she was born in India, Patricia Wentworth spent much of her childhood in England. In 1881 she with her mother and two younger brothers was at Tunbridge Wells, Kent, on what appears to have been a rather extended visit in her ancestral country; while a decade later the same family group resided at Blackheath, London at Lennox House, domicile of Wentworth's widowed maternal grandmother, Maria Rothney. (Her eldest brother, Malcolm, was in Bristol attending Clifton College.) During her years at Lennox House, Wentworth attended Blackheath High School for Girls, then only recently founded as "one of the first schools in the country to give girls a proper education" (*The London Encyclopaedia*, 3rd ed., p. 74). Lennox House was an ample Victorian villa with a great glassed-in conservatory running all along the back and a substantial garden--most happily, one presumes, for Wentworth, who resided there not only with her grandmother, mother and two brothers, but also five aunts (Maria Rothney's unmarried daughters, aged 26 to 42), one adult first cousin once removed and nine first cousins, adolescents like Wentworth herself, from no less than three different families (one Barrow, three Masons and five Dempsters); their parents, like Wentworth's father, presumably were living many miles away in various far-flung British dominions. Three servants--a cook, parlourmaid and housemaid--were tasked with serving this full score of individuals.

Sometime after graduating from Blackheath High School in the mid-1890s, Wentworth returned to India, where in a local British newspaper she is said to have published her first fiction. In 1901 the 23-year-old Wentworth married widower George Fredrick Horace Dillon, a 41-year-old lieutenant-colonel in the Indian Army with three sons from his prior marriage. Two years later Wentworth gave birth to her only child, a daughter named Clare Roche Dillon. (In some sources it is erroneously stated that Clare was the offspring of Wentworth's second marriage.) However in 1906, after just five years of marriage, George Dillon died suddenly on a sea voyage, leaving Wentworth with sole responsibly for her three teenaged stepsons and baby daughter. A very short span of years, 1904 to 1907, saw the deaths of Wentworth's husband, mother, grandmother and brothers Malcolm and Edmond, removing much of her support network. In 1908, however, her father, who was now sixty years old, retired from the army and returned to England, settling at Guildford, Surrey with an older unmarried sister named Dora (for whom his daughter presumably had been named). Wentworth joined this household as well, along with her daughter and her youngest stepson. Here in Surrey Wentworth, presumably with the goal of making herself financially independent for the first time in her life (she was now in her early thirties), wrote the novel that changed the course of her life, *A Marriage under the Terror*, for the first time we know of utilizing her famous *nom de plume*.

The burst of creative energy that resulted in Wentworth's publication of six novels in six years suddenly halted after the appearance of *Queen Anne Is Dead* in 1915. It seems not unlikely that the Great War impinged in various ways on her writing. One tragic episode was the death on the western front of one of her stepsons, George Charles Tracey Dillon. Mining in Colorado when war was declared, young Dillon worked his passage from Galveston, Texas to Bristol, England as a shipboard muleteer (mule-tender) and joined the Gloucestershire Regiment. In 1916 he died at the Somme at the age of 29 (about the age of Wentworth's two brothers when they had passed away in India).

A couple of years after the conflict's cessation in 1918, a happy event occurred in Wentworth's life when at Frimley, Surrey she wed George Oliver Turnbull, up to this time a lifelong bachelor who like the author's first husband was a lieutenant-colonel in the Indian Army. Like his bride now forty-two years old, George Turnbull as a younger man had distinguished himself for his athletic prowess, playing forward for eight years for the Scottish rugby team and while a student at the Royal Military Academy winning the medal awarded the best athlete of his term. It seems not unlikely that Turnbull played a role in his wife's turn toward writing mystery fiction, for he is said to have strongly supported Wentworth's career, even assisting her in preparing manuscripts for publication. In 1936 the couple in Camberley, Surrey built Heatherglade House, a large two-story structure on substantial grounds, where they resided until Wentworth's death a quarter of a century later. (George Turnbull survived his wife by nearly a decade, passing away in 1970 at the age of 92.) This highly successful middle-aged companionate marriage contrasts sharply with the more youthful yet rocky union of Agatha and Archie Christie, which was three years away from sundering when Wentworth published *The Astonishing Adventure of Jane Smith* (1923), the first of her sixty-five mystery novels.

Although Patricia Wentworth became best-known for her cozy tales of the criminal investigations of consulting detective Miss Maud Silver, one of the mystery genre's most prominent spinster sleuths, in truth the Miss Silver tales account for just under half of Wentworth's 65 mystery novels. Miss Silver did not make her debut until 1928 and she did not come to predominate in Wentworth's fictional criminous output until the 1940s. Between 1923 and 1945 Wentworth published 33 mystery novels without Miss Silver, a handsome and substantial legacy in and of itself to vintage crime fiction fans. Many of these books are standalone tales of mystery, but nine of them have series characters. Debuting in the novel *Fool Errant* in 1929, a year after Miss Silver first appeared in print, was the enigmatic, nautically-named *eminence grise* Benbow Collingwood Horatio Smith, owner of a most expressively opinionated parrot named Ananias (and quite a colorful character in his own right). Benbow Smith went on to appear in three additional Wentworth mysteries: *Danger Calling* (1931), *Walk with Care* (1933) and *Down Under* (1937). Working in tandem with Smith in the investigation of sinister affairs threatening the security of Great Britain in *Danger Calling* and *Walk with Care* is Frank Garrett, Head of Intelligence for the Foreign Office, who also appears solo in *Dead or Alive* (1936) and *Rolling Stone* (1940) and collaborates with additional series characters, Scotland Yard's Inspector Ernest Lamb and Sergeant Frank Abbott, in *Pursuit of a Parcel* (1942). Inspector Lamb and Sergeant Abbott headlined a further pair of mysteries, *The Blind Side* (1939) and *Who Pays the Piper?* (1940), before they became absorbed, beginning with *Miss Silver Deals with Death* (1943), into the burgeoning Miss Silver canon. Lamb would make his farewell appearance in 1955 in *The Listening Eye*, while Abbott would take his final bow in mystery fiction with Wentworth's last published novel, *The Girl in the Cellar* (1961), which went into print the year of the author's death at the age of 83.

The remaining two dozen Wentworth mysteries, from the fantastical *The Astonishing Adventure of Jane Smith* in 1923 to the intense legal drama *Silence in Court* in 1945, are, like the author's series novels, highly imaginative and entertaining tales of mystery and adventure, told by a writer gifted with a consummate flair for storytelling. As one confirmed Patricia Wentworth mystery fiction addict, American Golden Age mystery writer Todd Downing, admiringly declared in the 1930s, "There's something about Miss Wentworth's yarns that is contagious." This attractive new series of Patricia Wentworth reissues by Dean Street Press provides modern fans of vintage mystery a splendid opportunity to catch the Wentworth fever.

Curtis Evans

Chapter One

JIM MACKENZIE came into the bare room with the office table set on one side of it to catch the dingy light of the winter afternoon. It was only two o'clock, but the sky was dark with snow clouds and the air tense with frost. The room was cold in spite of the stove in the corner, but the place from which Jim Mackenzie came had been colder. The icy chill of it was in his bones, and the horrible rank stench of it in his nostrils. This cold, bare office room felt warm as he came into it—warm, and full of clean air. His eyes went to the patch of leaden sky before he looked at the man behind the office table.

A yard inside the door he stood still, because the men on either side of him stood still. He wished that they would stand farther off, because the reek of the prison was upon them, as it was upon him. He wanted as much clean air as he could get. He had had ten days of the sort of prison which is reserved for political offenders in Russia, and now he supposed that he was to be shot. He stood still with his guards on either side of him and watched the man at the office table.

A small man, rather like an ant, with an ant's big head and an ant's restless activity. He had taken no notice of the opening door or of the prisoner's entrance. He wrote with feverish haste, snatching one paper after another from a pile on his left, scribbling some marginal note, and then thrusting the paper upon a growing pile to his right.

Jim was wondering why he had been brought here at all. It was ten days since he had been arrested, a week since he had been told that he was to be shot without the formality of a trial, a week since he had written to Laura. He wondered whether she would ever get the letter. He had been assured that it would reach her. If the assurance was worth anything, the letter might very well have reached her by now. His brows drew together in an involuntary frown of pain. His heart said "*Laura*"; and all at once it was as if she was there in the cold, bare room, bringing with her all those things from which a Bolshevist bullet would presently divorce him.

A man's senses are sharp on the edge of death. To Jim Mackenzie, Laura Cameron was for that instant exquisitely and unforgettably present. There was a sweetness, and a something that was like the bloom on light. There was the way she smiled, and the turn of her head. She did not smile like any other woman that he had ever known. Her eyes smiled first; you could watch a kind of dancing joy come up in them like light coming up through dark water. And then her lips quivering, and the smile come and gone before you could catch your breath. He caught it now. The sense of her presence was strong. It pierced him with an agony beyond anything he had known. To die with Laura waiting for him, with their wedding set for a bare week ahead! To leave her comfortless! He had a strange irrational feeling that it would not be so bad if he could be there to comfort her. He rocked for a moment on the verge of the impossible—

The little man at the table thrust a paper violently upon the right-hand pile, and said without looking up,

"Come nearer—I can't speak to you over there."

Jim advanced. The guards advanced. They stood still again, all three of them, about a yard from the table.

The little man looked up, pen in hand. His eyes, behind powerful lenses, were small, intent, and highly intelligent. The tip of his nose moved, sniffed.

"Those prisons are insanitary," he said in an irritable voice.

"Undoubtedly," said Jim Mackenzie.

The eyes focused on him. At a sign the guards fell back towards the door.

"You are James Mackenzie?"

"I am."

"You are a Russian subject."

"Certainly not."

The little man plucked a paper from an open file, slammed it down on the desk in front of him, stabbed at it with a quivering finger, and repeated,

"You are a Russian subject!"

"I am a British subject," said Jim Mackenzie.

Both men spoke Russian. Both men spoke it as men speak their own language.

The little man banged a fist on the paper before him.

"You were born in Russia—your father was born in Russia—your grandfather and your father were married in Russia. You are a Russian subject!"

"I haven't got a drop of Russian blood in my veins!" said Jim Mackenzie. He stood up straight and stuck his chin in the air.

It was a blunt chin. All his features were blunt and rather heavily moulded. He had fair hair that curled thickly, and a short fair stubble of eyelash and eyebrow. His strong neck rose from powerful shoulders. He had not been able to shave or wash since his arrest.

You cannot turn a Scot into a Russian by arranging for him to be born in Russia. Jim Mackenzie was at this moment full of the Scot's arrogant contempt for lesser nations. Inwardly he said, "And be damned to you!"—and for twopence he would have said it aloud. There was a bullet waiting for him anyhow. He smiled rather grimly, then shut his lips and let his eyes speak for him.

The little man made a marginal note.

"You are a Russian subject. You have been engaged in counter-revolutionary activities."

"I have not!"

The little man made another marginal note.

"You have been engaged in counter-revolutionary activities. The sentence is death. You were informed of this a week ago."

The room was as cold as a tomb. The patch of sky was leaden dark. The little man leaned sideways and touched a switch; a bright unsparing light stripped the room to its bare, ugly bones. Jim Mackenzie faced it impassively. The eyes behind the strong lenses watched him.

"The sentence is death," the little man repeated. "In certain circumstances it is possible that the sentence might be commuted." He paused, and then darted a sharp question. "You do not say anything?"

Jim Mackenzie stood like a rock. The sudden assault of hope tried his defences high, but he stood. He thrust the thought of Laura down, down, into those depths which were secret even to himself. He faced the white light and the keen intelligent eyes and smiled.

"Is there anything to say?"

The telephone bell rang sharply. The little man picked up the receiver. There was a buzzing and a thrumming from the instrument.

The little man said, "Yes;" and after a while, just before he hung up the receiver, he nodded and said in an emphatic manner, "Immediately—I understand." Then he pushed away the instrument and once more fixed his eyes on Jim Mackenzie.

"This morning you saw Mr Trevor?"

"Yes."

"He made a report on you," said the little man.

"Did he?"

He had been surprised that they had allowed him to see Trevor. The interview had not lasted more than two minutes. He had been unable to conceive its purpose, but Trevor had promised to write to Laura—to give messages—

The thought broke off as a jerked thread breaks. The little man was speaking.

"The special circumstances have arisen. You are free to go."

The blood rushed to Jim Mackenzie's head. He could feel it pounding against his ears. He said in a hard voice which he himself could scarcely hear,

"What do you mean?"

"Your sentence is commuted—on conditions. You are free."

There was some snag then. The pounding lessened. He said,

"What conditions?"

"You are to leave Russia."

A gale of inward laughter shook his self-control. It wavered. What would happen if he burst out laughing in the Insect's bespectacled face?

"That is one condition." The little man was speaking. "You are to leave Russia. And the second condition is this. You will go straight to Berlin, and from Berlin you will telephone to a lady who is anxious to have news of you."

Jim Mackenzie's self-control gave way. He said, *What?* in a voice that caused the guards to make a tentative step forward.

The little man waved them back impatiently.

"You will telephone to Miss Laura Cameron," he said.

Chapter Two

LAURA CAMERON stood looking at herself in the slender mirror which had belonged to her great-grandmother, another Laura Cameron. It hung between two tall and slender poles. The poles were gracefully fluted, and their feet were shod with old dim brass. The mirror was of an oblong shape with brass corners and a very narrow line of gilding between the glass and the mahogany frame. Laura had brought it out of her bedroom and set it at the far end of the sitting-room.

Very little light came through the sitting-room windows. A yellowish fog hung across them like a curtain. The houses opposite were blotted out. Laura had switched on both the lights, the one in the alabaster bowl, and the one in the reading-lamp with the orange shade. These two colours of light, warm white, and glowing, filled the mirror and shone on the image of Laura in her wedding dress. Behind her to the right and left, sometimes in the picture, and sometimes merely in the room, were the figures of Amelia Crofts in her black dress and white apron, and of Jenny Carruthers in her bridesmaid's frock, which had a tight green bodice and a very long and spreading green skirt. The green was shot with a silver thread which repeated the colour of Jenny's ash-blonde hair.

By every canon of the heart Laura Cameron was beautiful. The very air of beauty surrounded her, and under its influence classic standards were discarded. Her face was oval, the dark line of her eyebrows like slender wings, her nose of a charming irregularity, lips sensitive and deeply coloured parting over teeth that were very white and a little uneven. Her ears were beautifully shaped, and beautifully set on a gracefully carried head. Her eyes had dreams in them. Her skin was soft with a downy bloom and quick with colour. All this the world could see. The tender sweetness of Jim Mackenzie's Laura was for him alone.

Laura stood and looked into the mirror. She saw herself in the white cloud that was her veil. It hid her hair, and the line of her slender shoulders, and the young curve of her breast. It came down in a faint foam about her feet. She lifted it with both hands and looked over her shoulder to say to Jenny,

"It's too long—isn't it?"

The white, veiled Laura in the mirror moved too. The veil floated out, the long straight dress shimmered through it—a silver dress like a silver sheath. Jenny stepped out of the picture with a whisk of her apple-green skirt.

"*Much* too long—*bulgy!*"

Amelia Crofts sniffed. She had a thin pale nose, and could convey practically any shade of meaning in a sniff. She considered that Miss Laura looked a perfect h'angel, and that bulgy wasn't no sort of word for a young lady to use. Her sniff made both of these things perfectly clear.

"I should have a good foot off it," said Jenny. She tilted her head. "Or two—or three. It makes you look exactly like a parcel done up in white tissue-paper."

Laura laughed—softly, because her wedding dress made her feel as if she was in church. She held the veil out like wings and turned to the mirror. There was something unfamiliar about the Laura who looked back at her. It was the veil of course; it hid her hair and made her look like a nun. She pushed it back a little and released a soft dark curl on either side.

"Is that better, Jenny?"

Jenny looked over her shoulder and nodded in the glass.

Amelia said, "Oh, miss, that's lovely!" and Laura turned to smile at her.

She saw herself as she turned, the smile in her dark eyes—eyes neither grey nor brown, no-coloured eyes full of a soft darkness—her bloom heightened, the carnation springing to her cheeks. And as she turned, the bell of the flat rang with a hard buzzing sound.

Amelia sniffed—a sniff of pure aggravation. This was perhaps the most enchanted moment of a rather drab life, and it was just bound to be broken into by that there dratted bell, as if there wasn't twenty-three other hours in the day for *them* to come a-banging and a-ringing—the dratted nuisances. Her pale nose twitched angrily as she went out of the room, shutting the door sharply behind her.

Jenny stood on tiptoe listening.

"It's a man."

Laura's colour sprang up.

"It can't be Jim! To-morrow's the very earliest, and I haven-'t heard—"

"Of course it's not Jim. He wouldn't stop at the door." She pounced on Laura and pulled her towards the bedroom. "And I don't care who it is, they're not going to see either of us. Quick—she's letting him in! I'll murder Amelia for this!" She whisked Laura and Laura's train into the bedroom and banged the door. "Tell Amelia I'll come back and murder her in the middle of the night—slowly—something lingering, with boiling oil in it!"

"Tell her yourself!" said Laura, laughing.

And then the door opened and Amelia came in with a card in her hand.

"He says he must see you, miss."

"But, Milly—I can't!"

Laura took the card, frowning a very little. She read: "Mr Basil Stevens"; and, pencilled above the name, the words: "Very urgent business."

"But I hardly know him," she said.

Jenny was half out of her bridesmaid's dress. She wriggled free and threw it over the end of the bed.

"Who is it?" she asked.

"Basil Stevens. I've met him—I don't really know him. I can't imagine why he wants to see me."

Jenny slipped into a dark blue day-frock and crammed on a hat.

"Send him away if you don't want to see him. Golly! It's late! I'm meeting Kathie for a matinée, and she'll be wild. Where's my coat, Amelia? It's a perfectly foul afternoon! I'll leave the dress here. So long, Ducky! Snub Basil if he gets fresh!"

"I didn't know you knew him."

"I don't," said Jenny at the door. *"Au revoir!"*

Laura smiled vaguely at the closing door.

"I must change if I've got to see him," she said; and then, "What is it, Milly?"

Amelia's hands were shaking; she held her apron, but they shook. Her nose twitched, and her long upper lip.

"Oh, Miss Laura!"

"Milly—what is it?"

Amelia put up a trembling hand and touched her smooth grey hair.

"I don't rightly know—it come into the flat with him."

A cold air blew upon Laura.

"What, Milly?"

"Trouble," said Amelia Crofts. She blinked with reddened eyelids.

Laura stood still for a moment. It was a moment in which she forgot everything except that word trouble. Trouble meant bad news, and bad news meant Jim. She forgot all about being in her wedding dress. When the moment passed, she opened the door and went into the sitting-room with Basil Stevens's card in her hand and an icy fear at her heart. She lifted her train, closed the door again mechanically, and then stood still.

Basil Stevens came to meet her.

"How do you do, Miss Cameron? I must apologize—"

Laura interrupted, first with a movement of the hand, and then with a quick,

"What is it?"

He had left his hat and stick in the hall. He stood before her bare-headed—a good looking man of five or six-and-thirty with widely set eyes of a bright hazel colour, brown hair, and a face that narrowed from the rather high cheek-bones to a pointed chin. He held his tall figure a little bent forward as if he were ready to bow over the hand which Laura had not extended.

She kept her eyes on his face and repeated on a hurrying breath,

"What is it, Mr Stevens?"

Perhaps he had not expected this ready alarm. Perhaps the wedding dress and veil, which she had forgotten, were not without their effect upon him. He was, for the moment, silent; and in that moment Laura came nearer and laid a hand upon his arm.

"Mr Stevens—is it anything about Jim?"

Basil Stevens recovered himself. He said,

"I think we had better sit down."

Laura took the chair which he offered her. She was glad of it, because, when he did not answer her question, she had felt the floor move under her feet. She sank down into the chair and said piteously,

"Is it Jim? Won't you tell me? I'd rather—know—" And there she stopped, because some bottomless pit seemed to open as she said the words, and out of it there came up the shadows of the things that she might have to know—Jim ill—Jim dying—Jim dead....

Basil Stevens saw the last of her colour drain away. She had been pale and startled when she came into the room, but now even her lips were white. He had no wish to have her fainting on his hands. He said sharply,

"Mackenzie's alive and well."

The change came so quickly to her face that it astounded him. Colour and life rushed back to it. She closed her eyes for a moment, and then looked at him with a kind of gentle reproach.

"You frightened me dreadfully."

"I'm sorry—I had no wish to frighten you. May I ask when you last heard from Mackenzie?"

"I haven't had a letter since Saturday."

"And this is Wednesday."

Laura smiled a little tremulously. Relief had deadened her perceptions.

"Yes—but he may be home to-morrow. I don't think he will, but it's just possible, and he said I could *count* on Friday."

"I'm afraid you mustn't count on anything."

Laura's head lifted. She could be angry now. How really impertinent of him to be talking like this!

"Will you tell me what you mean, Mr Stevens?"

"I am going to tell you. I am afraid you must not count upon Mackenzie's return. It is unfortunate that he should have allowed himself to become involved in a political difficulty."

"I don't understand what you mean," said Laura.

"I will explain. Mackenzie was arrested a week ago."

Laura turned startled eyes upon him. They were not terrified yet, but somewhere under the surface terror stirred. She repeated his word under her breath.

"Arrested—"

Basil Stevens said, "Yes," and waited.

"But why?"

He could only just hear the question.

"I am afraid he has been extremely imprudent. Imprudence is a very dangerous complaint in Russia just now."

"Where is he?" said Laura.

"In prison."

"But they *can't*! He's a British subject—they can't do anything to him!"

"They can shoot him," said Basil Stevens.

Laura thrust away the terror that had come nearer.

"A British subject—" she said.

"In Russia he is not considered to be a British subject. I am afraid you must face the fact that he is in an extremely dangerous position. He is, in fact, under sentence of death."

Laura said, *"No!"*

She heard her own voice saying it. The sound seemed to fill the room. Then she heard Basil Stevens say,

"I am afraid it is a shock. If you are to help him, you must believe me."

Sensitive people very often have a great deal of courage. Laura called on hers. The words "If you are to help him," spurred it. She said,

"How can I?" And then quickly, "How do you *know*?"

He was ready for this.

"I will tell you in a minute. But I should like first to ask you a question. I should like to ask you what you know about me."

She looked at him with a rather piteous vagueness. Her mind was so full of Jim that it was very difficult to think about anyone else. For the moment, Basil Stevens was as impersonal to her as the telegraph boy who brings a message of disaster.

He repeated his question.

"What do you know about me, Miss Cameron?"

She forced herself to consider—because he would not ask her such a thing unless it had somehow a bearing upon what was happening to Jim. She said in a hesitating way,

"I don't know…. I met you at the Harrisons'…. You're an engineer, aren't you?"

He nodded.

"An engineer may have connections with many countries. I have connections with Russia. Did you know that?"

Laura said, "No."

Her hands lay in her lap; they held one another tightly. Her eyes looked steadily at Basil Stevens.

"How have you heard—this—about Jim?"

He shrugged his shoulders very slightly.

"I have just told you that I have a connection with Russia."

A little colour sprang into her cheeks.

"How do you know—that is true?"

A curious look passed over his face.

"My dear Miss Cameron, I should certainly not have come to you with a piece of hearsay gossip."

"How can you prove it?"

He put his hand into an inner pocket and took out a pocket-book, which he laid upon his knee. Very deliberately he opened it and took out an envelope, which he handed to Laura.

She took it, and sat there looking at it. It was a square white envelope with her name written on it in a strange hand: "Miss Laura Cameron"—just that and nothing more.

"What is it?" she said in a bewildered voice.

"There is a letter from Mackenzie inside."

Laura's hand tightened on the letter.

"It's not his writing."

"The letter is inside. He was allowed to write to you, but"—he shrugged again—"they don't supply envelopes in prison."

Very slowly Laura tore open the envelope. She tore it without looking at it, and, still without looking, she drew out the enclosure. Then her eyes went to it—quickly. It was a letter, and it was from Jim, but it was written in a pencil scrawl on a crumpled half sheet. She saw her name, and the words that followed it: "Laura—they're letting me say good-bye." And then she couldn't see any more, because there was a darkness between her and the page. She looked up, her eyes wide, and remained like that whilst she drew half a dozen difficult breaths.

Basil Stevens got up and walked to the window, where he stood with his back to her, looking out at the fog.

When Laura could see again, she went on reading Jim Mackenzie's letter:

> "They are letting me say good-bye. I'm to be shot to-morrow. It will be over by the time you get this. I'm making you unhappy, and I'm cursing myself for it. I hope you won't be unhappy for longer than you can help. I don't want you to be

unhappy about me. You've made me gloriously happy. I didn't know that there was anyone like you in the world. We've loved each other very much. No one's going to take that away from me. You know how much I love you. I can't say the things that I would like to say—I can't get them into words. I don't want you to wear black for me and be unhappy. Good-bye, my darling.

Your

Jim."

Chapter Three

LAURA SAT for a long time with the letter in her hand. The words had left the paper and were in her heart. She could hear Jim's voice saying them to her. It said them over and over again. It went on and on.

Then there was a movement by the window. Basil Stevens returned to his chair.

Laura came back. She stopped hearing Jim's voice, and she saw her own hand with the letter in it, and, a little farther down, the folds of her silver train. Then she heard Basil Stevens say in his rather deep voice,

"Don't look like that, Miss Cameron—he hasn't been shot." He made quite a long pause, and then added, *"Yet."*

The letter shook in her hand. She put out her other hand to steady it, but that shook too.

"Miss Cameron—I give you my word that he's alive."

"How—do you—know?"

"It is my business to know. I have come here on business. I want you to pull yourself together. Have you any wine here?"

She shook her head.

He brought her a glass of water, and she drank a little. The first impact of the shock was over. She was numbed by it, but her head felt clear.

"You're better? You can listen to me?"

"Yes."

"You've read Mackenzie's letter. He wrote it under the impression that his sentence would be carried out next day. It has not been carried out—it need never be carried out."

Laura's mind was clear, but her thoughts moved slowly; they had a heavy, clogged feeling.

Basil Stevens repeated his last words.

"The sentence need not be carried out." He paused, and then said very distinctly, "Whether it is carried out or not depends on you."

The words came into Laura's mind. Her thoughts stood round and stared at them. They made nothing of them. She said,

"I don't understand."

"Please try and understand, Miss Cameron. Mackenzie is under sentence of death. His fate is entirely in your hands. If you do one thing, he will be shot—if you do another, he will go free. Do you understand that? He will go quite free. There is no question of prison or anything of that sort."

Laura looked at him.

"I don't know what you mean."

"But you know what I've just been saying. It's for you to say whether Mackenzie is shot, or whether he goes free."

Laura went on looking at him.

"How can it be?"

"I suppose that you would be willing to make some sacrifice to save his life?"

"Yes," said Laura—just the one word in a soft failing voice. All her life and strength seemed to be drawn inwards about her consciousness of Jim. Her voice failed.

"Well, you can save him if you want to," said Basil Stevens.

Laura said, "How?" and it seemed as if he hesitated.

At last he said, "Mackenzie can be—how shall I put it?—exchanged. He has been condemned to death for counter-revolutionary activities. The Russian Government considers that they have a claim against his life. They will press the claim unless it is to their advantage not to press it. Now it happens to be in your power to be able to offer them something which would be more to their advantage than their claim against Mackenzie."

Laura leaned forward, her clasped hands upon the letter. A quick colour came and went in her cheeks.

"*I?*"

Basil Stevens nodded.

"Yes. It is fortunate for Mackenzie—isn't it?"

"*I?*" said Laura.

"You. You have it in your power to release him."

"Mr Stevens—"

"Yes, I am going to tell you how. It is a business matter. The Russian Government have, as you may know, embarked upon a great scheme of industrial and agricultural expansion. They want machinery, railway plant, aeroplanes, agricultural implements, like tractors—you will have seen things about it in the papers, and you will have heard Mackenzie talk about it. His firm has a contract to supply tractors."

"Yes."

Basil Stevens made a gesture that cut across his explanations.

"I cannot go any farther until I have your assurance that you will treat what I am going to say as confidential."

Laura's eyes dwelt on him.

"What do you mean by that?"

"I mean that you are not at liberty to take what I am going to tell you to some friend whom you wish to consult—or, shall we say, to the Foreign Office? I am willing to give you some confidential information, but I am not willing that you should pass it on." He smiled slightly and added, "You need not be alarmed, Miss Cameron—I am not going to tell you anything that will burden your conscience—it is merely a matter of trade secrets. You need have no objection to giving me your promise."

"What has all this to do with Jim?" said Laura in a grave, slow voice.

"I will tell you when you have promised that you will not repeat—to anyone—what I am going to say."

"I hardly know you," said Laura. "I don't know what you are going to say. I can't promise."

His straight, short eyebrows drew together in a frown. Then he made a gesture with his right hand.

"Very well, I won't ask you to promise—I will only tell you that if you talk, you will kill Mackenzie. That is not a threat—it is just a plain statement of fact."

"Yes," said Laura. "Will you tell me please?"

Basil Stevens leaned back in his chair.

"Do you know the name of Bertram Hallingdon?"

Laura had wondered what he could possibly be going to say. His question took her completely by surprise. Her lips parted in an involuntary exclamation.

"You know the name, Miss Cameron?"

"Yes."

"Did you know the man?"

"No, I don't know him. Everyone knows him by name."

"Yet he is a relation of yours."

"A distant one."

"Your grandfather's half brother. That is not such a very distant relationship."

"I've never met him—there was a family quarrel—I don't suppose he knows of my existence."

Basil Stevens smiled slightly.

"Have you any objection to telling me what you know about Bertram Hallingdon?"

"I really know very little—just what everyone knows."

"Go on, please, Miss Cameron."

"Well, there's nothing to tell. He's very—rich. He's the head of a big engineering firm, isn't he?"

"The head of the Hallingdon combine. That means a little more than being the head of an engineering firm. Hallingdons controls a number of firms engaged in various branches of engineering. Is that all you know about Bertram Hallingdon?"

"I think so."

"You did not know that he was dead?"

She was startled, but without knowing why.

"No—I didn't know."

"He died this morning. He had been ill for some time."

He was regarding her intently, and something in this regard set her heart beating. She waited for him to speak with a curious sense of fear.

"You are Bertram Hallingdon's heiress," said Basil Stevens.

Laura's heart beat so hard that it shook her.

She said "No!" and saw that he was smiling again.

"You succeed to a very important position, Miss Cameron. May I be the first to congratulate you?"

Laura recovered herself.

"How do you know this?"

"Does that matter? I can assure you that my information is correct. Now, Miss Cameron—a little while ago you asked me what all this had to do with Jim Mackenzie? Do you begin to see what the connection may be?"

She said, "Go on."

Basil Stevens went on.

"I told you that it was in your power to offer something which would induce the Russian Government to give up their claim against Mackenzie. The head of the Hallingdon combine has certainly got it in her power to make it worth their while to let Jim Mackenzie go. That's plain talking—isn't it?"

Laura lifted her hands and pressed them against her breast. A brilliant flame of colour sprang into her cheeks. She did not speak. Her eyes searched his face.

"It only remains for you to come to terms with them," said Basil Stevens.

She spoke then in a voice that trembled with hope.

"What do they want?"

"Well, they want their *quid pro quo*—trade facilities, credits, and all that sort of thing."

Laura stretched out her hands.

"And they'll let him go? You're sure?"

"Yes—quite sure."

"Then of course—" she stood up, pushing back her veil—"whatever I can do—only it ought to be done quickly—he's in prison!"

"Please sit down, Miss Cameron. It is not quite as simple as that. There are conditions. I am afraid you will not like them. Will you please remember that they are not of my making?"

She sat down again.

"What conditions?"

"You will remember that I asked you whether you would be prepared to make a sacrifice."

"You needn't have asked me that."

Why did he waste time? If what he had told her was true, did he suppose that these business details mattered? Did he think that she was going to haggle over Jim's life? The whole Hallingdon combine might go up in smoke so long as Jim was safe.

"You may think it a big sacrifice," said Basil Stevens.

"Tell me what it is."

"There is a condition attached that you should agree to nominate a person approved by the Russian Government to the boards of the various firms in the Hallingdon combine."

Laura's eyes widened.

"Could I do that?"

"Certainly." He hesitated for a moment, and then said, "I have seen Mr Hallingdon's will."

"I am to nominate *Russians*?"

"You are to nominate a person approved by the Russian Government. This person is to have a seat on the board of every company in the combine."

"But that would take time," said Laura in a puzzled voice. "It would take a long time, wouldn't it? The will would have to be proved—I know that takes months—and Jim—Jim can't be in prison for months."

"You would be required to nominate your husband," said Basil Stevens.

Chapter Four

LAURA STARTED SLIGHTLY. Her bewilderment increased.

"My husband?" she said. "They want me to nominate Jim?"

"Mackenzie is not your husband, Miss Cameron."

Laura looked down at the silver of her wedding dress. She even smiled a little. He must be rather dense—

"Well, we're to be married next week," she said.

"Mackenzie would not be a suitable nominee—I think you must see that yourself."

Laura looked up again, puzzled, but not yet afraid.

"But you said—"

"I said your husband—I didn't say Jim Mackenzie."

"What do you mean?" said Laura in a voice between fear and anger.

"Haven't I told you? You must nominate your husband. Mackenzie is not eligible for the position."

Laura stood up.

"Mr Stevens—you don't realize what you're saying!"

"I am afraid it is you who do not realize, Miss Cameron. I am going to speak plainly. Your husband and your nominee must be a person approved by the Russian Government. Mackenzie scarcely fulfils that condition."

As he rose and took a step towards her, she backed away from him, her hand on the chair rail, the long train about her feet. He took no more than the one step, and she stayed, leaning on the chair and looking at him.

She was beginning to understand. The blank puzzled look in her eyes was changing. He saw it flash into anger, whilst the brilliant colour flamed in her cheeks.

"How dare you?"

Again that fleeting smile.

"Easily, Miss Cameron! You see, I am trying to do you a service. The whole thing is, naturally, a shock to you. I am afraid that is unavoidable. You see, there is no time to beat about the bush and come gradually and tactfully to the point. It is a question of Mackenzie's life He is in prison at this moment, and he will be dead to-morrow unless—" He paused weightily.

The room filled with a horrible silence. Laura stood in it, and felt numb. It was like standing in ice-cold water—at first one felt the cold, and afterwards one felt nothing. The power to feel was gone, the words "he will be dead to-morrow" were frozen in her mind.

Basil Stevens broke the silence rather sharply.

"Are you faint?"

Laura shook her head.

"I will go away and leave you to think the matter over. I can give you an hour, not longer, or we should be running things too fine—there's the difference in time to consider, Mackenzie has got till to-morrow. But it will be to-morrow in Russia some hours earlier than here."

Laura gripped the chair rail.

"How do I know you're speaking the truth?" she said.

"In what particular?"

She said, "How do I *know*?" and caught her breath.

He spoke in the same courteous and formal tone which he had employed throughout.

"If there is any point on which you are doubtful, I think I can suggest a way in which you can check what I have told you."

"How?"

"You could ask the Foreign Office to cable for information. You need offer no further explanation than your very natural anxiety. You have had a letter telling you that Mackenzie is under sentence of death. You will not, of course, say how the letter came into your hands, and you will not mention my name. I think Mackenzie has a friend at the Foreign Office?"

"How did you know? Yes—there's Peter—Peter Severn—I could ask him—" Her voice trailed away.

"You can ring him up," said Basil Stevens. "Perhaps you would like to change your dress first."

Laura's frozen calm broke up. She threw out her hands with a wild gesture as if she were beating him away.

"You've come here with everything planned!" she said. "You know that Jim's in prison—you know that Mr Hallingdon is dead—you know that he has left me his business—you know about Peter Severn. You've got the whole thing planned out!"

"And if I have?"

She stood there trembling with her passionate impulse.

"And if I have, Miss Cameron—does that make Mackenzie's danger less—or more?"

The passionate impulse failed. Jim—she had to find out about Jim. She went over to the little writing-table where the telephone stood and picked up the instrument.

Basil Stevens watched her with a faintly satirical look. He could have wished that she had been of some other type. She reminded him of a car that he had once driven—a touch on the steering wheel, and you were in the ditch; another, and you were across the road. He liked a woman who was good company and ready for anything—an easy, sensual woman. With Laura Cameron's type you had to walk on egg-shells, and that did not amuse him in the least. He watched her seat herself, push aside her veil, and lean forward listening. Her profile was turned to him. There was a little pulse of colour in her cheek.

"I want to speak to Mr Severn."

Then she shut her eyes and stayed there motionless, with the cloud of her veil failing about her.

Basil Stevens came to her elbow and said quietly,

"You must be careful what you say."

She spoke into the telephone again.

"I want to speak to Mr Peter Severn.... Miss Laura Cameron. It is very urgent."

After that they waited. It seemed a very long time. Laura had a picture of Peter walking towards her down an endless cold corridor—his footsteps echoed in it, but he never came any nearer. And all the time Jim was waiting to be shot. When Peter's voice came suddenly along the wire, she started violently, and her heart beat so hard that she could not hear what he was saying at first. Then she heard her name.

"Laura—is that you?"

Her "Yes" told Peter Severn that at least he would not have to break anything to her.

"What is it, Laura?"

"I've had a letter—from Jim."

"Yes?"

"He's—in prison."

There was a silence. Laura caught her breath.

"Peter—is it true?"

"I'm afraid it is."

"He says—he says—"

"When did you hear?" said Peter Severn.

"Just now." She forced her voice. "He says they're going—to shoot him."

Another silence.

"Peter—is it true?"

"I'm afraid—"

"Tell me what you've heard."

"We had a report from Trevor yesterday. We wired at once. There was an answer half an hour ago. I was coming round to see you."

"They *haven't*!" Laura's tone was sharp with agony.

"No—not yet."

"When?"

"Trevor says to-morrow. He's doing all he can. But they're claiming him as a Russian national. His grandfather took out papers in order to get some concession or other, and both Jim and his father were born in the country. It's a most damnable business. We're—we're doing all we can, Laura."

Laura drew a difficult breath.

"Do you think there's—any—hope?"

"We're doing all we can," said Peter Severn. There was no hope in his voice.

She stayed silent, her eyes fixed, her hand rigid on the receiver. At last she said,

"Are you sure—he's still—alive?"

Peter's answer came quickly.

"Oh yes. Trevor was to see him to-morrow. We've got till to-morrow."

After a pause Laura repeated his words: "We've got till to-morrow." Then she said,

"Thank you, Peter. You'll let me know if you hear?"

"Shall I come round?"

Basil Stevens laid a hand on her arm. She looked up and met an emphatic shake of the head. She bent again to the mouthpiece.

"No, don't come—ring up."

She hung up the receiver and turned.

"He said—"

"I heard what he said—he has a very good telephone voice. Well? Are you convinced?"

"Can you save him?" said Laura with sorrowful simplicity.

"Yes," said Basil Stevens.

"How do I know?" She put her hand to her head. "I can't think—but I must—I must think!" She covered her eyes for a moment, leaning her elbow upon the little table.

"Perhaps," said Basil Stevens, "you would like me to repeat the terms of the—exchange. It is natural that you should be feeling a little confused. This is the position. Mackenzie will be shot to-morrow unless you can offer the Russian Government a sufficient inducement to let him go free. You are able to do this, but it involves a sacrifice that you find painful. You cannot marry Mackenzie, because you will be required to marry some one to whom the Russian Government can entrust their trade interests. When you are married, it will be natural for you to nominate your husband to the boards of the various companies controlled by Mr Hallingdon. I am very sorry to have to press this upon you, but you can see for yourself that there would be no guarantee of permanency unless the Russian nominee was your husband."

Laura's hand dropped from her eyes. She looked up wildly.

"I can't marry—anyone—but Jim!"

"You cannot marry Jim if he is shot to-morrow," said Basil Stevens.

Laura flinched as if he had struck her. She said *"Don't!"* in a quivering voice.

Basil Stevens shook his head slightly.

"Just consider for a moment. You have not to choose between marrying Mackenzie and marrying—well—me. You cannot in any case marry Mackenzie now. You can let him be shot, and remain Miss Cameron—or you can enter into a business arrangement with me, and have the satisfaction of knowing that you have saved his life."

"You?" said Laura in a tone of horror.

Basil Stevens made her a queer, un-English bow.

"I, Miss Cameron."

"Oh, no, no, *no!*" said Laura.

Basil Stevens flung up his hands. It was exactly as if he were throwing off the polite formality which had clothed him. He made a guttural sound of anger.

"Ah! Do you suppose that I have a passion for you? Do you? Then I will tell you that you do not appeal to me in the least! I will tell you that this is a matter of pure business! Will that make you see reason? Listen to me! Did you ever see a play called *Hassan*? There is a woman in it who behaves exactly like you. If she will marry the Sultan, she can save her lover from death. Does she want to save him? Does she act like a sensible human being? Not in the least! She requires him to die with her by lingering tortures. And the young man—" he waved his arms in a vigorous gesture and laughed loudly—"the young man, does he thank her?—does the prospect enchant him—has he the least desire to die with her?" He laughed again, more loudly still. "He is—what is the word—fed to the teeth! It was a play that amused me very much because it was so true to life. You women are all sentiment, but a man thinks about other things. Do you think that Mackenzie wants to die? He is in love with you—that goes without saying. He wishes to marry you, and he will suffer when he finds that you have married some one else. But he will get over it—he has other interests in his life—he has youth, and health, and some money, and an invention for which he has great hopes. In a little while he will be very grateful to you. At the first it will be a blow. But that kind of blow will not kill him—it is not like a bullet. One can recover from a broken engagement, but not from an encounter with a firing-squad."

Laura had turned in her chair, her wide horrified gaze upon his face. At the brutality of his last words she shrank back as far as she could. The man who had poured out this rapid tirade was some one she had never seen before; his manner, his intonation, the movement of his hands were no longer those of an Englishman. But this change went far to accomplish its purpose. Whilst she was speaking to Basil Stevens, whom she had met at the Harrisons, English like herself, an engineer like Jim, a man who had taken her in to dinner, with whom she had danced, the things that he had said had somehow fallen short of that final reality from which there is no escape; but this man with the savage un-English inflection in his voice—all at once he made her feel that the thing was true. Jim was going to be shot. It wasn't too bad to happen—it was going to happen unless—unless—

"Who are you?" she said.

He burst out laughing.

"Why do you ask me that?"

"Because I must know. You must tell me the truth—nothing else will do. You're not English."

He was still laughing.

"I am a British subject, Miss Cameron. You find that funny? Well, so do I. I am Vassili Stefanoff—and in English that is Basil Stevens. I have not one drop of your English blood, I am pleased to say; but I am a British subject, because my father was a Tsarist exile, and I was born in England. In some ways, you see, my situation resembles Mackenzie's. I find that amusing. But I am in a more favourable position than he is—I am not expecting to be shot."

Laura did not flinch this time. Something had happened to her. At the touch of that inescapable reality her confusion and her tremors had passed. She had reached the point at which a man turns and, with his back to the wall, prepares to sell his life as dearly as he may. It is the point at which, hope being dead, courage takes its place.

Laura folded her hands in her lap. She sat up straight and pale, and said what she had to say in a quiet voice that no longer shook.

"If I do what you want, I have got to be sure about Jim. You can't expect me to trust you." She used no sarcasm; it was a mere statement of fact.

She was recollecting a terrible little story of the French Revolution read years ago in some forgotten book of memoirs. There was a girl who had sold herself to one of the Terrorists to save the father whom she adored, and when she had made her sacrifice she was shown his head. Laura's mind was cold and clear. There should be none of that.

Basil Stevens had stopped laughing.

"Now we talk business!" he said, and took a chair.

"I must know that Jim is safe before I do anything," said Laura.

"My dear Miss Cameron—be reasonable! When Mackenzie is safe, how do we know what you may do?"

Laura took him up with a quickness he had not expected.

"And when I have done what you want, how do I know that he will be safe? You might come to me and say that there has been an accident—that you were too late. No! I don't trust you—you can't expect me to trust you!"

Basil Stevens had resumed that reasonable, formal manner of his.

"If you think, you will see that you can trust us. The marriage is only the first step. In itself, it does not help us at all. You trust us by taking the first step—then we trust you, because we release Mackenzie. It will be some months before we reap any real advantage, because it will be some months before Mr Hallingdon's will is proved and you can obtain any effective control of his affairs."

"How do I know that you will release Jim? I won't trust you!" she said.

Vassili Stefanoff emerged with sudden violence.

"You will, and you won't! You bargain—you make terms! You do not trust! Do you think it is for you to make terms like that? You may be thankful if you get Mackenzie's life! I say you may be thankful!"

When he shouted at her, Laura's resolve hardened.

"I shall be thankful when he is safe," she said. "I won't do anything till he's safe. I've got to know that he's safe before I do anything."

"You propose that he shall be a witness to the marriage, perhaps!"

Her pallor and her calm were unbroken. She said quite gently, "You mustn't speak to me like that." And then, "I have thought of a way."

"Well—what is it?"

"He must be out of Russia before I do anything. If he was in Germany, I should know he was safe. He could telephone to me from Berlin—he has done it before. When I have spoken to him—when I am sure that he is safe—I will do what you want."

"And be made fools of? That's a very nice plan—for you!"

"No," said Laura. "I'll keep my word—when he's safe."

There was a curious silence. Laura was aware of a pressure, an insistence, but it was outside the walls of her mind. She was aware of it only as an outside thing. It had not the slightest power to touch her thought or turn her purpose.

All at once Vassili Stefanoff sprang up.

"You will swear to go through with the marriage?"

"I'll give you my word."

He made a quick gesture.

"You will swear? What is there that is sacred to you? Are you religious? Have you a Bible?"

"If I give you my word, I shall keep it."

"Oh, naturally you do not wish to take an oath. But you will take one!"

"If you like," said Laura—"it makes no difference."

She got up, went into the bedroom, and came back with her Bible in her hand. Her silver train whispered behind her. The folds of her veil fell all about her as she put the book into his hand.

"What do you want me to say?"

He dictated the oath. His vehement tone left her unmoved. It was no more to her than her word would have been. She was giving her word to marry Vassili Stefanoff as soon as she knew from Jim himself that he was free. She laid her hand on the Bible and took tremendous words upon her lips. The whole thing was no more than something that had to be done for Jim.

Vassili Stefanoff put down the book.

"You have your way," he said. "You will bear in mind that if you do not keep your oath, no place in the world will be safe for Mackenzie. You will not expect to hear from him for thirty-six hours. There are formalities—and he will have to reach Berlin. This is Wednesday. He should be able to ring you up on Friday morning. We shall be married at the Chelsea registry office that afternoon. I have made all the necessary arrangements."

He bowed ceremoniously and went out of the room.

Chapter Five

LAURA CAMERON remembered neither her father nor her mother, and with the exception of the cousin, whom she called Aunt Agatha and who had brought her up, she had no near relations.

Miss Agatha Wimborough, last survivor of an old Virginian family, was an acid, upright, competent lady, handsome in person and decided in her views. Feminism was her religion. Man was vile, and woman his suffering victim. That Laura should contemplate marrying, actually marrying, a man, was almost past her powers of belief—Laura, brought up from infancy to look upon marriage as a degrading survival of the days of woman's subjection—Laura, her pupil, accustomed to hear daily, almost hourly, of woman's wrongs and man's depravity. Alas, it is possible to hear a thing so often that the mind develops a callous and refuses to respond. When Laura at eighteen began to meet young men, she looked at them with a kind of horrified curiosity. But this very soon wore off. She found them pleasant, and most undoubtedly she pleased them. Before she knew where she was, she was making friends with the monsters and beginning to think that Aunt Agatha might be mistaken. Man might be capable of anything; but Buster, and Freddy, and Dick, and Bimbo were not Man with a capital "m"; they were her friends—and Laura could never believe anything but good of a friend.

She was twenty-three when she met Jim Mackenzie. In the first hour he had her trust, in a month her friendship, and six months later her love. Laura's affections were strong, delicate, and deep. She would never tumble into love headlong. With her, love must grow, and it must be firmly rooted in friendship and in trust. Passion would come to her as a fusing of these three things, and it would burn with a white and steady flame.

She presented an immovable front to Miss Wimborough's reproaches. They could wound her to the quick, but they could not shake her. She came to a point where she stopped being wounded and felt a deep, sweet compassion for the woman who knew so little about love. When, after a year's engagement, the date of her marriage was fixed, it was a real grief to her that Miss Wimborough, announcing that nothing would induce her to attend the sacrifice, departed upon a lecture tour in the United States—her theme "Some Crying Evils of our Social System." It was a grief, but also something of a relief. It would have been nice to have Aunt Agatha if Aunt Agatha could have brought herself to be nice to Jim; but if she couldn't, it was perhaps just as well that she should be saying the sort of thing she did say, on a lecture platform, and not in the flat she shared with Laura.

Since Miss Wimborough was some three thousand miles away, it could not be known how she would have dealt with Mr Basil Stevens. She was undoubtedly a woman of great force of character and exceedingly competent. Living through the thirty-six hours which separated her from the moment when she would hear Jim Mackenzie's voice on the telephone telling her that he was free, Laura was aware of a desperate, lonely longing for Aunt Agatha. No one could do anything; there was nothing that anyone could do. But at the back of all her thoughts was the irrational conviction that if Agatha Wimborough had been here, the impossible would have been done.

Thursday passed like a long, slow dream. Laura maintained a despairing composure. She waited for only one thing—to hear Jim's voice. Beyond that she did not allow her thoughts to pass. All through the hours of Wednesday night she lay and listened. Would Jim still be in prison? How long would it take to put in motion all those wheels which must turn before he could be free? As long as she thought about Jim being set free, it was easier; but as soon as she stopped thinking about that, she had the terrible feeling that she was on the very edge and brink of void, empty space, and that with her next movement she would fall, and go on falling, down, down, down.

All through the hours of Thursday she sat and waited. When Amelia set food before her, she ate it. When Amelia spoke to her, she answered in a gentle toneless voice. Then she went back to listening for the telephone bell. It would not ring before Friday morning—she knew that. But she could not help listening. Sometimes it rang so loud in her head that she took the receiver off and sat leaning forward, straining for the sound that wasn't there.

The bell actually did ring more than once. The first time it was some one who wanted to know what she would like for a wedding present. And then Peter Severn rang up to say they had had another cable from Trevor, and that there was practically no hope. Peter wanted to come round and see her. Laura said, "No—please don't." When she had rung off, there was a strange agonized happiness in her heart. Peter said there was no hope—but he didn't know. She knew that the wheels were turning, and that Jim was going to be free. Jim was going to be safe. For a moment the joy leapt right up through everything. Nothing mattered if Jim was safe.

Then Jenny rang up about her bridesmaid's dress. Did Laura think that the bodice could bear to be the least thing tighter? Jenny had waked up in the night and wondered about it. Laura's answer was quite gentle and composed. She thought the dress was very nice as it was. She didn't think it would be worth while to alter it.

At seven o'clock Peter Severn rang her up again.

"Laura—"

She knew at once from his voice that he had news. Her heart seemed to lift and turn over.

"Laura—we've had another cable from Trevor! Marvellous news! I say, I can't break it, or anything—but he's free! They've let him go! It's the most amazing thing—because I don't mind telling you now that nobody thought there was an earthly chance. It's great—isn't it?"

"Yes," said Laura—"it's great."

"Won't you let me come round? Are you all right?"

There was something in Laura's voice that Peter had never heard in a voice before. He didn't know what it was, and it worried him.

"I say—*are* you all right?"

"Quite all right, Peter."

Laura hung up the receiver.

Jim was safe. Jim was free. It was true—but not quite true until she had heard him speak. It would be another twelve hours before she could hear his voice.

She lay all night in the dark and waited. The hours went slowly. She lay quite still with her head turned towards the open sitting-room door. At the first sound of the bell she must be ready. She couldn't look beyond the moment when her bell would ring. She never thought once of how she would answer Jim Mackenzie when he spoke to her.

It was between seven and eight in the morning that the bell rang.

Laura's hand was quite steady as she pressed the receiver to her ear. There was a thrumming noise on the wire. The operator said,

"Are you there? Berlin wants you."

Laura said, "I'm here."

Then she heard Jim Mackenzie say, "*Laura.*"

Chapter Six

AFTER THE LAST SOUND of Jim Mackenzie's voice had died away, Laura sat on by the telephone for a long time. She continued to hold the receiver in her hand and to stare fixedly down at the table on which the instrument stood. There were no conscious thoughts in her mind. Everything had come to a dead stop.

Presently Amelia came in. She said, "Oh, Miss Laura!" and sniffed and said, "Oh, Miss Laura!" again. She had been crying and her eyes were red and looked smaller than ever.

Laura had not shed a single tear. When Amelia came in she got up, went into her bedroom, and dressed herself. She was rather slower than usual, but she did all the things that she was accustomed to do. She put on a dark plain dress and then went back into the sitting-room.

Basil Stevens found her sitting in an upright chair with her hands folded in her lap.

"She's not fit to see anyone, unless it was a doctor," said Amelia in the hall. "What's been a-happening to make her look like this? That's what I want to be told."

Basil Stevens turned a hard look on her.

"You had better ask her," he said, and walked past her.

When he had shut the door, he stood looking down at Laura with a frown. Her appearance alarmed him. She looked as if she hardly knew that he was there. He spoke in a loud, abrupt voice.

"Well? Has he rung up? Has Mackenzie rung up?"

Laura had not moved when he came in. She looked past him and said,

"Yes." There was no expression in her voice.

"He rang up from Berlin?"

"Yes."

"Well, that reassures you—doesn't it? I can tell you he's lucky to be alive. So that's all right. And now for our arrangements. Have you packed?"

A light tremor passed over her.

He repeated his question in a raised voice.

She made an effort then and looked at him.

"Why should I pack?"

"Are you proposing to stay here? Have you forgotten that you are marrying me?"

Into Laura's tragic eyes there came a startled look.

"But not really!" she said.

"What do you mean?"

"I couldn't marry you *really*. You know that. You said it was—a matter of business."

"Yes—yes, of course. Don't imagine that I have the least desire to force myself upon you. It's a matter of business. But you can't stay here—you must come away with me."

"Why?" said Laura.

He threw out his hands with one of those sudden gestures of his.

"Do you, then, want to stay here and meet Mackenzie?"

She quivered as if he had struck her, and at once he spoke soothingly, his one concern now to get her through the marriage without a breakdown.

"Come! Don't you see that it will be easier for everyone? I have a house in the country where you can be quiet. You do not want just now to meet people, to answer questions."

Laura shuddered.

She said, "No," and looked down at her clasped hands.

"*Now,*" he said—"have you written to Mackenzie?"

She moved her head slightly,

"You haven't. But I think you must write."

Laura said, "I can't!" He could barely catch the words.

"I will tell you what to say," said Basil Stevens briskly. He pulled her chair round until it faced the writing-table. "I think you must write—it will be kinder to him. Besides, unless he hears it from yourself, he will not believe it."

A frightful pang pierced Laura's numb heart. She had not felt anything for a long time—not since the last sound of Jim's voice had died away; but now for a moment she felt again, Jim trusted her so much that only she herself could kill his trust. That was the last and most dreadful pang.

Basil Stevens patted her shoulder.

"Since it has to be done, it is better to do it quickly."

For the first time there was some kindness in his voice. He was, in fact, sorry for her, and very anxious lest she should collapse and be unable to go through with the marriage. He put a pen in her hand.

"You can make it quite short," he said.

Laura stared down at the block before her.

"There's nothing to say."

"I will tell you what to say. Write, 'I am marrying Basil Stevens to-day at the Chelsea registry office.' Yes, write the date first. There! You see that is quite easy. And now sign your name."

Laura wrote the words: "I am marrying Basil Stevens to-day at the Chelsea registry office." Then she wrote, "Laura"; and whilst Basil Stevens reached for an envelope, she added three shaky words below the signature and turned the page so that he should not see what she had written.

When she had addressed the envelope, Basil Stevens said,

"Now you will write to your aunt. You will say the same thing. It is all that is needed—except that you can say, if you like, that you are hoping to see her when she returns."

Laura wrote mechanically. When she had finished, Basil Stevens rang the bell.

"What have you told your maid?"

"Nothing."

He turned to meet Amelia with a shrug.

"Your mistress is going away. Pack what she will require for a month."

Amelia sniffed.

"Miss Laura!" She sniffed again. "Miss Laura! You're *not* a-going away!"

Laura turned with an effort.

"Yes. Will you pack my things."

Amelia ran to her.

"*Miss Laura*—what's the matter? What's he been a-doing or a-saying to make you like this?"

Laura put her hand to her head.

"I can't talk about it," she said. "Will you pack my things, Amelia. And when Mr Mackenzie comes, will you give him this letter."

Amelia stared at the letter. The tears began to run down her cheeks.

"Oh, Miss Laura!" she said. "What are you a-going to do?"

"I'm going to marry Mr Stevens," said Laura in a distant gentle voice. "Now will you please go and pack my things for me."

Laura Cameron was married to Basil Stevens at a little after noon. He had found it possible to advance the time. When Laura was asked whether she took him for her husband, she remained silent for so long that the registrar repeated the question. He was accustomed to all sorts of brides. Sometimes they blushed, and sometimes they giggled; sometimes they looked happy and sometimes they looked bored; often they appeared to be impenetrably stupid. He was quite accustomed to having to repeat his questions, but as he repeated this one, something stirred in him. Laura was looking past him with a blank lost look which he found disquieting. He coughed, raised his voice, and put his question sharply. This time Laura answered it, her voice quite clear and steady.

It is the easiest thing in the world to be married in a registry office. It needs so few words, so very few words, to swear a life away.

Laura received a marriage certificate, which she put into her handbag. Then she came out of the room and into the street. There was a car waiting there. She got into the car, and as Basil Stevens followed her and shut the door, she leaned back into the corner with a rushing noise in her ears. It was like the rushing of a tremendous sea. She went down into it and it closed over her.

Chapter Seven

JIM MACKENZIE arrived in London at about eleven o'clock on Monday morning. It was one of those days that halt between frost and fog. The gloomy yellow sky appeared to touch the housetops. The air was stinging cold.

Jim rang the bell of the flat, and waited with the most exquisite thrill of anticipation for it to open. To come back to Laura was about the best thing on earth at any time, but to come back to Laura from prison and from the sordid edge of death was something that simply couldn't be put into words. And in four days more they would be married.

The door was slow in opening, slow even after it had begun to move and draw in. Amelia looked round the edge of it with reddened eyes. Something caught Jim Mackenzie by the heart. He had talked to Laura on Friday, and this was Monday. Nothing could have happened since Friday.

"Where's Miss Laura?" he said sharply.

Amelia sniffed, gulped, and opened the door a little wider. He pushed past her into the hall, and the first thing that he saw was an orange envelope on the table.

"Is that my telegram? Where's Miss Laura?"

"I don't know, I'm sure, sir."

He tore open the telegram, looked at it, and threw it down. "Yes, it's mine. Is she out?"

Amelia gave a most rending sniff.

"Went away Friday," she said.

Jim Mackenzie stared.

"*Went away?* What do you mean?"

"Went away Friday," said Amelia, and choked.

A horrid cold feeling began to creep over Jim. There was some mistake. Laura couldn't have gone away when she was expecting him. Not unless—

"She isn't ill?"

"Not as I knows of—but I shouldn't wonder." She had her apron at her eyes now, and the sentence ended on a sob.

Jim put a hand on her shoulder and shook it.

"What's all this? Can't you say?"

Amelia twitched away from him.

"I got a letter for you, sir."

He held out his hand, took the envelope, and after one glance at the writing walked away from her into the sitting-room. He left the door open, and Amelia, fluttering and weeping, saw him go over to the window and open the letter. As he unfolded the paper, he was conscious of bitter disappointment, and behind the disappointment—fear. What could possibly have taken Laura away when he was coming home?

A bleak light fell on what Laura had written. He looked at those few unbelievable words, and his mind rejected them. He went on looking at them in the cold foggy light:

"I am marrying Basil Stevens to-day at the Chelsea registry office." Then her name: "Laura". And written below it, written hastily, three shaky words: "Don't be unhappy."

In some horrible way the words were effecting an entrance into his mind.

He turned abruptly and called to Amelia. The thing was impossible, a stark lie. But then—she must be ill—she must be. He took hold of Amelia by the arm.

"What's all this? Where is she?"

"Oh, sir, I don't know—I don't indeed!"

"But she's gone away."

"Oh yes, sir."

"When?"

"Friday morning, sir, and no address left, only a bank, and the letter for you, which I'd rather have died than give it you, sir—and—and—what *h'ever* come over her, 'eaven knows, for I don't."

"She's—*married*," said Jim Mackenzie.

"If you can call it married—in a registry, and no wedding dress nor nothing."

He said it again as if he had not heard her,

"She's *married*—" Then, very suddenly, "No! My God, no!" And with that he let go of Amelia's arm and went reeling back against the wall.

After a moment he groped for a chair and sat down.

The tears ran down Amelia's cheeks.

"She was trying on her wedding dress when he come, and I hadn't no more than opened the door, when I knew that what he brought with him was trouble for Miss Laura. I hadn't no more than got the door ajar, when I felt it. And when he come in, he brought it with him, and I says to Miss Laura—"

Jim Mackenzie lifted a hand that felt as heavy as lead.

"What are you talking about?"

"Him," said Amelia. "Him that put the trouble on Miss Laura and stole her away, with his registries, and his banks, instead of a lawful address like any honest gentleman would have."

"Basil Stevens—" said Jim Mackenzie slowly.

"I never seen him before. Mr Basil Stevens was the name on the card, and when I took it to Miss Laura, she looks at it and she says, 'But I hardly know him—' just like that she says it. And in two days they was married—and in a registry office, which I wouldn't have believed if the Archbishop of Canterbury had taken his Bible oath on it—no, I wouldn't. And whath'ever Miss Wimborough's a-going to say when she hears, I don't know, but 'eaven help me when she does, for she'll be neither to hold nor to bind."

Jim Mackenzie kept his grey face turned towards her.

"She's—*married*—" he said again.

"I wouldn't go and see it," said Amelia—"not if she'd begged and prayed me, I wouldn't. And she only says, just like she might have said she was a-going to the post, 'I'm a-going to marry Mr Stevens,' she says. And 'eaven knows why I didn't drop."

"You didn't—*see* her married?"

"I couldn't have brung myself to it. But it's no good you a-building on that, for when I'd had my cry out and put her room to rights, I went round to the registry and ast the clerk, I couldn't have faced

Miss Wimborough if I hadn't a-made sure—and 'eaven knows how I'm a-going to face her now. But married they was and gone away in a private car, so the clerk could tell me."

"Why?" said Jim Mackenzie. "Oh, God! Why?"

He was not speaking to Amelia, but she had an answer for him.

"I don't know no more than the babe in h'arms, except that it was something to do with money, sir."

"Money?" he said. *"Money?"*

Amelia sniffed, the sniff of a superior being in grief.

"It's a 'orrible thing for money to come between two loving 'earts—but something to do with money it was, for I 'eard what he said with my own lawful ears." She sniffed again, deprecatingly this time. "I'd scorn to listen at a door, but I was a-folding up Miss Jenny's dress—'er bridesmaid's dress what she'd been a-trying on, and skipped out of the other door when Mr Stevens come in. Well, there I was, in the bedroom, a-shaking of it out and a-folding of it up, and I 'eard him say a gentleman's name, as plain as plain I 'eard it—Mr Bertram Hallingdon—and there's been enough about him in the papers since to make me sure that I didn't make no mistake."

Jim Mackenzie stared at her.

"Bertram Hallingdon?"

"Him that's died and left a mint of money. Well, I 'eard that Stevens say, 'Mr Bertram Hallingdon', and I 'eard him say, 'He's dead.' And I 'eard him say, 'You're his heiress.' And I didn't 'ear no more, because it wasn't my business—and I shouldn't have stayed all these years with Miss Wimborough if I didn't know how to mind my own business and let other folk mind theirs." She went on talking. There were words and there were sniffs, and sometimes there was a sob.

But Jim Mackenzie was not listening. He scarcely knew there was anything to listen to. He sat sunk down in his chair with an elbow on the arm of it and the hand across his eyes. Amelia's plaintive voice went by him, and her many words. He had gone into the secret place which belonged to Laura. It was a place in which he had always found her waiting for him. It was lighted by her eyes and sweetened by her smile. It was romance, and home, and his very heart. When he had waited for death in the Bolshevist prison, he had been able to go into this secret place and find Laura there. He was in it now—and it was empty. It was more dreadful than if Laura had been dead; because if she had been dead, he would still have been able to find her there. She was not dead—she had never been alive. It was all a cheat and a lie. There wasn't any Laura.

He got up out of his chair and walked past Amelia, and so out of the flat. He walked with a most careful steadiness; he even remembered to shut the door. It closed quite gently. There wasn't any Laura. He had shut the door upon the place where she had ceased to be.

Chapter Eight

LAURA DID NOT know how long she had been ill. All the familiar divisions of time had vanished. There was a darkened room, and sometimes a shaded light, and sometimes a cold streak of daylight at the edge of a blind. Sometimes there was a whispering in the room, and sometimes there was a voice that wearied her until she opened her lips and drank what she was told to drink. She did not want to eat, or to drink, or to open her eyes; she wanted to be let alone; she wanted to sink deeper and deeper into the weakness and lethargy in which she was drowning, until they closed over her and blotted her out. Instead, they began to recede, and as they receded, it came to her to wonder where she was. There was more light in the room, but it showed her nothing that she had ever seen before—nothing, and no one. She was in a strange place, and served by strangers. This latter fact was most comforting.

The room had drab walls, but when the light fell on them, you could see that they were not really drab, but covered with a close pattern of little flowers in dingy shades of mauve, and pink, and blue, and green, and yellow. The effect ought to have been gay, but it wasn't; the colours all ran together in a fog. The other things in the room fitted in very well with the paper. The windows had dark green blinds and faded crimson curtains that were not meant to draw; they were just strips of stuff with an edging of woolly balls. There was one strip across the top of each window, and one on either side of it, and the strips at the sides were looped back with crimson cords. There were two windows, and between them a bow-fronted mahogany chest of drawers. Laura's milk, and Laura's Benger, and Laura's beef-tea stood on the top of this chest, and over it there was a framed engraving of Queen Victoria's marriage, with lots and lots of beautiful bridesmaids in flowery wreaths, bare shoulders, and billowing skirts.

On the opposite side of the room there was a gloomy wardrobe and a very large double wash-stand with a marble top, and china patterned with roses as big as peonies and of a most insistent pink.

For a long time Laura couldn't see the carpet. As she came up out of the waters of lethargy, she thought about it vaguely and wondered what it was like. The first time she really saw it, she received a most curious shock. It wasn't at all the sort of carpet that you would expect to find in that sort of room. It had been woven in Persia a very long time ago, and it made Laura think of princesses and bulbuls, and fountains and enchanters, and the scent of attar of roses. It was very old and very much worn, but it had been beautiful, and the ghost of its beauty haunted it. It was as much out of place amongst repp curtains and ball-fringe and brightly patterned china as Laura herself.

The bed in which Laura lay stood facing the wardrobe, with the windows on its right. On the left of the bed was a single upright chair with a cane seat, and a screen covered with crimson repp to match the curtains. Behind the screen was the door, and through the door there came and went the three people who made up Laura's world. Only two of them really counted; for the third was the wooden-faced tow-headed girl who did the room, tearing at the old carpet with a merciless broom and flapping dust off the furniture with a bright yellow duster. She wore a dirty cap and a washed-out print dress that was too tight for her and had split under the arms. She made a surprising amount of noise at the wash-stand without actually breaking anything. She didn't count.

The people who counted were the woman and the man.

The woman was a deft and competent nurse, which was surprising, because she looked more like a *Vogue* fashion-plate—a rather dashed and not quite up to date one, but still a fashion-plate. Her shiny black hair fitted her head like a cap; her eyebrows, plucked to a single line, made a queer pointed arch over very brilliant black eyes. She used a greenish face-powder, an orange lipstick, and some out of the way kind of scent. As Laura got better, the woman puzzled her. She wore such odd clothes—*outré*, elegant garments that had seen better days. Her stockings were sometimes laddered but always silk, and her slender elegant feet trod the floor of Laura's sick-room in rubbed satin slippers. She spoke English, but not the English of an Englishwoman. She made no mistakes, and she had no accent, yet from the very beginning Laura knew that she wasn't English. Laura called her "Nurse," and came to have a secret appreciation of the incongruity.

The man, Laura supposed to be a doctor. He was young, with fair hair inclining to be red, sharp features, and a trick of studying his nails. He came twice a day, looked at her, felt her pulse, conversed in a low voice with the woman, and went away again. What they said trickled past Laura's ears as running sound. She never heard a word she knew; there was just a sound of speech.

Laura began to grow stronger. The tide had turned, and every day it rose a little higher. She was not unhappy. Everything that had happened to her seemed a long way off and a long time ago. Between her and the twenty-five years of her life there was a great gulf fixed. She had passed over the gulf, and all the bridges behind her were broken down. The things that she had done, and said, and thought on the other side of the gulf she would never think, or do, or say again. She had no part in them any more for ever. They were gone; the bridges were broken down. Presently she would begin to live through another twenty-five years. The events, the thoughts, and the feelings which belonged to this new part of her life were hidden from her. She was content that they should be hidden. She did not want to look back, and she did not want to look forward. She stayed in a kind of truce of God—a truce which compelled the complete cessation of thought and feeling. Laura's mind was quiet and quite clear. She knew that she had been torn by feeling, ravaged almost to the point of death. She knew that she would feel again, and that for her, feeling and suffering would go hand in hand; but during this time of illness and convalescence there was a truce in which she neither felt nor suffered.

She began to be propped up in bed. Everything looked different. She could see the carpet, and she could see a great bare bough not a yard away from the left-hand window. On a windy day thin fingering twigs reached towards the pane. Laura used to watch them and wait to hear whether they would tap against it or, just falling short, strain creaking in the wind. She could watch a thing like that for hours—clouds piling up against a shower; or mist gathering, thickening, coming up to the windows and blocking them. She liked to wake in the night and see a star like a bright thought in the black waste places of the sky. She liked to see the cloudwrack hurrying past before the wind.

She never saw Basil Stevens, and no one mentioned his name.

There came a day when the man whom she supposed to be a doctor departed from his usual routine. As a rule, after spending a few minutes beside her bed, he crossed the room, conversed with the woman, and then went away. This time he did not go away. He came to the foot of Laura's bed, frowned a little, and said,

"Well—you're better."

Laura said, "Yes."

She was sitting up in bed with three pillows behind her. There was a fire in the room, but the screen hid it and the air was not very warm. The woman had wrapped Laura in a silk shawl which had been a Christmas present from Agatha Wimborough a year ago. It had a deep amber fringe, and shaded yellow embroideries on an ivory ground. Laura took a special pleasure in the soft feel of the silk and the beautiful delicate work.

The man pressed his lips together for a moment. Then all at once he smiled.

"Do you know who I am?" he asked.

"A doctor?"

"Oh yes. Well, you're not going to need a doctor much longer—but I shan't want to be dismissed when you're well. Trina tells me you don't talk—you don't ask any questions. Why is that?"

A faint smile touched Laura's lips.

"Why should I talk—and what questions should I ask?"

"You might want to know where you are."

"Does it matter?"

"Well, I would rather you thought it mattered," Laura let the heavy fringe slip through her fingers. Its deep colour made them very white.

"You call Trina Nurse, and you call me the doctor—" He paused and then shot at her, "Don't you?"

Laura inclined her head.

"But we've got names of our own, you know." He turned half round. "Come here, *liebchen*—it's time you were presented in form. This is Miss Catherine Werner—called Trina by her friends. And I am Alexander

Stevens—whom my relations call either Alec or Sasha, according to whether they are in an English or a Russian mood. I am a first cousin of Vassili's—of your husband's. Our family is of Russian origin, you know, but we are quite Anglicized. As you are my cousin's wife, I hope I am permitted to call you by your Christian name. We are relations now, and though you won't want a doctor for very much longer, I hope we are going to be very good friends."

He had taken Trina by the arm when he said her name, and continued to hold her lightly, though his eyes never left Laura's face. He saw a little colour come into it, a pale ghost of the rich carnation which had made her beautiful, but she did not speak. Her hand trembled on the amber fringe.

"And still you do not ask me where you are, or why you are here," said Alec Stevens.

Laura shook her head.

"It doesn't matter," she said under her breath.

"And you do not ask me where Vassili is—or do you call him Basil? Doesn't that matter either?"

The colour faded.

"Where—is—he?" said Laura with white lips.

"You didn't really want to know. Don't turn pale like that—there's no need. He's in Paris, and Trina and I are looking after you. Come—we haven't done it so badly—have we?"

Laura's heart quieted again. It had begun to beat in a terrified manner, but now it quieted. Paris was a long way off. The truce held.

When she could speak, she said,

"You've been—very kind."

Trina said something in a low voice. Then she came round and shook up Laura's pillows.

"You have talked quite enough. Sometimes Sasha forgets that he is a doctor—but I remember all the time that I am a nurse. If he doesn't want to make you ill again, he had better leave you to me." Her voice grated a little; it had dark, hard tones in it.

Alec Stevens shrugged his shoulders and went out frowning.

After a few minutes Trina followed him. She came out of Laura's room on to rather a dark landing. Three other doors opened upon it.

A staircase descended from an upper story to one side of it and wound down to the ground floor from the other.

Catherine Werner went down the stair, pushed open the first door she came to, and entered a small room furnished as a study. Alec Stevens looked up from the writing-table as she came in.

"What do you want? I'm busy," he said, speaking English.

Catherine came up to the table. She rested the tips of her fingers on it and looked at him—hard.

"What did you want to talk to her like that for?" she said in Russian.

"Speak English!" said Alec Stevens. "You have improved, but you need all the practice that you can get. Even now you could not pass for English as I do. And you must not only not speak Russian—you mustn't so much as think Russian. Waking or sleeping, there must be nothing but English."

Her expression did not change in the least.

"I asked you a question, Sasha," she said.

"And you are not to call me Sasha."

Trina laughed.

"My dear Alec—I asked you a question. I asked you why you wanted to talk to Laura like that."

Alec Stevens laid down his pen and began to light a cigarette.

"Well, I didn't do it for fun, my dear. I wanted to see how she would react when I mentioned Vassili."

"I thought she was going to faint."

"But she didn't faint. She's much better. I am really quite satisfied— the experiment told me what I wanted to know."

Catherine leaned forward a little.

"I won't have experiments tried on her—she's my patient!"

Alec Stevens blew out a lazy cloud of smoke.

"And mine, *liebchen*."

"It's a dangerous game to pretend to be a doctor."

He inhaled comfortably.

"Where's the danger? She's getting well, isn't she? The whole of Harley Street couldn't do more for her than that. She's getting well like a house on fire. Vassili is in luck—she's a healthy creature as well as a beautiful one. When she gets her colour back, she'll be worth looking at.

Did you see her flush when I startled her? A wonderfully sensitive skin. But I don't suppose she has any temperament. What should you say?"

Trina's eyes flashed black lightnings.

"I should say you had better be careful. Vassili won't stand poaching."

"Bah! He isn't in love with her. She's not his sort—he likes a girl who'll sit on his knee. Besides, he's a long way off—and people who are recalled to Moscow don't always come back. They'll be wanting him before long."

"What do you mean?" she said breathlessly.

He made a gesture with his cigarette.

"Absolutely nothing. What should I mean? I like to score you off— you rise so easily. And there, my dear, I make you a present of two new idioms. You can practise introducing them into conversation. But remember a little idiom goes a long way. Overdo it, and you are the comic foreigner at once."

Catherine sprang back from the table.

"You will laugh at me once too often! Yes, I tell you so! I will not have it! And I will not be kept in the dark and made the catspaw!"

"*A* catspaw, my dear. The use of the definite article is a thing you've got to watch—it's a hopeless giveaway."

Catherine put her hands behind her.

"I keep my temper because I do not choose to compliment you by losing it. No doubt you are seeing how I shall react. Very well then— here I am—and I am warning you that you can go too far. I ask you now, seriously, why are you so interested in Laura's progress? Why do you test her? Has anything happened?"

"The lawyer wants to come down and see her," said Alec Stevens, frowning.

"Her lawyer?"

He laughed.

"He's her lawyer now. He *was* Bertram Hallingdon's lawyer. He wants to come down and see Bertram Hallingdon's heiress—and I want the exact psychological moment for letting him come. If she is too ill, he will not tell her anything, and he may be troublesome and want another opinion. If, on the other hand, she is too well—" He shrugged and made a gesture, "You understand—if there is valuable information going, there is no need that she should be able to take it in, and yet she must not be too obviously unable. And that is what I mean by the exact psychological moment."

"What are you going to do?" said Catherine Werner.

"I am telling Mr Rimington that he can come down to-morrow. You will have to put on that nurse's dress."

"It doesn't suit me."

"And what does that matter? He's not being had down here for you to get off with him, is he? Besides, you look very well in it—I told you so when you tried it on."

She made a face, turned with a flick of her red skirt, and went towards the door. But before she reached it she stopped.

"When is Vassili coming back?" she said.

Alec Stevens blew out a cloud of smoke.

"I don't know, and I don't care," he said.

Chapter Nine

"UNFORTUNATELY, MY COUSIN had to leave his wife almost immediately. He had business in France which could hardly be set aside. As the only possible treatment was a complete rest, it was really better for him to be out of the way. She is progressing very favourably."

Mr Rimington inclined his head.

"I am glad to hear it. And you think she will be able to attend to business?"

Alec Stevens pursed up his lips.

"Well, I hardly know what to say. You will have to judge for yourself. Don't tire her, and don't excite her. I think the nurse had better remain in the room, if you don't mind."

Mr Rimington lifted a large white hand an inch or two from his knee and let it fall again.

"I would rather see her alone," he said in his ridiculously soft voice.

He was a large man with a bald head and strongly marked black eyebrows. Everything about him was large except his voice. His smooth white face had no lines. His heavy white eyelids drooped over eyes of a most peculiar pale blue.

"Well, you'd better come up," said Alec Stevens, and led the way. "The nurse will be handy if you want her. She can wait on the landing."

Mr Rimington made no reply. He appeared to require all his breath for the quite easy ascent.

At the top of the stairs Alec Stevens turned and knocked upon a door. Catherine Werner opened it—but a Catherine who was hardly recognizable in her trim blue uniform and snowy cap and apron.

Alec Stevens led the way round the screen.

"Well," he said, "here is Mr Rimington. And I've told him that he mustn't tire you. You must say at once if you find you are getting tired—Mr Rimington."

Mr Rimington came round the screen and saw Laura in her embroidered shawl propped high against pillows. She made on him an instant and very strong impression. She had been ill, she was recovering, she was a singularly beautiful young woman; but behind and beyond these things there was something else; he did not quite know what it was, but it impressed him. He touched her hand, sat down on the chair between the bed and the screen, and heard Alec Stevens and the nurse go out of the room. He listened for the click of the latch, but the door closed quietly.

Mr Rimington nodded very slightly and turned to the bed.

"I am told that I must not tire you, so I will come to the point as quickly as possible. And as you have been ill, it will be best if I just run over the preliminaries, because, you see, I do not really understand how much you know."

Laura spoke in a soft fluttering voice.

"Dr Stevens said—you were—Mr Hallingdon's solicitor."

"Yes—his solicitor—and one of the executors of his will. I am here in both capacities." He paused, turned his head, and shivered slightly. "Dear me—what a draught! I feel sure that you ought not to be in a draught like this. I wonder if that door is shut." He pushed back his chair as he spoke, and disappeared behind the screen.

The door was not open; on the contrary it was closed. It was closed, but not latched. When a door is closed, it can very easily be pushed ajar; the merest touch will do it. The merest touch will latch it. Mr Rimington applied the flat of a large hand to the middle panel of the door. The latch clicked sharply, and he returned to his seat.

"Well, now we will begin. I am Mr Hallingdon's solicitor. And you are Mr Hallingdon's heiress. You know that?"

"Yes." The word was just audible. She was watching her hands and the amber fringe of her shawl.

"Yes," said Mr Rimington. "I wrote to you. You received the letter, of course?"

Laura did not answer. She heard Vassili Stefanoff's voice saying, "You are Bertram Hallingdon's heiress." She couldn't remember anything at all about a letter. A light shiver ran over her.

Mr Rimington went on speaking.

"I received a reply from Dr Stevens. He said that you had married his cousin, Mr Basil Stevens, and that you were lying ill at this address, with himself and a nurse in charge. He stated that your husband had been obliged to go abroad on urgent business, and he enclosed a copy of your marriage certificate. I take it that all this is correct?"

Very faintly Laura said, "Yes."

"I don't want to tire you, but I suppose you can listen to me for a little?"

He paused and looked at her with a half formed wonder as to whether his words were really reaching her. What kind of intelligence was there behind her pale unmoving features? The beautiful line of the lips did not change. The eyes were hidden by the down-dropped lids whose lashes lay dark upon the colourless cheeks. There was nothing to betray what she thought, or how much she understood.

Mr Rimington frowned and raised his voice.

"Mr Hallingdon was a very rich man." Then, abruptly, "That doesn't interest you?"

Laura's lashes lifted. He saw her eyes, beautiful and most forlornly indifferent.

"Not very much," she said. The line of her lips melted into the merest hint of a smile.

"That," said Mr Rimington, "is because you have been ill. When you are stronger, you will find that wealth has its compensations. Now there's not the slightest necessity for you to worry about anything at present. The will has to be proved, and these legal matters take time. If you want money, it will be at your disposal, but you won't have to trouble yourself about your responsibilities for quite a while to come.

You will, I hope, be completely restored to health before there is any need for me to trouble you with business matters."

A look of relief passed over Laura's face. The truce held. She had not to make any decision or to sign anything. It would be months before she could be called upon to fulfil her pledges.

Mr Rimington was opening an attaché case. He took out of it a long envelope with a bright green seal.

"My reason for coming down here this afternoon was not to trouble you about business, but to hand you this letter at Mr Hallingdon's request. His instructions were that I should give it to you personally as soon as possible after his decease." He laid the envelope on Laura's pale hands, closed the attaché case, and pushed back his chair. "I won't stay now. I hope I haven't tired you."

He touched her cold fingers and said good-bye. Then, as he was going, a thought appeared to strike him, for he turned back again.

"Does your husband expect to be away for long?"

The colour rushed into Laura's cheeks. The beauty which it gave her quite astonished Mr Rimington. It also conveyed a completely false impression to his mind. He had nieces of about Laura's age, and he was very fond of them. He imagined Laura's blush to be a tribute to Mr Basil Stevens, and thought him a singularly fortunate man. He regarded his young client with sympathetic admiration, and it would have required an affidavit to persuade him that her unexpected marriage had been due to anything except the haste of two young people impatiently in love.

He said good-bye again, added his best wishes for a speedy recovery, and left the room completely at his ease.

As soon as the door had closed behind him, Laura moved. The sealed envelope lay on the turned-down sheet, just touching one of her wrists. She moved, took it in her right hand, and looked at it. She saw an ordinary manila envelope heavily sealed with green wax. The seals were towards her. She turned it over and saw her lost name staring at her—Miss Laura Cameron. Something pricked at her heart. She felt a pang that turned her faint. And at the same moment the door of the room opened.

On an impulse which she did not understand, Laura pushed the envelope under the bed-clothes and leaned back with half closed eyes. Afterwards she thought that she had hidden the envelope because she could not endure that anyone else should see that lost name of hers. At the time she did not reason; she merely acted.

Catherine Werner came round the screen.

"Faint?" she said.

Laura made an effort and opened her eyes.

"Not now."

"He has tired you. Men are tiring—except when they are making love. They never know when to stop." She laughed a little. "I suppose he wanted you to sign a lot of papers?"

Laura shook her head.

"No."

"I thought a lawyer always made you sign papers—many papers."

Laura's head moved again.

"You did not sign anything?" said Catherine.

"No."

"Did he leave you any papers to sign?—because I will not have you troubled any more to-day. You can give them to me, and I will put them away until tomorrow."

A faint shade of surprise changed Laura's expression. She lay back upon the raised pillows, with the embroidered shawl spread about her and fallen a little open in front, so that her neck showed and the thin silk of her nightdress. Her hands lay palm upwards on the sheet. She could feel the envelope pressed against her right side. Her elbow held it there, and the bedclothes covered it.

Without any conscious reasoning Laura burnt her boats.

"There won't be any papers to sign until the will is proved," she said; and then, "I'm tired."

"I'll take away one of those pillows," said Catherine.

Laura held the letter close against her. She was glad to lie down, and for more than one reason. If Catherine thought she was going to rest, she would leave her alone. Laura wanted to be alone. She wanted to stop holding back the tears that were burning her eyelids, and to weep away the pain at her heart.

Chapter Ten

WHEN SHE WAS alone, Laura shed some very bitter tears, but after a while they ceased to flow and she fell into a light uneasy sleep. From this she waked with a start, to hear the clock in the lower hall strike three. It had a deep, booming note that left a tremor upon the air. Laura waked, turned a little, and felt the envelope which Mr Rimington had given her. For the first time she wondered what it contained. After a few moments she drew it out and looked at it, leaning on her elbow. What could Mr Hallingdon have had to say to her?

She turned the envelope over, and then, sitting up in bed, she opened it, without breaking the seals, by tearing the other end. There was rather a thick letter inside. She took it out and unfolded it, and as she did so, a smaller envelope fell down upon the fringes of her shawl. It was written in a decided hand upon greyish-blue paper, and it began:

"My dear Laura—"

There was something strange about getting a letter from a dead man whom living she had never known. Bertram Hallingdon was her grandfather's half brother, but he was only a name to her, and a stranger. He was only a name to her, but by a stroke of the pen he had broken her life in two. If he had not made her his heiress, she would have been Laura Mackenzie now—she would be Jim's wife. Perhaps he had signed his will with the very pen which had written, "Dear Laura."

Laura did not think these things consciously. They moved in the desolate places of her mind while she looked at the grey-blue paper and the words which Bertram Hallingdon had written. Then she began to read the letter:

DEAR LAURA,

By the time you read this you will be the head of the Hallingdon combine. Exactly what that means, you will find out by degrees. Put shortly, it involves great wealth, great power, and great responsibilities. I am afraid that I cannot allow you to suppose that it involves great happiness—and I am afraid that you are young enough to expect happiness as a right. My own expectation of personal happiness died nearly fifty years ago. However, I do not wish to force my philosophy on you. You may have a gift for happiness—some people have, and I have known it persist amidst the most untoward conditions.

I am writing this, not to philosophize, but to acquaint you with my reasons for burdening you with the responsibilities which I am about to lay down. The Hallingdon combine is composed of half a dozen firms handling what are commonly called munitions. They are engineering firms; but side by side with the inventions and products of peace they possess the plant, the knowledge, and the formulæ necessary to meet all the requirements of mechanized warfare. I am being as little technical as I can, because I do not wish to confuse you or to distract your attention from the main issue. This I now approach.

I am, and have been for the last thirty years, what is called a pacifist. That is, I believe firmly that no nation can either thrive by war or find any solution of its problems through war. After the Great War I set myself the gigantic task of assembling under a central control as many as possible of those firms whose plant was capable of being turned to the uses of war. The Hallingdon combine is the result, and I am leaving the direction of its policies to you, a young girl. It is a crushing responsibility, but I have my reasons. They are these.

I believe that the interests involved will be safer in the hands of a woman than of a man. I have been observing you carefully for some years. During the last year a weekly report has been submitted to me. I could turn to these reports and tell you just where you were, and what you were doing upon any given day. In addition to these reports, I have observed you myself, though I have taken pains that you should not know it. You resemble very closely both in body and mind my mother—your great-grandmother, who became Laura Cameron. She was the best and sweetest woman whom I have ever known, and in her youth rarely beautiful. I can think of no human being to whom I could more safely entrust the peace of the world—for that is what it comes to. You will have the controlling interest in six companies. You will have the power to appoint a proportion of the directorate. You will have, through interlocking trade relationships, a power and an influence extending far beyond this country. Use it in the cause of peace. I believe in the wisdom of the simple. I believe in the intuition of a good woman. I believe in Laura Cameron's great-granddaughter. If I have misplaced my faith, I shall not know it. But I will not believe that I have misplaced it. I have watched the man whom you are to marry. He has, I believe, the qualities which will make him your complement. Together, I have faith that you will fulfil my hope.

And now you may ask why we have never met. After much thought I decided against any personal contact. I did not wish to be biased by personal affection. In fact, my dear, I decided that it would be very easy to love you—and love is a disturbing factor, to the absence of which I have for many years accustomed myself.

Do not read the enclosure until you are quite alone.

God bless you, Laura.

BERTRAM HALLINGDON.

A faint steady colour came into Laura's cheeks as she read. Something in her rose to meet Bertram Hallingdon's trust. The reference to Jim Mackenzie stabbed deep, but the very pain of it helped to rouse her. Since these great responsibilities were laid upon her, she must carry them; and if she must carry them alone, she would need all her courage and all her strength. At the call, courage and strength began to rise. She had lain prostrate because, having made her sacrifice, there was no more that she could do. She had come to the foot of a frowning wall and there sunk down. Now, with a vehement grating of hinges, a door had opened in the wall, and all at once she was on her feet again and ready to go forward.

She read the letter again, and then, with the enclosure in her hand, looked anxiously at the clock on the chest of drawers. It was twenty past three. Catherine would not come near her till four at the very earliest. Bertram Hallingdon had said that she must read the enclosure when she was alone. She was alone now.

She opened the envelope, and there fell out a small thin packet wrapped in green oiled silk and fastened with a cord and sealing-wax. Laura broke the seal and undid the cord. When she had opened the packet, she found that it contained a small envelope and three sheets of paper folded separately. She picked up the first sheet that came to hand, and found it covered with Bertram Hallingdon's writing. She straightened the sheet and read:

My dear Laura,

When I wrote in the letter which you will have read already that I was leaving the peace of the world in your hands, you probably discounted the statement as a mere picturesque phrase. I used it because I wished to strike your imagination and to set you thinking. But it was more than a phrase. It has a basis in fact.

I am now going to tell you something that has never been public property. During the autumn of 1917 and the early months of 1918 the Government was earnestly seeking for something which would be a decisive factor in bringing the war to an end. To this end a number of confidential experiments were carried out. One series of experiments concerned what was known as the Sanquhar invention. The experiments carried convincing proof that the Sanquhar invention would give to the country employing it an overwhelming and decisive advantage. I do not propose to indicate the nature of this invention. You must take my word for it that the effect would have been staggering. But on the very eve of success a terrible disaster occurred. An explosion took place in which Mr Sanquhar himself, together with his two assistants, several mechanics, and three highly placed officers of the Navy, Army, and Air Force all lost their lives. A fire followed the explosion, wrecking the plant and destroying—as it was believed—Mr Sanquhar's notes, plans, and formulæ. No one survived who possessed sufficient knowledge to enable the invention to be reconstituted. Fresh experiments yielded nothing. A few months later the war ended.

The papers were, however, not destroyed. They were stolen. I have reason to believe that the explosion was designed to cover the theft. After the Armistice they were offered to me for sale in circumstances into which I do not propose to enter. I was, and am, determined that the Sanquhar invention shall not be thrown into the arena where armament contends with armament and each lethal invention provokes another still more deadly. At the same time, I dare not destroy what might prove the salvation of my country in a time of danger. It is inconceivable that this country or the United States of America should ever willingly enter upon another war; but they may be called upon to stand together for peace. The future is to the young. I am leaving the Sanquhar invention to three trustees, of whom you are one. They are all young. Your mother was American, and this fact links you with the United States.

These papers, plans, and formulæ are deposited in a safe the whereabouts of which are known to only one person. This person has also the key of the safe, but has no idea of what it contains. For the moment I will designate this person as Z. Z knows where the safe is, and Z has the key.

Now I come to your part. You are only one of three persons amongst whom I propose to divide the responsibility of deciding whether the Sanquhar invention is ever to be used. You are, in fact, trustees. Each one will receive separately the torn third of a five-pound note. The note entire constitutes an authority which Z will recognize. When this authority is presented, Z will inform whoever presents it of the whereabouts of the safe and will hand over the key. Nothing less than the whole note—that is, the three torn pieces reassembled—will be recognized by Z. Should a crisis arise comparable to the world crisis of 1914, you may confer with the holders of the other thirds. Should you all three be agreed, you may approach the Prime Minister of the day.

Read what follows very carefully.

You, Laura, will know the holders of the other two thirds; but they will not know each other, and they will not know you. The ultimate responsibility therefore lies with you, since without you the divided note cannot be reassembled.

The enclosure marked I will give you Z's identity. The enclosure marked II contains your third of the torn note. The enclosure marked III will give you the names of your co-trustees.

Memorize and instantly destroy enclosures I and III, but preserve enclosure II.

There was no signature.

Laura pushed the letter under the bed-clothes and picked up the first enclosure. It had the figure "I" on the outside and was fastened with a little dab of green wax. She opened it and read:

My housemaid, Eliza Huggins, has been with me for thirty years. She is a very sober, industrious, and honest person.

Laura stared at the words. She turned the paper, and saw the figure I on the back of it. "Enclosure I" was to give her the identity of Z. If words meant anything, Z was Eliza Huggins. Eliza Huggins knew where Bertram Hallingdon's secret safe was, and had the key of it.

Laura laid the paper down and took up the second enclosure. This was an envelope bearing the figure "II" and was sealed like the other. It contained an irregular fragment torn from the middle of a bank-note. She put it back into the envelope and took the enclosure which was to give her the names of her co-trustees.

As she broke the seal, such a tremor passed over her that the paper almost slipped from her hands. She straightened it out, and saw the names, very black on the blue-grey sheet:

James Moiran Mackenzie.

Basil Stevens.

Chapter Eleven

LAURA DID NOT FAINT. She looked at the two names in their unnatural conjunction, and saw them recede to an immense distance and then come rushing back.

James Moiran Mackenzie.

Basil Stevens.

She felt as she might have felt after a blinding lightning flash, or some immeasurable shock of thunder. Nothing in her mind functioned. The names were in front of her, and she was looking at them. Then, as she looked, she saw that there was some more writing—just a faint pencil scribble. She turned the paper towards the wintry afternoon light and read:

I need not introduce Mackenzie. I have a very high opinion
of him. Stevens has been one of my private secretaries for the
past three years.

Laura's mind became quite suddenly very clear. Basil Stevens
had been one of Bertram Hallingdon's secretaries for three years. It
was as Hallingdon's secretary that he had come to know that she was
Hallingdon's heiress. Had he also somehow come to know that he, and
she, and Jim were the three trustees to whom Bertram Hallingdon was
committing the Sanquhar invention? In the clear, cold place where her
thoughts moved, it seemed to Laura that he must have known—known,
or guessed; it did not matter which. He had moved the levers that were
to his hand, and disaster had rushed upon her like a flood, parting
her from Jim. That was all past and gone and done with. She was
Basil Stevens's wife. But she was also Bertram Hallingdon's trustee.
Everything in her lifted to meet the trust.

The first thing that she had to do was to destroy Bertram Hallingdon's
letters and two of the three enclosures. She looked about her. It wasn't
going to be easy. If she burnt those papers, there would be questions to
answer. And yet, what could she do except burn them? She pushed the
envelope containing the torn bank-note under her pillow, gathered all
the other sheets of paper together, and picked up the broken fragments
of sealing-wax, putting them carefully into the manila envelope. Then
she pushed back the bedclothes and sat for a moment on the edge of
her bed. Her legs felt as if she had not used them for a long time. She
steadied herself by the bed-post and stood up.

Catherine kept the matches on the chest of drawers with the spirit-
lamp. From where she stood Laura could see the lamp, and her milk,
and her Benger—but there weren't any matches. She turned to the
wash-stand. There were no matches there either.

Holding on to the side of the bed, she reached its foot. From here
she was able to look round the screen. She saw a part of the room that
she had not seen before—the door, with an odd blue glass handle, and
between the door and the corner of the room the fireplace, with a low
chair standing beside it. Laura's first thought was, "How stupid! Of
course I don't want matches—there's the fire." But in the next moment
she saw that the fire was dead. Catherine had made it up before she left

the room, and the weight of the coal had smothered it. There were three black forbidding lumps of coal on a bed of grey ash. She gave it up. Her eyes searched the mantelpiece, but there were still no matches.

If there weren't any matches, she must manage without. She sat down on the edge of the bed and tore all the sheets of paper as small as possible. The manila envelope was very difficult to tear. There was a clean handkerchief under her pillows. She put all the bits of paper into the handkerchief and made an adventurous crossing from the foot of the bed to the wash-stand. She dipped the handkerchief full of torn-up paper into the water-jug and held it there.

With her first efforts at walking a wave of heat had flowed over her. Her shawl had fallen from her shoulders and lay across the bed. Now as she stood in her thin night-gown dabbling her fingers in icy water, the cold of the fireless room closed about her and she began to shiver. She needed both her hands to squeeze and soften the paper. It seemed to take a long time, for when she opened the handkerchief a little, words were still legible upon the torn fragments. Finally she spread the handkerchief upon the wash-stand and shredded and tore them until they were mere pulp. She had still to get rid of them.

Her feet were like ice now and she was trembling with the cold. She scraped all the paper off the handkerchief and kneaded it into a ball. Then, with the ball in her hand, she made her way to the window. A sash window she could not have opened; but this was a casement, and the latch moved easily at her touch. There came in a stinging breeze and the smell of frost. She looked down, into a garden with a neglected lawn, and beyond the lawn a tangle of evergreens and the tall masts of leafless trees. A heavy cloudy sky hung low, and the dusk was falling. There was no other house in sight.

Laura leaned out as far as she could and threw the paper ball with all her might. It fell amongst the bushes on her left. She drew back panting and shut the window. She was tingling in every limb. Her first feeling of weakness and giddiness was gone. She walked back to the wash-stand, secured the wet handkerchief, and sat down once more on the edge of the bed. This time she pulled her shawl round her.

She had got rid of Bertram Hallingdon's letters. But what in the world was she to do with the envelope containing her third of the torn five-pound note? Basil Stevens had one piece already. She was Basil

Stevens's wife. She was in his house, surrounded by his people. She knew now what he had married her for—not for Bertram Hallingdon's money, though he would use it; and not for a seat on the directorate of Bertram Hallingdon's companies, though he would use that; but for the torn scrap of paper which would help to give him access to the Sanquhar invention. If he could get her piece, he would have two thirds of the note. A terrible light broke upon her. He must never gain possession of her third, for if he did, only Jim Mackenzie and his third would stand between Basil Stevens and the invention.

Her heart beat quickly as she looked towards the head of the bed. There, under the tumbled pillows, was the envelope containing her third—her trust. It must be hidden, and securely hidden, before anyone in this house guessed that it had reached her.

And where was she to hide it? The question asked itself despairingly, and she had no answer. An invalid has no rights and no privacy. She could lock neither her door nor her box—the latter, indeed, had been removed. Her very toilet was assisted by Catherine, to whom each drawer, each shelf, in chest of drawers or wardrobe, was open.

She bent down and felt the under side of the bed, but her fingers touched a mesh of woven wire. She might push the envelope between the wire mesh and the mattress, but she had a settled conviction that if she did so, Catherine would decree that it was high time the mattress was turned and shaken.

She thought of the top of the wardrobe; but she had seen the girl who did the room routing at it with a mop. If she had drawing pins, she might fasten the envelope underneath the chest of drawers; but she had no drawing-pins. She might just as well say, "If I had wings, I would fly."

It came to her then that she must hide the envelope in another room. If suspicion were aroused, it would be this room upon which it would focus. If he thought that she had received the envelope, Basil Stevens would make a very thorough job of searching the room in which it had been delivered to her; but neither he nor anyone else would dream that she had been able unassisted to reach another room and conceal it there. Yesterday she had not been able to raise herself in bed. Even to-day, even a couple of hours ago, she had clung to Catherine's arm whilst she was being propped up.

As she remembered her weakness, Laura trembled. Could she reach another room, find a hiding-place, and retrace her steps? If she fainted or fell, if she failed either to hide the envelope or to get back to her room without being seen, there would be an end of everything. She was surprised at the warm courage with which she knew that she would neither faint nor fail. She took the envelope from under the pillow, caught the long embroidered shawl about her, and opened the door. The amber fringes brushed her cold bare heels.

She looked out upon the unfamiliar landing. She had a vague recollection of having been lifted and carried, but she had not consciously seen any part of the house except the room in which she had been ill. The landing was empty. In the far corner a stair descended from an upper floor, and a yard to her left continued its descent to the hall below. There was a door opposite her own, and two in the right-hand wall. The opposite door was open, disclosing a dim interior. She discerned piled-up boxes, the foot-rail of a bed, and a row of men's boots.

Laura decided that she would not hide the envelope in what was obviously Alec Stevens's room. She turned her attention to the doors on the right. They were both shut. That Catherine's room was next door to hers, Laura knew; and it came to her now that the other room was empty, because Catherine had said, "When you get better, I can move you into the room on the other side of mine—it gets more sun." Catherine wouldn't have said that if the room hadn't been available.

Laura had at first opened a mere crack of the door, but now she widened the opening and stood on the threshold, holding to the jamb and listening. There was not any sound in the house; it was heavily, unnaturally still. It might have stood empty for years. The stillness had a paralysing effect upon Laura. It seemed impossible to break it by moving from the shelter of the doorway. And then she knew that this was the beginning of faintness. With a desperate effort she took her hand from the jamb and made a wavering step forward. The linoleum which covered the landing was cold to her bare feet. She held her shawl together across her breast with the hand that grasped the envelope. One of its sharp corners ran into her. She found a red mark afterwards, but at the time she did not notice it.

She came across the landing to the door beyond Catherine's and opened it. The first thing that she saw was the uncurtained window staring at her. It was nearly dark on this side of the house, but the window was not so dark as the room. It hung on the dusk like the picture of a fog. Laura could see nothing beyond, neither house nor tree, only this pale picture of fog hanging there in the dark. There was something frightening about it.

A little of the light from the landing followed her into the room. It wasn't really so dark when she was well inside. There was a second window, but the blind was down, a dark blind that let nothing past. Laura could make out the shape of the bed on the left of the door, and between the windows the dressing-table, with a faintly glimmering glass. The room felt unused, the air stuffy and cold. She went to the bed and felt beneath it as she had done in her own room. This time she touched canvas, and her heart jumped. The bed had a box-spring mattress, and the under side of it would make the best hiding place she could think of. Nobody turns a box-spring mattress. She could pin the envelope to the under side, and no one would ever think of looking for it there. Only she must have pins. She wanted four pins so as to be able to pin it out quite flat.

She got up and looked about her. The room seemed quite light now that she was more accustomed to it. On the dressing-table, in front of the glimmering mirror, stood a pale, prim pin-cushion. Laura's heart beat as she passed her hand over it. There were three pins and a needle. She pricked her finger on the needle, and was much too thankful to care. Next moment she was kneeling by the bed pinning the envelope to the under side of the box-spring mattress as near the middle of the bed as she could reach. She had pulled herself up to her feet and had almost reached the threshold, when a heavy door banged violently downstairs.

Laura took another step and stopped, shocked with an utter inability to move or think. From the hall below came the sound of Basil Stevens's voice.

She stood, and felt rushing waves of terror break upon her. She could only stand quite rigid and let them break. A thick darkness seemed to have fallen upon the landing, so that she could not see, and she could hear nothing except the drumming of her own pulses.

She did not know how long this lasted, but all at once sight and hearing returned. A light which seemed blindingly bright showed her the landing and the descending stair. Some one had switched on the light outside her room. She could hear voices in the hall—Catherine's voice, Alec's voice. And then Basil Stevens's voice, angry and excited. She found herself running across the landing under that blazing light, and into the safe darkness of her own room.

And then, as she pulled up trembling and panting, she looked back and she saw that she had left the other door open. She couldn't go back and shut it. She must go back and shut it. What you must do you can do. She went back slowly, shut the door, and then came slowly back again. The most terrible moment was when three steps more would take her into safety. If whilst she was taking those three steps, anyone were to begin to come upstairs, she would be seen. She took the three steps, came stumbling into the dark room, and, closing the door, leaned there shaking from head to foot. The closed door shut her off from light and sound again.

A horror of the door opening suddenly to admit Catherine sent Laura groping towards the bed. When her hands touched it, she fell forward half fainting, and it was not until some minutes later that she moved, pulled the bed-clothes about her, and lay cold and spent, yet with a faint triumph at her heart.

Chapter Twelve

VASSILI STEFANOFF came into the house and banged the door behind him. There was nothing of the controlled, rather formal Basil Stevens in his look or manner. He tore off his coat, flung down hat and gloves, and precipitated himself in the direction of the study, demanding, "Sasha!" in loud insistent tones.

The study door opened before he reached it. Alec Stevens appeared in a cloud of cigarette smoke, and from behind him Catherine's voice inquired,

"What is it then—another war?"

Vassili Stefanoff rushed into the room and flung the door to behind him.

Catherine was sunk in a deep chair with her legs crossed. She still wore her nurse's uniform. She waved a cigarette in half mocking greeting and said lazily,

"What! It is only Vassili? I thought at least that a bomb had gone off."

"Am I in time?" said Vassili in a choked voice. "That cursed fog! The instant I received the telegram I started—and we are delayed hours, hours, *hours*! I say, am I in time—am I in time—*am I in time?* A thousand million curses! Will no one tell me whether I am in time or not?"

Alec Stevens had seated himself carelessly on the edge of the writing-table.

"My good Vassili," he said, "pull up your socks! When you are excited, you give yourself away very completely. Do you imagine that at this moment even a half-witted person would take you for an Englishman?" He threw back his head and laughed, showing very even white teeth. *"A thousand million curses!"* He laughed again. *"Learn to swear in English—Basil."*

Vassili rushed forward and took him by the shoulder.

"Dog!" he said.

"Englishmen don't call each other dogs."

Vassili's grasp tightened. Then suddenly he stepped back, his hands fell.

"Will no one tell me if I am too late?" he said in a voice of suppressed fury.

Catherine shrugged her shoulders.

"Too late for what, my dear?"

"The lawyer," said Vassili—"Hallingdon's damned lawyer—that cursed Rimington! Has he been here? Will no one tell me whether he has been here?"

"It's the first time you've asked us," said Catherine.

Vassili rapped out a Russian oath.

"*Has* he been?" he asked.

"He has," said Alec Stevens.

Vassili swore again.

"When?"

"This afternoon."

"When did he go?"

"An hour ago—no, an hour and a half."

Vassili controlled himself. His passion changed to a sort of savage impatience. He kept his voice low.

"Did he see Laura?"

"Of course."

"Alone?"

"He insisted," said Alec Stevens.

"And you let him have his way?" His passion strained at its bonds again.

Alec Stevens shrugged his shoulders.

"You think it would have been wise to give him the impression that Laura was not at liberty to see her solicitor?"

Vassili made an abrupt gesture.

"No—no—of course not! I am distracted! I don't know what I'm saying, Sasha! No—no—you were right. But you've seen her since. What passed between them? Did she tell you?"

"Trina saw her."

All this time Catherine had been lying back in her chair smoking with every appearance of idle ease. Her long dark lashes hid her wary eyes.

Vassili turned on her.

"Well? Why don't you speak? You saw her after Rimington had gone. What did she say? What did you say? How did she look?"

Catherine blew out a cloud of smoke and watched it rise and blur the light of the electric pendant.

"What do you want to know?" she said.

"What she said—whether there were any papers. Did the lawyer bring her any papers?"

"How should I know?" said Catherine Werner.

Alec Stevens watched them both.

"You can answer what I ask! Were there any papers? Did you see any papers?"

"Do you think some one is writing her love-letters? She is pretty enough."

He put a hand on either arm of her chair and, bending down until his face was close to hers, he said in a slow, deadly voice,

"Did you see any papers—any letters?"

"No," said Catherine.

He remained bending over her.

"You saw no papers of any kind?"

"No."

"Why did you not listen?"

"Because he came to the door and shut it. I had left it ajar. You would have been pleased if I had been caught—*hein?*"

He took no notice of the question.

"How long was he there?"

"A few minutes—oh, not more than five."

He straightened up with a jerk.

"That is long enough."

"For what?"

"To give her a letter—papers." He turned and began to pace the room. "I had a man in his office who was to cable. I could have come by air if necessary. Then Sasha was to cable if Rimington made an appointment. I got both cables within an hour, and I had plenty of time—*plenty*. How could I tell that there would be a fog?" He made a wild gesture and flung round upon Catherine. "When you went in afterwards—you did go in—how did she seem?"

"As usual."

"As usual! What is that? Have I been here, that I should know what is her usual?"

Catherine shrugged.

"I left her propped up in bed, and when I went back—there she is, still propped up—she has tilted back her head and shut her eyes—she has the air of being tired. When I ask what Sasha tells me to ask, she says 'No.' 'Has he brought you any papers to sign?'—'No, there are no papers. The will is not proved. There will be no papers till the will is proved.' She has the air of being exhausted. I arrange her pillows, and I leave her to rest."

"You should have searched the bed."

"For what?"

"She has had the letter."

Alec Stevens broke in with an air of cool mockery.

"And still you do not tell us what this letter is, or why it excites you so much. Now if you had given us a little more of your confidence, my dear Basil—you know, really, you should be blaming yourself and not

Trina—" He broke off, and then resumed with a complete change of tone. "So Rimington came down to bring her a letter?"

"Yes—yes—yes!"

"One yes would do. Well? What letter is it? And why does it matter? What is in it?"

"There is a piece of paper in it."

Alec Stevens burst out laughing.

"You don't say so! How original!"

"A torn piece of paper—and it must be found. She has been alone an hour—two hours. She would not destroy it, but she might try to hide it. Can she walk? Can she get out of bed?"

Catherine shook her head.

"She is as weak as a baby. When I lift her up her head swims and she is ready to faint."

Vassili Stefanoff made a gesture of relief.

"Then it cannot be far away. I will go up and see her."

Upstairs Laura lay motionless. The dusk had turned into darkness; she could just see the shape of the window and distinguish the sky from the black wall of her room. The room was very still and very cold. She herself was very cold. She had straightened her night-gown and the bed-clothes. She still wore the embroidered shawl wrapped close about her. She was so tired that she felt as if she were falling down and down and down. Everything that had been happening seemed remote.

When the door opened and the light flashed on, she was shocked back to consciousness. With startled eyes she saw Catherine come round the screen and stand looking at her.

"Well, I have neglected you—but I thought that you would sleep. Have you had a nice rest?"

She did not wait for an answer, but went to the window to draw the curtains across it. Then, turning, she exclaimed,

"Your fire is out! No wonder the room is like ice. Are you cold?"

Laura said "Yes" in a faint voice.

At once her hands were felt and exclaimed over.

"They are like stones! I will get you a hot-water bottle and some tea. Now wait whilst I pull your pillows up a little. And I had better comb your hair. I wish mine would curl of itself like yours. Has anyone ever told you that you have hair like a black mist? It is not fair really, because you would be quite good looking enough without it. There! Now I will tell you that you have another visitor. What will you do, I wonder? Blush, or turn faint? It is Vassili, so you should do one or the other."

Laura did neither. She leaned her head against the freshly piled pillows and set her face in a pale composure.

Catherine laughed, patted her shoulder, and went out swinging the hot-water bottle; and at once Basil Stevens came round the screen.

He was Basil again, not Vassili—a quiet, rather formal person, more like a doctor or a solicitor in his manner than an engineer. He stood at the foot of the bed and said,

"Good afternoon, Laura. I hope you are better."

Laura had thought that she could control herself. She had not known that his presence would instantly bring back all that her illness had blotted out. At the first sound of his voice an agony of loss and longing swept over her. She clenched her hands under the folds of the shawl, and was silent from a sheer inability to speak.

"You are better?" said Basil Stevens.

This time Laura managed a weak "Yes." Looking at her, he wondered if it was true.

He left the foot of the bed and took the chair beside her.

"I understand that you were well enough to see Mr Rimington this afternoon."

Again Laura said, "Yes,"

He went on speaking in a cold business-like manner.

"I am sorry that I was not here. Alec tells me that you are far from fit to attend to business—indeed I can see that for myself. I should be glad to save you as much as possible."

Laura said nothing. Her hidden hands clung together. Her black hair was like a cloud against the pillow. Her black lashes hid her eyes and made her cheeks look even whiter than they were. He had a sudden fear lest she might die and rob him.

He said "*Laura—*" with the impatience of alarm, and the lashes rose a little. "I don't want to trouble you, but I think I ought to know why Mr Rimington came down."

"To—see—me."

"Naturally. But I want to know what passed between you. If he left any papers, I must ask you to show them to me." He smiled slightly. "I can save you a lot of trouble."

She made an effort and said,

"Mr Rimington said there would be no papers until the will was proved."

"No? And yet he brought some papers with him—did he not?"

The lashes sank again.

"I didn't sign—anything."

"No? All papers do not have to be signed. Come, Laura—do not fence with me! He brought you a letter?"

She was silent.

"Did he not bring you a letter?" He leaned forward, dropping and hardening his voice. "Did he not?"

The door opened, and there came in Catherine with a shovelful of red embers. The acrid smell of smoke filled the room. The slammed door, her hurried footsteps, and the sound of the fire being violently stirred and lumps of coal split up came cheerfully into the silence and shattered it.

A black frown brought Basil Stevens's brows together.

Catherine gave the fire a final poke and came round to the far side of the bed.

"That will burn up in a minute," she said—"and I've put on a kettle. Now don't let him tire you. Do you hear that, dear Basil? I do *not* nurse my patients in order that some clumsy man may come and give them a relapse. Yes, frown as much as you like. It does not make you very handsome—but perhaps you do not mind about that—perhaps she loves you for yourself alone. Does she?" She laughed, kissed her hand to Laura, and ran out of the room.

Basil Stevens waited until her footsteps had died away on the stairs. Then he leaned forward again and continued as if there had been no interruption.

"He brought you a letter. Where is it?"

Laura's eyes opened, dark and full.

"I—destroyed it."

He started, and said harshly,

"That is not true!"

Laura closed her eyes again.

"How did you destroy it—how could you destroy it? It is not true! You will tell me what you have done with it—at once!" His hand shot out and fell upon her wrist.

With a violent shudder Laura pulled her hand away.

"Give me the letter!" said Basil Stevens. "Do you hear? Give me the letter with the torn paper in it! Give it to me, I say!" He had sprung from his chair and was bending over her. "You know very well that I must have that letter. Will it do you any good to make me angry? If you give me the letter, I will let you alone." His voice suddenly shook with rage. "*What?* Must I search you for it?"

Laura shrank away from him. The room shook and darkened about her. Through her faintness and confusion she heard the door open again, and Catherine's voice coming from a long way off.

"Now here is your hot-water bottle, and here is your tea. Now you will be warm. And whether Basil has finished talking to you or not, out he goes."

She put down the tray, slipped the bottle into the bed, and became aware that Laura was trembling.

Basil Stevens had resumed his seat. He frowned at her, and she met the frown with a snap of her fingers.

"Out of this room, my dear—and quick! If you do not want to know just what I think of you, be off! I tell you she is fainting. Blockhead! Will it suit you if she dies? Tell me that! Yes, I said *dies*. Yes, that makes you think, does it? Borrow some brains and go on thinking! And get out of this room before I lose my temper! Men are beasts—one knows that— but they needn't be idiots too!"

She shut the door sharply on him, came back to the bed, and slipped her arm round Laura.

"What did he do to you... Nothing? Then I shouldn't cry about it. Drink your tea, silly!.... Oh yes, I won't let him come back—I promise you.... Stay with you? Yes, of course I'll stay with you. I never came across a man yet that knew when he wasn't wanted.... Yes, yes—I've said I'll stay with you, haven't I? And now you'll eat some bread and butter and have another cup of tea."

Chapter Thirteen

Catherine Werner came into the study about an hour later, shut the door behind her, and surveyed Basil Stevens. She had changed into a very tight silk dress of the shade called fuchsia. There was a fine green bloom upon her pale skin, and her lips were the colour of orange-peel. It is safe to assume that she would have scandalized Mr Rimington.

Basil Stevens was at the table writing furiously. He looked up as she came in, wrote a little more, dipped his stylograph unnecessarily, wrote again, and finally flung the pen to the other side of the table.

"Why do you look at me like that?" he inquired angrily.

Catherine's single line of eyebrow made an exaggerated arch.

"A cat may look at a king," she said, separating the words like a child learning to read. "And that, as Sasha would say, is another English idiom. Do you find that I have come on with my English?"

"Why do you look at me like that?" He rapped out an angry oath. "You'd better be careful! You will go too far some day!"

Catherine tilted back her head and laughed.

"You are a fine lord of creation, are you not? Listen to him—so clever, so superior, and with so much tact! Oh, my dear Vassili, you have really too many accomplishments! You are too clever! Now, if I had had to manage this affair—"

"I will *not* be sneered at, I tell you!"

"But who sneers? You shock me, Vassili. I *appreciate*—I *admire*—I say to myself, 'How bold—how dashing!' Now, if I had wanted to find out whether Laura had had a letter, I should not have been bold and dashing like you—oh no!"

"Some people are too clever to live," said Basil Stevens in an unpleasant tone. He pushed back his chair and came round the table. When he was close to her, he took her by the shoulders and held her facing him. "Well now—if you are so clever, you can find that letter. It's got to be found—make no mistake about that."

Catherine snapped her fingers under his nose.

"Got to be found? And you begin by scaring the life out of the girl! Now listen to me! I will not have her scared—and I will not have her made ill again. I'll help you to find the paper if you behave like a rational being, but not otherwise."

His grip relaxed.

"What do you propose?"

"To bring her into the other room. She will jump at it, because I can leave the door open into mine, and that will reassure her—she needs it badly. I can't congratulate you on her feeling for you at present. No, my dear Vassili, you need not glare at me. I am not Laura—I am very tough."

"You want to move her?" he said, frowning.

"I have said so. You will have to help me carry her, but you will be a beast of burden and no more. You are not to speak. I will guarantee that she takes nothing out of the room she leaves, and you may search it until you have found this terribly important letter. That, I think, will be better than frightening her into a seizure."

He let go of her and stepped back.

"Yes," he said—"yes. That is a good plan. The letter must be found. She would not destroy it—no, that would be impossible. And afterwards—"

"What?"

He flared into sudden anger.

"What is that to you?"

Laura was carried over the landing which she had crossed on her own bare feet an hour or two before. Catherine had been quite frank.

"He wants a paper which you have—or which he thinks you have. Why can't you be sensible and let him have it? He is not a good person to get bad with—is that right? Never mind, you will know what I mean. If he wants a thing, he must have it. He is like that. If you make him angry—" She shrugged her shoulders. "You want him to leave you alone, don't you? Very well then, give him the lawyer's letter, and get well in peace."

Laura looked at her with a wide, clear look.

"I can't give it. It wasn't from the lawyer—it was from Mr Hallingdon—and I destroyed it."

"Why?"

"He asked me to."

"How did you destroy it?" said Catherine. She was sitting on the bed, and as she asked the question, she leaned on her hand so that her face came close to Laura's. She saw a bright flush change it.

"Well, my dear—*how?*"

Quite unexpectedly, Laura laughed.

"Don't tell him—and don't scold me. I crawled out of bed and I soaked the pieces of the letter in the water-jug and made them into a ball, and then I got to the window somehow and threw it out. That's why I was so cold."

Catherine pressed her lips together and made an inarticulate sound.

"Well," she said after a moment, "we're going to move you. Shall you like a change of room? He's going to search this one for the letter you say you've destroyed. And I'm going to search you to see you haven't got it on you."

When they carried her into the other room, Laura had a moment of panic. Just this way she had come with the paper that must be hidden, and through this doorway, and so groping to the bed—to this bed where they were laying her now. She kept her eyes shut because she did not dare to meet Catherine's eyes or Vassili's. She kept her lids down and her lips close.

When they went out of the room and shut the door, she drew a long breath of relief and opened her eyes. The mysterious dusk was gone from the room. It was all hard and clear in the light that was over the bed. The blinds were drawn down over both the windows—cream-coloured blinds with a broad edge of string lace. A newly lighted fire burned on her left. The fire-place had bright blue tiles and an overmantel set with looking-glass. In the opposite wall on her right was a door which led into Catherine's room.

Laura lay and looked at this door. It stood for safety and protection. Gratitude welled up in her, and with it hope and a sense of returning strength. She was tired, and presently she would sleep. She would ask Catherine to leave the door open between the rooms.

She lay with her cheek on her hand, and all at once a soft ripple of laughter shook her. She could hear a distant creaking sound from her old room. They were moving the bed, perhaps even the heavy chest of drawers and the wardrobe. She wondered whether they would take the carpet up. Probably. The ripple of laughter came again. She hoped

Vassili was taking up the carpet. And all the time the envelope with the torn scrap of paper in it was pinned under the box-spring mattress on which she lay.

Laura slept all night. The door stood open into Catherine's room. She slept a deep, tranquil, dreamless sleep and woke refreshed.

Chapter Fourteen

THE PAPER BALL that Laura had thrown desperately from her window was found two days later. It would have been found before but for the fact that it had never reached the ground but had lodged in a rhododendron bush.

Vassili Stefanoff spent a couple of hours in an endeavour to extract from the sodden pulp some hint of what Bertram Hallingdon had written. He had it dried to start with, and then, very delicately, he separated fragment from fragment. In almost every instance the writing was a mere smear of ink, with here or there the shape of a letter just discernible. On one fragment the word "war" could be read. Another long-shaped piece actually bore two consecutive words that were legible. He read: "will receive", and looked up frowning as Catherine Werner came in.

"I am busy," he said curtly.

Catherine came round the side of the table.

"Well?" she said. "Do you make anything of it? For my part I think you are wasting your time."

"I am busy," repeated Vassili.

"You are busy about the wrong things. What is wrong with you, my dear, is that you have no psychology. You will spend hours looking at little bits of torn paper through a magnifying glass, but it does not occur to you to spend even half an hour in making friends with your wife. Yet those pieces of paper can tell you nothing, and Laura, if she chose, could tell you all that you want to know."

"Women have been known to lie."

"You think everyone tells lies. You did not believe Laura when she said that she had destroyed the letter. You did not believe that she had made it into a ball and thrown it out of the window. She said she had done this, so of course you did not believe her. It seems that after all she spoke the truth. Now I tell you that Laura will not tell a lie unless she must—and then I do not think that she will tell it very well. I knew quite well that she was telling the truth when she said, 'I have destroyed the letter—I have made it into a ball and thrown it out of the window.' I told you that two days ago. But of course you do not believe me either—it is a weakness of yours. And now that I have told you all this, perhaps you will tell me something."

She was leaning on her hand bending over the table, her face close to his. She lost nothing of the flash of annoyance with which he said,

"What do you want to know?"

"What you are looking for," said Catherine deliberately.

"That is my business."

She lifted her hand from the table and brought it down again sharply.

"Your business! Oh, my dear Vassili—what a very big fool you are! Am I perhaps to see what you are looking for, to have it under my eyes, and not to recognize it just because it is your business?"

He pushed back his chair impatiently.

"I have told you—it is an envelope."

"All this fuss about an envelope—or about what is in it? Why can you not tell me what is in it?"

He frowned at the littered table.

"There is a torn piece of paper in it."

"Oh—a torn piece of paper—" She flicked one of the desiccated scraps with a reddened finger-nail. "Like this?"

He shook his head, frowned more deeply, and then all of a sudden pulled out a pocket-book and, opening it, produced a square folded envelope.

Catherine watched him with a queer veiled eagerness. It lurked behind those long lashes of hers, looked out when Vassili's eyes were on his pocket-book, and was gone when he turned back the flap of the envelope and produced an odd triangular piece of paper.

"That?" she said, and stared at it. She saw a thin white piece of paper with strong black lettering and a torn edge.

Her brows came together.

"What is it?"

"Part of a five-pound note."

"And you think she has another part?"

"Perhaps."

"All this fuss for five pounds?" she said, and laughed.

Vassili said nothing. He slipped the paper back into its envelope and replaced it in the pocket-book, which he then put carefully away into an inner pocket.

"There is no paper like that here," She touched the pieces on the desk, turning them over with her finger.

"No. Leave those pieces alone!"

"Are you sure she had it—a torn piece like yours?"

He banged with his fist on the table. It was the sudden, uncontrolled action of a furious child.

"No, I am not sure! I am sure of nothing—*nothing!* I guess—and when I have guessed, I guess again! I guess that it is she who will have this paper—but I do not know—it may be another person. Sometimes I think that Hallingdon would not put all his eggs into one basket. And then I think, no, it will be she—it must be she—and I go on guessing. I guess that the lawyer will come and see her—and there I guess right, and I make friends with his clerk before I go away, and I give him twenty pounds to send me a cable when Rimington makes any appointment that has to do with the Hallingdon affair. And then, after all, I am late—late—and I am left guessing! The clerk knows only that Rimington took an envelope out of the safe and brought it down with him—a manila envelope—here are the pieces of it." He indicated a little pile of discoloured scraps. "But of the other paper there is no trace. She would not destroy it. But did she have it—or is it still to come? Of all this—" He made a gesture that included the carefully separated shreds of paper. "Of all this that was a long letter I can read only three words." He picked up two of the fragments and set them upon a spade-shaped palm. "Here is the first." He tapped it menacingly. "It says: 'war'. Hallingdon wrote to her of war. That is one word, and again it leaves me guessing. And on this piece"—he tapped the second fragment—"there are two words, and they say: 'will receive'. Now what is it that she is to receive? Is it the paper that we are looking for? If it is, then she has not had it yet—she has only had a letter to tell her that she will receive it."

He dropped the fragments back upon the desk and looked past her with strained, brooding eyes.

Catherine straightened herself with a shrug.

"That seems evident," she said.

He turned his gaze on her then.

"You think that?"

"It is quite plain. If you will take my advice, you will put all this rubbish in the fire and make yourself more agreeable than you have been these last two days."

"What do you mean?"

She snapped her fingers.

"What do I mean? I have already told you that you have no psychology. I advise you to break your magnifying glass and take up psychology instead. Seriously, Vassili—will you tell me that Laura is nothing at all to you but a card that you play in this game of yours?"

"Why should she be?"

Catherine laughed.

"She is young. She is—" she paused—"rather beautiful. Some men might think of her—differently—*some men*." She came suddenly nearer and put a hand on his arm. "You have married her. Why don't you make friends with her—why don't you make love to her?"

"Those are two different things. To be quite frank, women don't interest me as friends, and Laura doesn't interest me as a woman."

Catherine's hand tightened on his arm. It tightened until its pressure was painful.

"She doesn't interest—*you*."

"What do you mean? Look out—you're hurting me!"

She released him with a jerk.

"My dear, you're not the only man in the house."

"*Sasha?*" he said with a staring look of surprise.

Catherine stamped her foot.

"Do you want Sasha to step into your shoes? Anyone would say that you did. He wants very little encouragement—I can tell you that. Do you really not care? No—it is only your wife, and that does not matter. If it were your precious piece of paper, that would be another affair—wouldn't it?" She laughed and walked to the door, but before she reached it she looked over her shoulder with a smile for his angry face. "All this time you have not told me what that paper is. Perhaps, like you, I have been guessing."

With a couple of strides Vassili was beside her. Her hand was already on the door when he caught her by the shoulders and pulled her round.

"And what have you guessed?" he said quite low.

Catherine looked into his dangerous eyes and said lightly between smiling lips,

"The Sanquhar invention."

The door opened and Alec Stevens came into the room. There was a moment of breathless silence. Then Alec Stevens said,

"Are you—rehearsing? Is this a scene from a play?"

Vassili pushed Catherine away. The movement was rough and uncultured in the last degree; his voice and look were those of a peasant as he said,

"I wasn't making love to her!"

Catherine's plucked eyebrows rose in a fantastic arch. She put two fingers to her orange-tinted lips and blew him a kiss.

"Thank you for the compliment, my dear."

Vassili turned upon his cousin.

"I thought you had gone to town."

"I missed the train," said Alec Stevens. "And as I had half an hour to wait, I came back for my stick, which I had forgotten."

"And that is why you came in here?"

Alec nodded.

"I left it over there in the corner."

He crossed the room, took up a stick with a heavy knob which was leaning against the book-case, and came back swinging it.

"When are you coming back?" said Catherine.

"I've no idea. Come and kiss me good-bye at the door."

He slipped an arm about her, walked her into the passage, where he bent to kiss her, called a pleasant good-bye to Vassili, and was gone with a resounding bang of the front door.

Catherine strolled towards the stairs, but before she could reach them Vassili caught her by the arm and pulled her back into the study. He shut the door and put his back against it. Then,

"Where did you hear that?" he said.

"*I?* What have I heard?" said Catherine, laughing a little. She went back as far as the desk and leaned upon it with her two hands. She pointed her foot in its shabby satin slipper and swayed a little with a faint rocking motion.

"Do not pretend to misunderstand me! Where did you hear what you said?"

"But what did I say?"

He lifted his arm in a threatening gesture.

"You said, 'The Sanquhar invention.' Where did you hear that?"

"Oh—the Sanquhar invention?" said Catherine. "Where did I hear it?"

His arm fell again. A dull colour rushed into his face.

"Where did you hear it?"

Catherine burst out laughing.

"Why, I heard it from you."

"You heard it from me?"

She blew him another kiss.

"My dear Vassili—your face! Yes, I heard you say it."

"When?"

"Last night."

He shouted, "That is a lie!" and she took her hands off the table and dropped him the funny broken curtsey which Germans call a *Knix*.

"*Danke schön!*" she said and laughed.

"If you say you heard me speak of the Sanquhar invention last night, I tell you you lie!"

"Don't be rude, my dear! Do you always know what you are saying when you are asleep?"

He stared at her, his flush fading.

"When I am asleep? I spoke of it in my sleep?"

She nodded, watching him.

"And how did you hear what I said? Where were you?"

"I was coming back from my bath. I woke up and I thought I would have a bath—there is always plenty of hot water. That is one thing about this house, there is always hot water."

He struck one hand on the other.

"Can't you keep to the point? You were coming back from your bath?"

"I was coming back from my bath, and when I came by your door it was a little open and I heard you call out."

"Go on—go on!"

She shrugged her shoulders.

"How impatient you are! I pushed open the door, because I thought perhaps you wanted something, and you said quite loud, 'The Sanquhar invention'."

"I said that? You swear it?"

"My dear Vassili, how else should I have heard it? Be rational!"

"What else did I say?"

"Nothing else."

"You are sure?"

"Of course I am sure. You said, 'The Sanquhar invention.' And when I knew you were talking in your sleep I shut the door and came away."

"Did you know what it meant? Had you heard of it before? Had anyone said those words to you before I said them?"

She said, "No," quite seriously.

"Did you think to yourself what it might mean?"

She answered him without any hesitation.

"But of course! I thought—well, I thought that the Sanquhar invention must be on your mind for you to talk about it in your sleep. And I thought perhaps this lost paper that you are looking for everywhere had something to do with it. Has it?"

He came across the room and stood frowning down upon her.

"You must not speak of it! Do you understand?"

"No. Why should I understand, when you have told me nothing?"

"I am not going to tell you anything. Do you understand that you are not to speak of the Sanquhar invention? Do you hear? It is not to be spoken of—not to me—not to Sasha—not to anyone."

"And why?"

He made a contemptuous gesture.

"Women always ask why! In this case I can give you a very good reason. If you speak of it, you will probably not live to speak of it again. That is why—Catherine Alexandrovna."

At this form of address, which so deliberately reminded her of her Russian nationality, Catherine turned pale under the greenish powder which covered her skin. She took a step away from him and put her hand to her head.

"The penalty would be death," he said.

Chapter Fifteen

CATHERINE SAT in the dark and waited. She had heard the big clock in the hall strike twelve, and one; she was waiting to hear it strike two. She had undressed, but she wore a wadded dressing-gown over her pyjamas, and her feet were warm in slippers lined with fleece. She sat by the window with an eider-down tucked round her. In spite of her warm clothing she shivered, and her hands were like ice.

She looked out of the window and could see nothing except the gradations of the dark. The sky was not visible as sky, but it was not so black as the formless blackness of the trees. Catherine knew these for a towering mass of evergreens. They had now the very blackness of night itself. She knew where the wall was, but she could not see it, or trace the stone pillars which supported the heavy door. Behind her, her room had the soft even darkness of an enclosed place.

When she heard the clock downstairs strike two, she rose to her feet, let the eider-down fall upon the floor, and with her hands stretched out before her felt her way to the door which stood open between her room and the one where Laura lay asleep. She stood for a moment on the threshold. The room slept—Laura slept. The air was peaceful, warm, untroubled. She wondered if it was Laura's dream that breathed this calm, untroubled air. She stood on the threshold of the dream, and felt it barred against her.

She closed Laura's door very softly and went out through the door that gave upon the landing. Absolute darkness here—but no dreams.

Catherine walked with light certainty to the head of the stairs and began to descend them. She could hear the clock ticking in the hall. It had a deep, slow, heavy tick that halted a little. The ticking grew louder and louder until she reached the hall.

She was not a yard from the front door, when it opened. She saw the darkness move, a whole black wedge of it. The faintest footfall sounded, and the black wedge moved again. The door shut as soundlessly as it had opened. A little bright pencil of light jabbed at Catherine and went out.

Alec Stevens put a hand on her shoulder and pushed her towards the study; but instead of entering it they went past it and through the baize door. Here he switched on his torch, and they came along a short passage to the kitchen and put on the light.

Catherine sprang into sight—a bizarre, attractive figure in orange pyjamas and a heavy wadded coat of wine-coloured silk belted with green. The slippers which warmed her feet were of scarlet leather worked in gold. She had washed the make-up from her face, and without it her skin had the tones of Chinese ivory. Not a hair of her sleek black head was out of place. She looked like something out of the Arabian Nights, and spoke like any woman whose man has come home late.

"Do you want anything to eat?"

He nodded.

"Presently. We'll talk first."

"Tea or coffee?" said Catherine, putting out cups.

"Oh, tea—and make it strong, I don't really want anything to eat. Brr! It's cold! You know, I wondered when I was half-way here what I was going to do if you hadn't tumbled to my assignation."

"It's not the first time," said Catherine composedly.

"I only had that moment when I kissed you—he was watching us through the door, you know. However, thank heaven you understood what I wanted. I had to see you—and I had to see you without his knowing that I'd seen you."

Catherine put a kettle on the oil stove.

"It won't take long," she said.

"Never mind that! Come here!"

He was sitting on the kitchen table, one leg swinging. When she came to him he locked his hands about her shoulders.

"Now, *liebchen*! What about it?"

She leaned back as far as she could.

"About what, Sasha?"

"About the Sanquhar invention?"

"What do you know about it?" said Catherine.

"I heard you say it, just like that, 'The Sanquhar invention', exactly half a minute before I opened the door. It didn't take me half a minute to decide upon this little rendezvous."

"Why?"

"Because, my love, the Sanquhar invention is a pretty big proposition, and I'd like to know what you know about it, and what Vassili knows about it."

Catherine lifted her eyes and looked him straight in the face.

"Vassili says it is death to know about it," she said in a low, steady voice.

"Oh—Vassili says that. But he is alive, and you are alive—and I am very much alive."

Catherine leaned forward.

"What do you know? Tell me."

"Ladies first," said Alec Stevens. "How do you come to know that there is, or was, such a thing as the Sanquhar invention?"

She leaned against him and spoke in a rapid undertone.

"I'll tell you. Last night, in the middle of the night, I felt that if I did not have a hot bath, I should die—*you* know. And when I was coming back, there was Vassili's door a little open, and I heard him call out, so I went to see if anything was the matter, and he was talking in his sleep. And that is what he said—'The Sanquhar invention'."

"In his *sleep*?" said Alec Stevens.

Catherine nodded.

His arms dropped. He had been holding her lightly; now he set his hands on the table and leaned back so as to get the light upon her face.

"He said it in his sleep? In his sleep? Did he say anything else?"

"*He* asked me that," said Catherine composedly.

"And what did you say?"

"I said no—to him."

"And to me?"

"Yes—yes—*yes!*" The words came with a sudden eagerness.

Alec Stevens sat up.

"What did he say? Take your time and be accurate."

She nodded.

"He said first, 'The Sanquhar invention'—like that. Then, whilst I waited to see if he would say any more, he began to speak very quickly, the words all tumbling over themselves, and he said, 'It must be somewhere. Look, look, look, look, look! Go on looking! We must find it. If she has it, we must find it—if she has it.' Then he stopped for a moment. And then he said, not so quickly, 'I have told you—a square envelope, and it is inside—Hallingdon put it there. A square envelope—the torn note—Laura—Hallingdon.' And then he began to mutter. I was just going, when he said very loud, 'Two pieces—three—four—how do I know?' That was all."

He made her say it over again, and she never varied a word. He wrote down the words as she said them. Afterwards he looked at them, frowning.

"Two pieces—three—four—what does he mean by that?"

Catherine spoke quickly.

"He has one piece himself in a square envelope—he showed it to me. What he is looking for is another piece to fit on to it. I think—I think he does not know how many pieces there are."

"He showed it to you? What is it like? Describe it."

Catherine held up her hands and indicated a size.

"Like this. It is a piece of a five-pound note, and there is one side torn, like when you tear something into bits."

"A note! Did you see the back? Was there writing on it?"

"No."

"You are *sure*? No figures? Nothing like a formula?"

She shook her head.

"No—no—nothing at all."

He fell into a silence, staring at the notes he had taken. In a little he burst out.

"If there was no writing on the note, it couldn't be the formula of the Sanquhar invention. That wouldn't be a matter of two, or three, or four bits, but of a whole pile. The note must be a clue to where the papers are—the key of a hiding-place. And Vassili has one part, and he thinks that Laura has one part, and he thinks that there may be another part, or parts, but he is not sure. The parts are of no use by themselves, but if anyone can put them together, he will get the Sanquhar invention. That is what I make of these things."

Catherine nodded.

"What is the Sanquhar invention?" she said.

Alec Stevens moved her out of his way and got down from the table.

"My dear, you had better not know."

"I wish to know."

"Your kettle is boiling."

She made the tea and set it to draw.

"Sasha—what is the Sanquhar invention?"

He threw back his head and laughed.

"Vassili says it is death."

Catherine took up a knife and began to cut a lemon.

"And you say that we are all alive," she remarked.

He came up to the tray and poured himself out a cup of tea.

"It is at least dangerous stuff, *liebchen*, and you'd better leave it alone."

Catherine put lemon into his cup.

"What is the Sanquhar invention?" she said.

Alec Stevens sipped his tea.

"I can't tell you because I don't know. Nothing makes one so discreet as not knowing."

"Tell me what you know," said Catherine.

"Yes, I suppose I had better. You mustn't blunder though. You must keep your head and remember just where you are with Vassili—*and* with Laura."

"That is easy. With Laura I know nothing—with Vassili only what I have told you. Now what do *you* know?"

He drained his cup and set it down.

"I don't know very much. Vassili knows more—I would like to know as much as he does. But I will tell you what I know. In 1918 this Sanquhar was making experiments for the British Government—I believe he had had a stupendous success. Then there was an explosion and everybody was killed. Do you understand? *Everybody*. The War Office experts who were witnessing the experiment, and Sanquhar, and all his assistants—they were all wiped out. No one remained who knew anything, and all the papers were supposed to have been destroyed. As a matter of fact the explosion was arranged by our people, and the papers had already been removed. But here's the rub—they disappeared. The agent who removed them disappeared. It was believed at the time that he had been fool enough to get caught by the explosion. Our people wiped the whole thing off the slate. And then three years ago—" He stopped. "Give me some more tea."

Catherine took the cup with a steady hand, filled it, added lemon, and gave it back to him. Then she said,

"Three years ago?"

He hesitated.

"Three years ago—well, you are *not* to know this, Trina—three years ago when I was in Chicago I met this man. I will not tell you his name. He is dead now. He was dying when I found him. He had been shot in a quarrel, and he told me his name because he wanted me to send money to his mother. He had plenty of money—too much. I remembered the old story, and I pressed him about this money. Well, he knew he was dying, and he told me. He took the papers about the Sanquhar invention out of the safe, and he hid them—to make his own profit. He hid them, and he hid himself. Then the Armistice came before he could make his bargain, and he sold the papers to the head of the Hallingdon combine—to Mr Bertram Hallingdon. I reported what he told me, and our dear Vassili became Mr Hallingdon's secretary. And now, my dear, you know as much as I do, and I'd better be getting along. I've got to think this over. I think Bertram Hallingdon had taken some pretty elaborate steps to prevent the Sanquhar invention getting into what he would consider the wrong hands." He broke off with a laugh. "What I want to know is, where do I come in? It seems to me that Vassili is getting more than his share. He gets Laura, and Laura's money; and now he's in a fair way to get the Sanquhar invention too. Do you know, it almost seems to me as if Vassili was getting more than is good for him." He smiled at Catherine pleasantly, and his eyes were bright.

"What are you going to do?" said Catherine. Her voice had a disturbed sound.

"Think things over," said Alec Stevens. "I think very well in a car. Go back to bed—and mind you don't make a noise."

Catherine washed the tea-things and put them carefully away before she went upstairs. She left everything in darkness and went slowly up the dark stair. She was tired and she was cold, and in the depths of her heart she was afraid. She went into her own room and opened the connecting door. Again that curious sense of peace came to her from the room where Laura slept. She could not enter this peace, but she was deeply aware of it. She got into bed, and fell into an uneasy sleep.

In the next room Laura lay dreaming a long strange dream. She had slept and wakened, and slept again and dreamed. She thought she was on a very wide and desolate moor in the hour between dusk and darkness. For as far as she could see there was no end to the moor. It climbed by a rough and precipitous ascent to some distant ridge as yet quite hidden from her, and as she climbed, she heard a great wind driving up behind her with a sound like all the winds of the world blowing together. It passed her with an unimaginable roar, and it beat upon the moor until a spark kindled there and was blown into a wide, tremendous sea of flame, and the voice of the fire joined the voice of the wind. But Laura walked on. Her feet were set on a straight pale path of light. It lay across the darkness of the moor like the track which the moon lays across the sea. It lay across the violent shock of the wind, and was not broken; and it lay across the devouring flame, and it was not consumed. As long as Laura walked upon it she was safe. She thought that her wedding veil was wrapped about her, and that the hem of it blew out against the fire. She put out her hand and caught it back again. The flame licked her hand and came up over her head like a golden tree that dropped sparks instead of leaves, but she was not afraid. She walked on her appointed path. There was a deep calm in her heart.

Chapter Sixteen

"I THOUGHT it was broken, but Sasha had the bright thought that it might be only the battery that was run down, so I went into the town this morning and here we are. It plays. See!"

Catherine put down a rather battered-looking portable wireless set upon the foot of Laura's bed and tapped the lid encouragingly.

"I got Paris just now. Some one was singing *Ciri biri bin*. It made me feel homesick."

"Is Paris your home?" said Laura.

Catherine sat down on the bed and began to twist the box this way and that.

"I have no home," she said. "Sasha would say that a sensible woman doesn't want one. In Russia there are to be no homes any more—they are individualistic and anti-Social." She broke off with a faint mocking laugh and said, "I was happy in Paris—once."

"Only once?" said Laura.

She was dressed for the first time and sitting in an old-fashioned basket chair with red padded cushions. It felt strange to be up. Her illness seemed to have set years between this afternoon and the last time that she had worn this dull blue jumper and skirt. They had come here in her box, and Catherine had warmed them at the fire and given them to her to put on. It seemed so long since she had worn them last that she could not help a queer recurrent feeling of surprise that they should still be in existence. It was like suddenly finding oneself dressed in the things one had worn at school. The jumper was very soft and comfortable. It had a little red and black and green embroidery at the wrists and down the front. She felt glad that it had come across the gulf with her.

A very faint, thin sound of music touched the silence. This too seemed to come from across a gulf.

"Some people are never happy at all," said Catherine. "Personal happiness is a mirage—you hope for it, you follow it, and you find yourself in a bog, my dear. There—that was Paris then. Well, I will leave it for you to play with. Vassili wants me to take the car down for petrol." She flung out her hand in a gesture. "I was in the town this morning and he said nothing, so I must go back. He has his nose in a report, or a letter, or a something—I do not know what—so it is Trina who has to go. My dear, I tell you it is a bad thing to be good-natured. I have a cousin who has such a bad temper that everyone spoils her. They speak softly, they never contradict, they run to do what she wants—and all because they must keep her in a good temper. Once long ago she was ill, and her doctor said, 'Do all that she wants—do not cross her.'" She stood up and stretched with her hands above her head. "Eh, my dear—what a convenient prescription! Anna has gone on having it made up ever since. I think I will have an illness and send for her doctor."

She lifted the small table beside the bed, put it by Laura's chair, and set the wireless down upon it.

"There—now you can reach it. I will be as quick as I can."

When she was gone, Laura began to move the controls. The set was one she did not know. She lost Paris, and could get nothing else. Then she remembered that a portable has to face in the right direction, and she pushed it this way and that. Where was Daventry? She stopped with her hand on the set. Where was *she*? For the first time it occurred to her that she did not know where she was. A sort of tingling shock passed over her. It was rather like being struck by a gust of wind. She had never asked where she was, and no one had told her.

She got up out of her chair and went to the nearer of the two windows. The house stood within a walled garden. She could see the gate from where she stood, a heavy wooden door between stone pillars. Dense evergreens masked the wall and hid the road beyond. There was no other house to be seen. Clearly, she was not in London. But except for that one fact the window told her nothing.

She stood still, looking out at the grey sky and the wet trees. She remembered writing to her bank and telling them to forward letters—but if she had done that, she must have given them an address. But she hadn't ever known the address, so she couldn't have given it to the bank. Her right hand closed hard upon itself as she made herself look back to her wedding day. She had signed a letter to the bank. Yes—but she hadn't written it. Basil Stevens—Vassili Stefanoff had written it, and she had signed what he had written. She looked back and saw herself signing the letter. There was a sheet of blotting-paper across it; she had neither known nor cared what she was signing. She must have given an address to the bank, because yesterday there had been a letter from Agatha Wimborough. A tremor passed over Laura as the words of the letter came pouring back into her mind—hot stinging floods of words. Agatha reproached, questioned, and demanded. Would Laura kindly explain her outrageous conduct—and *personally and without an instant's delay*?

An interview with Agatha would indeed be the last straw. Laura would have walked barefoot to the North Pole to avoid it. To stand in that torrent of words, to have every bruised place battered with questions—it was beyond her. She, who had never minded what Agatha said, now minded so much that she wondered whether any lapse of time would make it possible for them to meet. She had written in the fewest possible words to defer a meeting.

Her thoughts went from the inside of the letter to the envelope. Agatha must have written to the bank, and the bank must have forwarded the letter. Letter and envelope were both burnt. But she must have seen the envelope; and if she had seen it, she must have seen the address. Then all at once she had a little picture of it in her mind. There was the grey envelope, of the kind that Agatha always used; and there was the unfamiliar name, Mrs Basil Stevens. Well, if she could see that, she could see the address. But she couldn't. Why couldn't she? Because the address was blotted out. The picture completed itself—Mrs Basil Stevens, and then three rows of heavy black criss-cross lines.

She drew a long breath. So that was it—they didn't mean her to know where she was.

She stood quite still, thinking. She was not frightened. Things did not frighten her now. What was it that Catherine had said? "Personal happiness is a mirage." Well, hers was gone. But there were other things. She had to keep faith with old Bertram Hallingdon, who had trusted her with his fortune and with the secret of the Sanquhar invention. Strength and courage flowed into her. She meant to justify his faith.

The secret of the Sanquhar invention weighed heavily. Bertram Hallingdon's old servant, Eliza Huggins, knew where the papers were. To protect them, Hallingdon had devised an authority which Eliza would recognize. This authority was a five-pound note. He had torn the note into three pieces and given one part to Jim Mackenzie, one to Basil Stevens, and the third to Laura Cameron. Neither Jim nor Vassili was to know where the other pieces were. Only Laura was to know that. And Eliza Huggins would only give up the whereabouts of the papers to the person who could produce the complete note. Well, Laura had her piece, and so far she had it safe; but it could not remain pinned to the under side of her box-spring mattress indefinitely. Bertram Hallingdon's carefully devised plan had already broken down in one respect. Only Laura was to know who held the three pieces, but Vassili knew or guessed where two of them were. He had his own, and he knew, or guessed, that Laura had another. It was really vitally necessary to put this piece out of his reach.

All Laura's indifference was gone. She was full of a desire to know and to act. She wanted to know where she was. She wanted to see Mr Rimington again. If she saw him, she could give him the envelope with the torn fragment in it, and he could put it away in his safe or take it to the bank for her.

She began to think of an excuse for asking to see Mr Rimington, and the name of Eliza Huggins came into her mind. She could say that Mr Hallingdon had mentioned his old servant. She could ask what was being done about the servants. They couldn't prevent her seeing her lawyer. Or could they? She would have to see him—at least she thought so—before the will could be proved. No, not unless she was an executor. She remembered that she did not know who Bertram Hallingdon's executors were.

She turned from the window and went back to her chair. As she passed the table, she brushed against the wireless set, swinging it round. A long-drawn note came wailing into the room, and then a girl's voice—singing:

"Featherbeds are soft,
And painted rooms are bonny;
But I would leave them all
To go with my love Johnny."

Laura touched the chair with her knee. She sat down quickly. The voice went on:

"I know where I'm going,
And I know who's going with me.
I know who I love,
But the dear knows who I'll marry."

It was a slow and mourning voice, and a violin mourned with it.

Laura put up her hand blindly and felt for the switch. With a click the music stopped. She could shut it off with a touch of her hand, but it went echoing, echoing in her mind:

"I know who I love—"

She loved Jim, and she had given him back his life because she loved him. She loved Jim, and she had struck him to the heart. Her own heart said, "He would rather have died;" and something cold and far away said, "How do you know?" She stared into the fire, and did not hear a knock upon the door. It was repeated, and Basil Stevens came into the room.

Chapter Seventeen

LAURA TURNED at the second knock and saw Vassili just inside the door. She had known him as Basil Stevens, but she never thought of him now except as Vassili Stefanoff. As she turned, he spoke.

"May I come in? I want to talk to you."

Since he was already in, there was nothing to be said.

He crossed the foot of the bed and took a chair on the other side of the hearth. As he faced the windows, the grey afternoon light gave Laura every change in his expression, whilst she herself was in shadow. She set an elbow on the padded arm of her chair and leaned her head upon her hand. He was saying that he was glad that she was better. She said, "Thank you," very gravely, and watched him from under her hand.

He had returned to the formal manner which made him seem like some official. He sat rather stiffly upon an upright chair and spoke without looking at her directly,

"Now that you are better, there are some business matters which ought to be attended to."

Laura said nothing. This conversation was his affair, and these matters of business his. She waited.

He made a jerky movement with one hand.

"I want you to write a short letter to Mr Rimington. Are you able for that? If not, I will write the letter and you can sign it—but it would be better if you could do it yourself."

"What do you want me to say?"

"I want you to say that you are better, and that you are going away for a change."

"Where am I going?" said Laura with direct simplicity.

"We are going abroad. I think that you require a complete change. We shall be moving about, so you will give him the address of my agent in Paris."

Laura remained silent for a full minute. Then she said,

"I do not wish to leave England."

His brows drew together above the bright hazel eyes.

"We can discuss that presently—it is beside the question. What I want is that he should send you any papers that are in his care for you."

"What papers?"

His frown deepened.

"He brought you a letter from Mr Hallingdon the other day. Ask him if he has any other instructions for you—any other papers left to you by Mr Hallingdon. If he has anything, ask him to send it at once."

She waited again before answering. This time she said,

"Why?"

The formal manner vanished. A vehement hand struck his knee.

"Because I say so! Because it is part of your bargain!"

Laura lifted her head.

"I don't remember promising to let you have Mr Hallingdon's private papers."

"You do not? Then what did you promise?"

"I promised to marry you," she said steadily. "And I promised to nominate you as a director of Mr Hallingdon's companies. I will do what I promised, but I won't do anything more."

"Won't?" said Vassili in a low, dangerous voice. He got up out of his chair, and stood over her. "*Won't!* Do you think you can say that to me?"

"I won't write to Mr Rimington," she said.

Then in a moment he had her by the shoulders and had pulled her to her feet. There was such an iron strength in his hands that she could not move at all.

"You *won't?*" he repeated. "You won't write to Mr Rimington? You won't keep your bargain?"

"It's not in my bargain."

He lifted her clean off her feet, held her like that for a moment, and then put her down again.

"I am stronger than you thought. You had better take care. You have made a business bargain, and I am keeping my part. But if you break yours, Laura—if you break yours—why, then there is no bargain any more, because you will have broken it. And if there is no bargain— shall I tell you how you will stand? You will be my wife, Laura—just my wife. Do you want to be my wife, Laura?"

Laura turned faint. The pressure of his hands upon either side of her upper arm was bruising and intolerable. He thrust his face close to hers, and it was the face of a brutal peasant. The Tartar looked at her out of furious gloating eyes. She wrenched blindly away, and he let her go with a laugh.

"Think it over! Think it over, Laura! You can have it whichever way you like."

Laura had gone back unsteadily until she touched the foot of the bed. She leaned against it now and tried to control the tremor in her limbs.

Vassili stood on the hearth and watched her. He did not want her to faint or to have hysterics. He didn't want her at all, and never would. He wanted the torn piece of a five-pound note which he believed Bertram Hallingdon had left her. He wanted the Sanquhar invention, and if he could frighten her into giving it to him, he would have no scruple about doing so.

"Come back to your chair and sit down!" he said. "I won't touch you. I want you to realize your position. You are my wife, and I have certain rights over you. Well, I am prepared to waive them if you will allow me to supervise your business affairs. I will give you full personal liberty in return for business control. Do you understand? I will keep my part of the bargain if you will keep yours."

Laura came back to her chair, moving slowly and rather stiffly. She was trying desperately to clear her mind, to think. If she wrote this letter to Mr Rimington, could it do any harm? She did not think it could—she had already received and destroyed Bertram Hallingdon's instructions. The torn piece of the five-pound note which was the key to the Sanquhar invention was safely hidden. A moment ago, when she had leaned against the bed, it had been within a couple of feet of the hand which she pressed down upon the coverlet. She didn't see how it could do any harm if she were to write to Mr Rimington. She relaxed suddenly, leaned back, and said,

"Very well."

"You will write?"

"Yes."

"Then you had better do it at once."

He fetched a pen and block, laid a pillow across her knees for her to write on, and with a resumption of his official manner dictated what she was to say.

She wrote: "Dear Mr Rimington," and he stopped her.

"Your hand is shaking. That will not do."

Laura laid down the pen. He was looking at her reprovingly; he might have been a schoolmaster.

"Why are you so foolish? This hand shaking—this fainting—this getting ill—it is all most unnecessary. Get it into your head that this is a matter of business, and we shall get along very well. I do not wish to alarm you, I do not even wish to make love to you. As I said before, you do not really attract me. All I wish is to have a free hand in certain matters of business. Has your hand stopped shaking? Tear off that sheet and take another! Now begin!"

Laura looked up at him, oddly reassured.

"I don't know the address," she said.

He frowned.

"There is no need for you to know the address. You will write the date, and then you will begin, 'Dear Mr Rimington—'"

This time the letter was written. Laura informed Mr Rimington that she was better, and that they were going abroad as her husband wished her to escape the rest of the winter. She requested him to send all letters to an address in Paris. The last sentence of the letter ran: "If Mr Hallingdon left any papers that he wished me to have, or any written instructions, I am now quite well enough to attend to business and should like to have them sent to me without further delay." She signed herself, "Yours sincerely, Laura Stevens."

There was only the very slightest possible check between the Christian name and the unfamiliar surname. The pen wrote on quite steadily and legibly. Yet in that moment Laura's pride was stabbed to the quick. She had sold herself into slavery—she was a bondwoman, and she had just heard the crack of the whip. She wrote her owner's name and blotted it. She wasn't Laura Cameron any more. She looked at her new signature, and saw it dazzle and blur.

Chapter Eighteen

"THAT IS THE END of the second news bulletin, and stations will now give their own announcements."

Catherine rose to her feet and stretched herself.

"Shall I switch it off?" she said.

Laura was in bed, with the wireless set on the table by her side. The shaded lamp above the bed threw a warm circle of light upon the pillow and upon her left shoulder, which was covered by the embroidered shawl. The fringe gave back the light in a glow of golden amber. Above all this rich colour Laura's skin had a pale transparency which threw the blackness of her lashes and of her cloudy hair into strong relief—amber, and ivory, and that dusky shadowy hair. Her eyes had been closed, but at Catherine's question they opened a little blankly, as if she had been dreaming. She said,

"No."

Catherine laughed.

"You want to listen to shipping forecasts, and fat stock prices, and the New York stock exchange? Very well, my dear, you shall have them all to yourself whilst I go and write my letters. There is a talk presently—it does not say by whom, but it will be about unemployment, or debt settlement, or trade depression, or something else that is gay like that. So I will write my letters, and you shall tell me afterwards how soon we shall all be bankrupt."

She went out of the room, and Laura laid her head back against the pillow and heard all over again about the large depression that was approaching our western seaboard, and just how many kinds of unpleasant weather it was likely to bring with it. She was listening with a mechanical and forced attention. It gave her an extraordinary relief to hear the steady voice discoursing of things which had not the remotest connection with the tangle of thought and motive, the actions and interactions, which filled her mind. If she was listening to the probabilities of a gale in the Hebrides, she was not, for that space of time, calling herself a coward for having written at Vassili's dictation to Mr Rimington. She dreaded the moment when Catherine would put out the light and leave her alone in the dark to think.

Even whilst she followed the announcer's voice she was aware of an under-current of other voices. It was like another station coming through; but these voices were from within, from her heart and conscience. Abroad—she had written to Mr Rimington to say they were going abroad. Would he let her go without seeing her? Would Vassili let him see her? Would he be able to prevent him? Were they really going abroad? Why? *Why?* Dreadful to be a stranger in a strange land, with Vassili to say do this, or do that. Dreadful to be Laura Stevens— no, Stefanoff—Stefanova—Laura Stefanova—that was what she was really—Vassili Stefanoff's wife.

"That concludes the announcements, and the topical talk will follow immediately."

The voices began to come through again. If Vassili took her abroad, what was she going to do with the torn piece of the five-pound note which was the key to the Sanquhar invention? Vassili had one piece, and she had one piece, and Jim Mackenzie had one piece—and the three pieces put together were the key to the Sanquhar invention. And she knew where the three pieces were. And Vassili knew about his own piece, and guessed about hers. Did he guess about Jim's piece too? If he did, Jim ought to be warned—and how could she warn him?

The announcer was speaking again.

"Our talk to-night is on 'Twenty Years of Invention', and it will be given by Mr James Mackenzie, who is himself one of our rising inventors. Mr James Mackenzie."

Laura sat up with a strange quivering movement as if she had been struck. Her outstretched hand just failed to reach the loud-speaker. Jim's voice came from it quite quietly and naturally. He said, "Good evening," and the vibration tingled against the palm of her hand.

"'Twenty Years of Invention' gives me rather a large field to cover—"

Laura's heart began to beat so violently that she could hear nothing else. The sound of it drowned Jim's voice. Presently she found herself with her hands pressed hard against her breast, listening, listening, whilst that loud beating died down and Jim's voice filled her ears. After the first shock there came a rush of emotion. For a moment her mind swung back. He was speaking to her from Berlin, telling her that he was out of Russia, safe. Well, she had saved him—yes, she had done that— and the price that she had to pay was that he would never speak to her again. A most terrible wave of home-sickness broke against her heart. Just to see him—to tell him why she had let him down. Just to feel his arms round her once, and to hear him say her name. It couldn't be; she knew that. But if it could—if it only could....

When Catherine came back into the room she found silence and darkness there. The firelight made a little glow on the hearth. The bed was a grey blur. She stood hesitating, and then put up her hand to the switch, and at once Laura spoke in a kind of breathless whisper.

"Don't put on the light."

Catherine hesitated.

"I'd have been up before, but Vassili telephoned."

A pause. Then Laura said,

"Vassili telephoned?"

"Yes."

"I didn't know he was out," said Laura, still in that breathless dry whisper.

Catherine laughed.

"We talk of him so much—don't we? After he saw you he had the sudden idea that he would go to town. Or perhaps it was not sudden, perhaps he had already thought of it when he sent me to fill up—I do not know."

Laura thought, "He has taken my letter to town. It's gone—I can't call it back. I've been a coward." She said aloud,

"Why did he telephone?"

"To say he would be late—perhaps he would not be back to-night. He need not have troubled. I do not expect him until he arrives, ever. And you—I do not think it would have given you a bad night—eh, my dear? Well, we are two alone women—or three, if you can count that lump of a girl upstairs, who would go on sleeping if we all had the bright thought of murdering one another and did it very loud with revolver-shots and screams. I do not think that any of us would scream loud enough to wake her."

Laura picked one word out of this and repeated it.

"*All?*" she said.

Catherine laughed. Her laugh was so much deeper than her ordinary voice that it was always a surprise.

"You are trying to catch me because I said we should be just two alone. But Vassili might come back, and it is certainly he who would begin to shoot, and I who would scream. I have a very fine scream."

"And I?" said Laura.

"I do not know. Perhaps you would faint—perhaps you would throw yourself in front of me and take the shot that Vassili would mean for me. Yes, I think that is your rôle. You have that kind of complex—you are deficient in *ego*. It is a pity, you know."

Laura laughed faintly, and was at once sorry that she had done so, because the laugh had a catch in it. She said quickly,

"And Dr Alec—what is he to do?"

"Sasha?" said Catherine. Her voice changed, darkened. "Sasha will be left to pick up the bits—he is good at that." She yawned elaborately. "It is time you were asleep."

"Yes."

"Have you everything you want?"

"Yes."

Catherine had taken a step back, when she heard her name spoken only just above Laura's breath.

"Catherine—"

"What is it?"

"Will you—will you shut the door to-night?"

Catherine stared in the direction of the bed. She could see Laura lying on her right side, with her hair black against the pillow, and the edge of the bed and the curve of her shoulder dark against the glow of the sunk fire.

"Very well."

She went out on to the landing. A moment later Laura saw the light come on in the next room; the open doorway became a shining oblong panel. She put her hand across her eyes, but just before she did so she saw Catherine in the middle of the panel looking in. She wore a bright green dress, and the light beat on it.

Laura shut her eyes and sheltered them with her hand. In a moment Catherine had crossed the floor and was standing over her. A cool hand touched hers and then withdrew.

"I am to shut the door?"

"Please, Catherine."

"So that you may weep and make yourself ill?"

Laura said, "No;" but her voice broke.

"No? I think it is yes. What has happened? Why have you been weeping? Did you think I should not know? I leave you all right; and I come back, and you are in the dark, and I must shut the door so that you may weep yourself into a fever again. What has happened? Is it Vassili?"

Laura spoke in a muffled voice.

"No."

"What is it then?"

"Nothing."

Catherine moved back a step.

"You will not tell me. Very well, my dear, weep if you will—it is easier than when one has to laugh. But if you are ill to-morrow, I will go away and leave you to Vassili—so be careful and do not weep too much. Good night, my dear."

She went into her room and shut the door.

Chapter Nineteen

LAURA TOOK HER HAND away from her eyes and turned a little. The soft fire-shot dusk was comforting. She had wept, and she did not want to weep any more. She only wanted to be alone. The feeling that she and Catherine were alone in the house except for the tow-headed maid gave her a feeling of security. She could be alone without being afraid.

She lay quite still and let herself think about Jim. She had cried all her tears away. She thought of him as if they were parted by death, and as if it was she who had died, not Jim. In some strange way this comforted her. He was safe, and he was alive. All that mattered was that he should be kept safe. But to be kept safe he ought to be warned that Vassili was trying to get hold of the Sanquhar invention. If Vassili knew or guessed that Laura had been left one of those bits of a five-pound note which was the key to the invention, he probably knew or guessed that Jim had the third of the torn pieces. He had not been Bertram Hallingdon's private secretary for nothing. If he could get the three pieces of the torn five-pound note, it would give him the Sanquhar invention, and Bertram Hallingdon's trust would be broken.

She thought of the old man who had trusted her. And she thought of Jim, who didn't know that he had something a good deal more dangerous than dynamite in his possession. She wondered how much he did know. There had been a moment in his talk to-night when she had waited for the words, "The Sanquhar invention." Of course they had not come, but for an electric instant she had waited for them. How much did he know? He couldn't know about Vassili, and unless he was warned he must be in danger all the time. He must be warned. And how was she to warn him? Vassili had talked about supervising her business affairs. She was very, very sure that he would make it his particular business to supervise her correspondence. She must warn Jim. She couldn't write to him. She had to warn him. How?

Catherine's words slipped into her mind like an answer: "Vassili telephoned." Until Catherine said that, she had not known that there was a telephone in the house. But—Vassili had telephoned—and Vassili would not be back until late—perhaps he would not be back at all to-night.

Lying there in the dusk, Laura felt strength and determination flowing in upon her. She had asked Catherine to shut the connecting door because she wanted to be alone, to feel herself shut in with Jim. She had had no other thought. But that closed door was going to make it possible for her to find her way downstairs and telephone her warning. Not yet—not just yet. She must wait until Catherine was asleep.

She listened to Catherine's movements in the next room. The party wall was thin, and she could hear footsteps, a splashing of water, and presently the creak of the bed and the sharp click which meant that the light had been turned out.

It never took Catherine long to go to sleep. Laura made up her mind to wait until the clock in the hall below struck eleven. She waited, planning what she would say. She must be very quick—she must be ready with just the right words. And she must ask Jim to tell Mr Rimington to come and see her at once, before she could be taken abroad; then she could give him her piece of the five-pound note, and he would put it in a safe place. There must be a place where it would be safe. Mr Rimington would know what ought to be done.

When the clock began to strike, she got softly out of bed, wrapped her shawl about her, and opened the door that led to the landing. The cold of the unwarmed house met her. She steadied herself against the doorpost and looked out. The landing was quite dark, but towards the well of the stairs this darkness thinned away to dusk, so that she could see the stair rails like a row of black strokes from a copy-book. She stepped out of her room, and it was like stepping on to very smooth ice. The landing had no carpet, and the polished linoleum was the coldest thing that she had ever felt. She did not dare risk putting on slippers—a leather sole can never quite be trusted, and heelless slippers have a dreadful way of flapping on a stair.

Laura went barefoot to the stair head and looked down the well. There was a very faint glimmer in the hall. She left the linoleum for the thin scratchy stair-carpet and came to the half landing. She could see where the glimmer came from now. The hall was lighted by a gas pendant, and the gas had been turned down to a mere point which made nothing visible except its own pendant and the surrounding gloom.

She began to descend again. It was like going down into ice-cold water. All this part of the house was colder than she could have believed possible. A thin, edgy draught blew in from under the front door. For a moment, with her foot on the last step, it came to Laura that she could open the door and walk out of the house. There are waking moments when nothing seems more impossible than it does in dreams. For one of these moments Laura saw herself slipping back the bolt with velvet softness and turning the key, as every key should turn but never does. She saw the door, open; and the gate beyond it, open to the black and empty road; and herself, going barefoot down the road and away.

Before she could so much as get this picture into focus it was gone. She could not really walk down the road in her night-gown and without a penny. It came to her just like that, with the queerest shock of realization, that she was three parts a millionaire, and that she had not a single penny in her possession. Only that morning she had turned out her purse and found it empty.

She stepped off the bottom stair on to linoleum that was even colder and smoother than that on the landing above. And then it came to her that she had not the slightest idea where to look for the telephone. It might be in the hall, or the dining-room, or the study if there was one. Yes, Catherine had mentioned a study. It wouldn't be in the drawing-room—but then she didn't know which of the two front rooms *was* the drawing-room. The idea that the telephone might be in the hall was simply paralysing. But no, it couldn't be, or she would have heard the bell, and Vassili's voice when he telephoned.

She crossed the hall, opened the right-hand door, and felt for the switch. Thank goodness it was only the hall that was lighted by gas. Instantly the darkness was gone and she was bathed in a pinkish light. It came from a double pendant whose drops were heavily shaded by rose-coloured silk. Two pale chintz armchairs and a shiny chintz sofa stood about the hearth like icebergs. The grate contained nothing warmer than gilt shavings. Above it a mirror reflected the icebergs, and the walls were hung with reproductions of lightly clothed young women dawdling negligently upon marble terraces. The room was evidently the drawing-room, and there was no telephone.

Laura put out the light, shut the door upon the pseudo-Greek young women, and crossed the hall.

She found a dining-room with a mahogany suite and a good deal of bright brown lincrusta on the walls. There was a tantalus and a siphon of soda-water on the table. There was a black marble clock on the mantelpiece with its hands immovably fixed at a quarter to five. There were bright peacock blue tiles on the hearth. But there was no telephone.

Laura wondered where the study was. Her feet were so cold now that she could not feel them. Her fingers slid over the shiny wallpaper as she felt her way along the side of the hall. Presently they touched the jamb of another door. She opened it, switched on the light, and saw the study in a green glow. The light came from a rigid reading-lamp with a bright green porcelain shade such as one sees in banks and offices. It made the lower half of the room look golden, and all the upper air green and fluid like water. Laura shut the door behind her, and saw the telephone standing on the opposite side of the table from the lamp.

After all, it had been easy. She had come out of that horrible icy hall into this room which was quite warm and friendly, with the telephone ready to her hand.

She went round the table, sat down, and drew the instrument towards her. When she had given Jim Mackenzie's number she sat leaning forward with the light slanting across the empty table and touching the amber embroideries of her shawl. Vassili Stefanoff did not leave his papers about. There was a blotting-pad with leather corners;

there was a calendar, a pen-tray, and an ink-pot; but not so much as an inch of paper was visible. Laura thought of this afterwards; at the time her whole consciousness was listening for Jim's voice. It was curious that it should never have occurred to her that he might be out. She was quite sure that now—*now*, at any moment—she would hear him speak. A little click, an instant's pause, and then she would hear his voice. She had ceased to be aware that her bare feet were frozen and her whole body stiff with cold; she was aware only of something that was like the most terrible hunger. It was as if she had been starved for a very long time and then had come suddenly within sight of food.

A tremor ran over her from head to foot as there came along the line what she had been waiting for—a change of sound in the running current, and the little far-away click of the lifted receiver. And then Jim's voice.

He said "Yes?" and with the one word everything that Laura had planned to say was swept from her mind by a glowing rush of joy. She had been dead, and she was alive again. The past weeks had been blotted out. An electric current, a little wire, and a man's voice saying "Yes?" Odd stuff to make a miracle out of. Laura felt the golden joy flow through her and round her. It warmed and fed her. It filled her heart, and it filled the room.

"Yes?" said Jim Mackenzie in a tired, hard tone.

Laura spoke then.

She said, "Jim!" and some of the miracle was in her voice.

There was an utter silence. It came into the room like a darkness. The gold of Laura's joy was dimmed. The miracle began to waver and wear thin like a dream just ready to go.

Laura said his name again, insistently this time.

"Jim—*Jim*—"

Jim Mackenzie said, "Yes?" and then, after a pause, "What is it?"

It was the controlled hardness of his voice that made an end of the miracle. No one can blot out the past. There was an irrevocable separation between them. You cannot die and come alive again; you must stay dead. Jim's voice told Laura that she was dead. She was his dead love speaking to him, and not Laura Cameron, who had been alive and had loved him living. She was dead. But even dead, she had a message for him. She must say her message.

She heard him speak again through a mist of pain.

"What is it—Laura?"

She did not think that anything could hurt her more than she had been hurt, but when he said her name it was as if he had stabbed a wound. She caught her breath with the sheer anguish, and the sound reached Jim Mackenzie.

He said, "Laura—" again; and then, quickly, "Why have you rung me up?"

"To tell you, Jim—to tell you—"

Every time he spoke the pain stabbed again. His voice seemed to come from farther and farther away. She tried desperately to rally the things she had meant to say to him.

She said in a fluctuating voice,

"You're—in danger;" and heard his hard,

"Am I? Why?"

"The paper—the torn piece of paper—from Mr Hallingdon—don't keep it—put it somewhere safe—it's dangerous."

"I don't think I know what you're talking about," said Jim Mackenzie.

Laura caught her breath in dismay.

"The torn piece—"

"I can't discuss this sort of thing on the telephone."

A cold sense of failure froze her words. She remained silent, her head leaning upon her hand. After what seemed like an endless time the voice of the operator, bored and rather sleepy, inquired,

"Another three minutes?"

Laura did not speak. She waited for the click which would tell her that they had been cut off. Instead, Jim said quickly,

"Yes, another three minutes;" and then, "Are you there?"

Still Laura did not speak. She was like an actor who has lost his words.

"*Laura*—are you there?"

She said, "Yes."

"Are you ill? They said you had been ill."

"Not now."

"Where are you?"

"I don't know."

"You don't know?"

"They—haven't—told me. Jim—for God's sake—"

The hall door shut. Not loudly but unmistakably it shut. She had not heard it open, but she heard it close, and she heard footsteps crossing the hall. In a blind panic she thrust the receiver back upon its hook and, reaching sideways with her left hand, turned out the light. The dark was overwhelming in its blackness. There was no fire, no chink of light.

The footsteps receded. She thought they had come to the foot of the stairs and then turned back. After a terrifying minute she got up and felt her way to the door. She had remembered the tantalus in the dining-room. If Vassili were in the dining-room, it might be possible for her to reach and mount the stairs without being seen.

She began very slowly to open the door. The first chink showed a vertical bright line. The hall gas had been turned up. There would be no sheltering dusk to make things easier. A cold dread touched her at the thought of coming out into that bright, unsparing light. If she were to wait here, perhaps Vassili would go upstairs and leave darkness behind him. And then she remembered that she had left the door of her room standing open—standing wide open. She had not thought of shutting it. She had stepped out on to the smooth ice-cold linoleum without a thought of shutting the door behind her. There had been, perhaps, the half-conscious instinct to leave open a way of retreat.

Now she must get upstairs before Vassili. There was no longer any choice. To wait was to make disaster certain. She caught her shawl about her and passed out into the lighted hall with the drip of its amber fringe about her bare, cold ankles.

When she had taken three steps, Vassili Stefanoff came out of the dining-room. He saw Laura, tall and white, with her black hair pushed back and her eyes wide, and dark, and strange. They looked past him, and she came forward with a slow, rigid motion as if her limbs were frozen. Her hands held the shawl and were hidden in its folds. At the first sight of her he had taken an angry step forward. Words rushed to his lips and died there in a sudden shock of something akin to fear. She looked so strange, so blank, so deathly white. A superstitious shudder passed over him, and as she continued to move forward, he recoiled a step.

She crossed the hall and came to the front door, where she stood still. Then in a slow, wavering fashion one of her hands detached itself from the folds of the shawl and knocked upon the door,

Vassili stood upon the threshold of the dining-room and watched her. It was like watching some one knocking in a silent film. She was all white and gold—and that black hair like a cloud. Her hand went up three times, and made no sound. Then she turned, faced Vassili for a moment with an unseeing stare, and began to move in the same slow, rigid fashion towards the staircase. She had mounted three steps, when his hand fell on her shoulder.

She did not need to play a part any longer. A sleepwalker suddenly awakened would start and shudder just as she started and shuddered when without warning the hand fell. He must have moved as silently as an animal. With a gasping cry she stood still and felt the hand weigh on her.

"What are you doing here?" said Vassili.

Laura shuddered again. Once more there was no need to act; she had only to relax the effort she had made, to let her limbs tremble and her sobbing breath go free.

"What are you doing here?" said Vassili again.

She looked about her wildly.

"Where—am I?"

"You are on the stairs—in your night-gown."

All at once his hand burned her. A scarlet flush changed her from a ghost to a woman, alive and resentful of his touch.

He swung her round to face him as he stood on the stair below.

"What were you doing in the study?"

"I—don't—know."

"You'd better think!"

He had her by both shoulders now, and his hands were rough.

"Let me go!"

"What have you been doing downstairs?"

She shook from head to foot and gave a choking cry.

"Are you going to pretend you were walking in your sleep?"

"I don't know—"

From the landing above them came Catherine's voice with a yawn in it.

"If you must come in at midnight, Vassili, you need not wake everyone else."

Laura sat down on the stair with a sob, and Vassili let her go.

"She asks one to believe she has been walking in her sleep!" he said in a tone of unrestrained fury.

Chapter Twenty

CATHERINE CAME to the top of the stairs and began to descend. She wore orange-coloured pyjamas and her feet were bare. Her usually smoothly lacquered hair was a mere mop. Without make-up her skin was a pale smooth olive. Her eyes were still vague with sleep. She looked younger, more like a masquerading schoolgirl.

When she came to the step on which Laura sat she stopped.

"So you've been walking in your sleep. What made you do that?"

Vassili caught her wrist and swung it.

"She has not walked in her sleep at all! It's a damned lie—and she's a damned liar!"

Catherine unclasped his hand without apparent effort. She flung it back to him so that it struck the banister. Then she wiped her wrist carefully with her pyjama sleeve. In a small restrained voice she said,

"Moujik!"

Vassili flushed a dull red all over his face.

Catherine put her arm round Laura.

"Come back to your bed at once! You are like ice."

Then, as Laura caught at the banisters and pulled herself up, Catherine, from a couple of steps above him, over her shoulder spoke to Vassili in rapid Russian.

When she had covered Laura and stirred the fire into brilliant light, she came to the bedside and stood looking down at the white face on the pillow. Laura's eyes, which had been closed, opened and looked up at her.

"Were you really walking in your sleep?" said Catherine.

A quiver passed over Laura's face. In the shaded light it reminded Catherine of a reflection blurred by a little shivering breeze.

"Well?" said Catherine.

Laura drew a difficult breath.

"I was here—" she said. "And then—I was on the stairs—he touched me."

She had no need to simulate the sob that shook her. That moment
when Vassili's hand had fallen on her shoulder had been pure
nightmare. A cold dampness broke out upon her temples and the palms
of her hands at the mere thought of it.

"Hm—" said Catherine. "Well—the fat is in the fire, as Sasha would
say. Go to sleep if you can."

She went out of the room, picked up her dressing-gown, and went
on down the stairs and into the study.

Vassili was cramming the receiver back on to its hook. His face was
wild and dark; he had run his fingers through his hair. He looked the
savage peasant she had called him. When he had sworn at length, he
brought out angry fragments of speech interspersed with gross gestures.

"In her sleep! She asks one to believe that! The liar!" He flung
gutter names at Laura and swore again. "She had been telephoning, I
tell you!"

Catherine started, and came to the edge of the table.

"Are you sure of that?"

He banged on the blotter with his fist and shouted.

"No, I am *not* sure! The operator is a fool! He does not know—he
cannot say—he cuts me off!"

Catherine put both hands to her head.

"Can one think in such a noise? You make me tired. I am sorry for
any woman who has to live with you. Keep quiet and let me see what I
can do!"

She reached across the table, picked up the telephone, and put the
receiver to her ear.

Vassili stared, his hands lying on the stained blotting-paper—
square hands, with blunt finger-tips and spade-shaped thumbs.

Catherine was speaking softly in a dropped voice that might have
belonged to any woman.

"Exchange... I'm so sorry to trouble you. Can you remember that
number I asked for just now?.... Oh, I see... Yes—of course. I'm sorry."

She hung the receiver up and pushed the instrument back across
the table,

"Well?" said Vassili.

"He has just come on duty—he does not know anything at all. Why do you think people will tell you things if you swear at them?"

He beat on the table.

"That is enough!"

"For me—certainly. I am going back to bed."

"No!" he said.

"My dear!"

He leaned across the table and took her by the arm.

"You are to be serious! This is a most serious matter. You will not go to bed—you will pack! We shall leave this house before it is light. If we are off by five o'clock, we should be safe. I can give you no more time than that, and you must be ready—it is, after all, only twenty-four hours earlier than we intended."

Catherine disengaged herself, but quietly and gravely.

"And we go—where?"

"All the arrangements stand. You had better give her the sleeping-draught at once."

"Is it necessary?"

His uncontrolled anger had passed; he spoke now with hard authority.

"You will do as you are told—unless perhaps you wish me to make an adverse report on you. No? I thought not. Then you had better get on with what there is to do!"

"And Sasha?"

"I will ring him up."

Laura opened her eyes, to see Catherine leaning over her in the firelight.

"Are you awake? I want you to drink this hot milk."

The thought was a pleasant one—she was still very cold. She raised herself on her elbow and sipped from a tumbler that was almost too hot to hold. After the second sip she stopped.

"It tastes—funny."

"There is something in it to make you sleep."

"Oh—I'd rather not."

"You must drink it, Laura," said Catherine very seriously.

Laura sat upright in bed. She fixed her eyes on Catherine in a wide, startled look.

"Why?" she said.

"Because it is the best thing you can do, my dear."

Laura went on looking at her steadily and without any fear.

"And if I say I won't drink it?"

Catherine raised her eyebrows.

"I shall have to tell Vassili—and that will be unpleasant—for you."

A shade of something like horror troubled Laura's gaze.

"Why am I being drugged?" she said.

Catherine's foot tapped the floor for a moment. Then she went quickly to the door and opened it. The light shone brightly overhead. The landing was quite empty. She shut the door again and came back to the bed.

"Listen, Laura," she said. "You have been very foolish. You took a great risk when you went downstairs and used the telephone. No, you need not lie to me. The operator gave me the number that you asked for."

Laura faced her with courage. The hand that held the tumbler did not shake. Her lips said nothing; her eyes implored.

"No," said Catherine, "Vassili does not know. I lied to him. I think he had rung up the exchange and bullied the poor man who was there, so of course he told him nothing. But I pretended that I was you, and that I had forgotten the number I had asked for. He gave it me at once. To Vassili I said that the operator had only just come on duty, and that he knew nothing. Now will you drink your milk?"

Laura's lips were stiff. She tried to speak, and failed.

Catherine patted her on the shoulder.

"My dear, do not be so much of a fool. There is no poison in your milk—I would be very glad to drink it myself and lie down and sleep. That is all that will happen to you, you silly Laura—you will sleep, and you will wake up—somewhere else."

"Where?" said Laura in a dry whisper.

Catherine laughed lightly.

"Did not Vassili tell you that he was taking you abroad?"

Laura put the glass to her lips and then set it down again.

"Catherine—"

"What is it?"

"Catherine—you won't leave me?"

"No, I won't leave you."

"You—promise?"

"Would you trust my promise?"

Laura nodded.

"I can't think why," said Catherine. "But as it happens you can. Drink up that milk and go to sleep, and I promise you that you will wake again and wake safely, and that I shall be there."

Laura drank the hot curious-tasting milk. When she gave back the tumbler her heart was beating a little faster. She held Catherine's wrist for a moment.

"You've promised—you won't leave me?"

Catherine looked down at her with the faintest of mocking smiles.

"How fond of me you are! Yes, I have promised. Lie down and go to sleep. You are really very lucky. If I could go to sleep and miss a Channel crossing, I would do it—every time, as Sasha says."

Laura lay down on her side with her hand under her cheek. She watched Catherine turn out the light and go through the connecting door into her own room. The door remained a little open. When Laura's lids rose, she could see a broad ribbon of light. It reminded her of a ribbon because it seemed to move with a shimmering motion like a ribbon stirred by a breeze. When her lids fell, she could see it still. It was not golden any more, but red. Imperceptibly a black curtain came down and blotted out both the red ribbon and the gold.

Chapter Twenty-One

JIM MACKENZIE let himself into his flat and shut the door. When he had hung up his hat and coat, he went into the sitting-room and set the attaché case he was carrying on the table. When he had poured himself out a drink, he opened the case and took out the typescript of the talk which he had just been broadcasting.

"Twenty Years of Invention".... A good title and a good subject—and a rotten hash he had made of it. He began to turn the leaves, frowning. Everyone had seemed quite pleased. Being polite probably. But something had been said about another talk next month, so perhaps it hadn't been so bad. He might have made more of the Lumsden colour-process. But of course it wasn't possible to get twenty years of invention into a twenty minutes' talk—a minute a year. It was ludicrous.

He flicked over another page and frowned at a heavily blacked-out paragraph. Odd things happened. One of the oddest that had happened to him was getting old Bertram Hallingdon's letter just as he had finished typing that paragraph about the Sanquhar invention. Of course the paragraph had had to come out.

He threw down the typescript and finished his drink.

On his way back from Savoy Hill he had met Kennedy Jackson, just back from a year on the Zambesi. A hearty man Jackson, and as obtuse as a hippopotamus. He had slapped Jim on the back and congratulated him on his marriage, and it had taken about ten minutes to get it into his head that he was neither married nor going to be married.

He turned to fill up his glass. Whilst his hand was still on the siphon the bell rang. He went to the door and flung it open. If Jackson had followed him home, he thought he should probably heave him down the well of the lift. Other peoples' bones might break, but he was convinced that Jackson would bounce. It was doubtful whether he would be even conscious of having been rebuffed.

He opened the door, and Miss Agatha Wimborough stepped into the hall. Jim would have preferred Jackson.

She said, "How do you do, I want to speak to you," all in one breath, and walked straight into the sitting-room.

He followed her, and when she reached the table she turned, cast a look at his empty glass, and then directed the same glance at him. It was a challenging, accusatory glance, delivered by a pair of very handsome eyes dark grey in colour and admirably furnished with black eyelashes. Miss Wimborough most undoubtedly had what is termed a presence. She combined to a quite extraordinary degree a distinguished appearance and an air of authority. She wore a dark fur coat over a wine-coloured dress. Her burnished silver hair was uncovered.

Jim Mackenzie met her level gaze as he came in, and experienced a sensation of shock. He was himself in no pleasant mood. Of all things on this earth he least wished to meet Laura's aunt. He could not imagine any reason why she should wish to meet him. He came in with a hard grip on himself and met those cold handsome eyes fixed in an accusing stare. He shut the door behind him and, without preliminaries, received the first shot of the engagement.

"Where's Laura?"

Standing just inside the door, he took a half step back against it. What a nightmare! Was it possible that she didn't know what had happened? And had he—*he*—got to tell her? He said with a jerk,

"Don't you know?"

"If I knew, I should hardly be asking you."

The nightmare deepened. He stuck to his own line.

"Why do you ask—me?"

"Because I want to know."

"You know she's—married?"

Miss Wimborough turned an icy look upon him.

"Certainly."

"Then why do you ask me where she is?"

"Because I thought you might know. Do you?"

"No."

She made an impatient movement.

"Who is this man Stevens?"

"I believe he was Mr Hallingdon's secretary."

"Do you know him?"

"I've met him."

"Why did she do it?"

"I don't know."

"What's the good of telling me lies?" said Agatha Wimborough. "Laura does a thing like that—*Laura*—and you tell me you don't know why?"

"I tell you I don't know why," said Jim in a hard, restrained voice.

Miss Wimborough flared into passionate anger. Anxiety, suspense, and love for Laura combined to carry her beyond her own control.

"What devilry had you been up to? She found you out, I suppose. You're all alike, and I should be glad, *glad*, to think she had found you out. If she had stopped at breaking off with *you*!" She struck the edge of the table with her hand. "But why she should imagine that this Stevens is any better than the rest of you, is what I can't understand!"

"There was nothing to find out," said Jim.

Miss Wimborough laughed.

"That sort of thing is quite wasted on me. I have my opinions, and I can assure you that you will not alter them. However, it doesn't really matter what Laura found out. What does matter is that she should have taken this suicidal step and then have disappeared. The man is, of course, an adventurer. If he was Hallingdon's secretary, he knew that she was Hallingdon's heiress. I landed four days ago, and after verifying the marriage I went to the bank. Laura had left no other address, and when I asked where she was they refused to give me any information. I then went to the lawyer. He wouldn't tell me anything either. He did say he'd seen her, and that she had been ill. Well, I wrote a letter in his office. He forwarded it. And to-day I get this!" She opened her bag, took out an envelope, and thrust it at him.

He had not meant to take it, but he found it in his hand. He had not meant to open it, but he found himself reading the half sheet of paper that it contained. There were only a few lines upon it, and they were written in pencil:

DEAREST,

You mustn't trouble about me—I'm all right. I've been ill, but I'm better now. We'll meet later—I'd rather not just now. *Please understand.*

LAURA

The paper swam before his eyes. There wasn't any Laura—there never had been any Laura. But the Laura who had never been had written the words that swam and dazzled before his eyes. They were not written to him; but they might have been. *"Please understand."* The dream Laura—the Laura who wasn't true—might have written that to him. She had thrown him over callously on the eve of their wedding. She had married Stevens. *"Please understand."* There simply wasn't anything to understand.

He lifted a haggard face and gave the letter back. There wasn't anything to say. He said nothing.

"Did you quarrel?" said Miss Agatha with sudden sharpness.

"No."

She put the letter back in her bag and snapped it to.

"Well, whatever it was, you brought it on yourself. Unfortunately, Laura has punished herself as well as you. I've stuck up for women all my life, but they're fools. If they weren't damned fools, the men could just go to the devil their own way, like the Gadarene swine that they are. But the women are such fools that they don't let them go alone. There's no man who's so much of a beast that some woman won't throw herself under his feet and ask nothing better than to be trampled on. But that Laura should fling herself away!" A hard sob caught her voice and broke it. "Do you really not know where she is?" she said.

He shook his head. She was cutting him on the raw with every word. "No idea?"

"None."

"Then it's no good my staying."

"No," said Jim. He stood away from the door and opened it.

Miss Wimborough walked out of the flat with her head in the air and tears stinging her eyelids. She turned for a moment before the outer door was shut.

"If you hear from her—"

"*I?*" said Jim Mackenzie. He laughed.

"More unlikely things have happened," said Miss Wimborough.

"I shall not hear," said Jim.

He shut the door and went back into the sitting-room. It had a cold emptiness beyond all enduring. Agatha Wimborough's anger and contempt had swept through it like a fire and left it blank. He felt as if he had come to a dead end. There confronted him a nothingness more dreadful than pain.

He stood for a moment and looked about him. In the book-case, a gap where Laura's books had been—the row of little red Kiplings which they had given to each other—packed away because he couldn't bear to see them. The empty place on the mantelpiece where Laura's photograph had stood. The whole dreadful emptiness of his heart with Laura torn from it. He dropped into the nearest chair, flung out his arms across the table, and let his head fall forward on them.

He went down into a cold hell where there was no Laura, and never had been.

After a long time he heard the church clock over the way strike out eleven heavy strokes with a little catch like a hiccup before each. He looked mechanically at his own watch and found it five minutes ahead. That meant that he was right, because the church clock was always slow. He got up, fished a key out of his trouser pocket, and unlocked the leather-covered dispatch-case which stood in the corner behind the sofa. He had cashed a cheque after lunch, and had been carrying rather more money than he liked all day.

He put the notes away under the tray and stayed looking down at an envelope which lay beside them. It had his name on it and nothing else. After a moment he picked it up, lifted the flap, and took out a piece of thin white paper heavily marked with black—the torn left-hand corner of a bank-note. When he had looked at it, he put it back. He could not really have explained why he had looked at it at all, but he had had an impulse to see that it was safe.

The envelope was still in his hand, when from behind him in the corner by the book-case the telephone bell rang. He dropped the envelope into the box, went over to the wall, and took down the receiver.

"Yes?" he said.

Nothing came along the line except that faint pulsing flow of the current.

He said, "Yes?" again.

And then Laura spoke his name.

The shock was very nearly as great as if she had been dead and he had heard her speak. It was her own voice—a very warm, soft voice. He hadn't any words to answer that voice; it spoke across too wide a gulf. And as he stood there dumb, it spoke again with insistence.

"Jim—*Jim*—"

"What is it?" said Jim Mackenzie. His lips said this mechanically—one has the habit of answering when one is spoken to. He said, "What is it?" and then suddenly spoke her name, *"Laura,"* and, having spoken it once, repeated it. He added, "Why have you rung me up?"

"To tell you, Jim—to tell you—"

All the warm softness had gone out of her voice; it wavered and sank as if from lack of breath.

"What is there for you to tell me?" he said. *Nothing*—having told him that she had married Stevens. Why in God's name had she rung him up? She had said everything that there was to say. And now in a trembling voice she said,

"You're in danger."

"Am I? Why?" And if he were, would it matter to her?

"The paper—the torn piece of paper from Mr Hallingdon—don't keep it—put it somewhere safe—it's dangerous—"

And how did she know about Hallingdon's torn bit of paper? Hallingdon's torn bank-note and the Sanquhar invention—had she by any chance another piece of it?

He said, "I don't think I know what you're talking about."

Her voice again, full of dismay:

"The torn piece—"

"I can't discuss this sort of thing on the telephone," he said emphatically.

"Another three minutes?"

It was her call. He waited for her to speak. She said nothing. A frightful panic that with just a faint cold click she would be shut away brought hurrying words to his lips:

"Yes, another three minutes." And then, "Are you there?.... *Laura*—are you there?"

"Yes." A faint sound—a faint helpless sound.

"Are you ill? They said you had been ill."

She had been ill last year—for a week. He remembered the dark shadows under her eyes. He remembered his fear—tenderness—joy.

"Not now," said Laura. There was no joy in her voice.

What had they done to her for her not to care whether she was well or ill? Where had they taken her? His poor girl—his sick girl.... The old fear had him again.

"Where are you?"

"I don't know."

His heart gave a bound. His voice came in a shout:

"You don't know?"

"They—haven't—told me. Jim—for God's sake—"

The words were strung on a thread of terror, and with the last word the thread broke. There were no more words; there was no more current, no more anything. He might have been in another world.

He jerked at the hook, but the line stayed dead—jerked and went on jerking and saying, "Exchange!" in a harsh, unrecognizable whisper.

"Exchange—exchange—*exchange!*"

It was like the story of the worshippers of Baal. There was no voice, nor any that answered.

He went on.

After five minutes exchange came suddenly to life. No, they didn't know who had been calling.... No, they couldn't say what exchange it was.... No, there wasn't any way of finding out.

He pitched the receiver back upon the hook and strode up and down the little room. *Laura*. What had they done to her? *Laura*— frightened—ill....

The cold hell was gone. A devouring flame had burnt it up. His girl—his sick girl—frightened—not knowing where she was. The fire roared round him. It burnt up everything except the fact that Laura had called to him across the gulf which she had set between them. Where was she? Agatha Wimborough didn't know. But she had heard from her. The letter must have had a post-mark. If they really didn't want people to know where she was, it was easy enough to get a letter posted somewhere else. But the lawyer knew. If he knew, he could be made to say. Or if Rimington wouldn't say, he might have better luck with Stark. Clerks always knew addresses—though of course they weren't supposed to pass them on. That might be arranged—with Stark.

All at once he was full of a thundering, pounding energy. He laughed aloud, flung the tray back into his dispatch-box, slammed down the lid, and locked it, pocketing the key. Five minutes ago there had been no go in him; now he did not know what to do with this rush of strength.

What he did was to go down the steps three at a time and take the nearest way to the Embankment. There was half a gale blowing down the river; half a gale, and half a moon, with the clouds driving across it, and the water ridged with black and silver. He walked fast and far, making plans.

He would have to ring Agatha Wimborough up first thing in the morning. It would be better for *her* to press Rimington for the address. Rimington might give it if he was told that Laura had rung up. Yes, that was it. And there was no need for Rimington to know that it wasn't Agatha Wimborough who had been rung up. She could say that Laura didn't know where she was—that she was frightened. He didn't see how Rimington could refuse the address after that. As a matter of fact he couldn't imagine anyone refusing Agatha Wimborough anything that she had really made up her mind to have. She must have given up rather easily, or she would have got the address when she asked for it before.

He got back to the flat at one o'clock, went straight to bed, and slept as he had not done for the best part of a month.

Chapter Twenty-Two

JIM MACKENZIE opened his eyes. Some one was knocking on the outer door of the flat. He looked at his watch. Half-past eight. Good Lord! Then he had overslept—and that was Mrs Mabb!

He opened the bedroom door, called out, "All right—I'm coming," and went back for an aged dressing-gown of Turkish towelling which had once boasted a rather loud red pattern on a purple ground. The purple and the red had long ago mingled in the wash, but it could still preserve Mrs Mabb's respectability from the shock of encountering him in his pyjamas. Mrs Mabb was very respectable indeed.

She came in coughing a little and averting her eyes from the dressing-gown. She herself wore a Burberry some half dozen sizes too large for her, and the relics of an orange-coloured feather boa. A black felt hat sat on the back of her head. She had hay-coloured hair, a long pale face, and very few front teeth. She said, "Good morning, sir," and vanished into the kitchen.

Jim went into the bathroom and struck a match. If he started the geyser now, he could shave whilst the bath was running. He would let it hot up a little before he took his shaving-water. And just as he got to that point Mrs Mabb screamed.

She was leaning against the open sitting-room door with both hands clutching at her side and a dustpan and brush at her feet. As soon as she saw Jim she screamed again.

"Oh—sir!"

"What on earth—" said Jim, and then stopped short, because he could see past her into the room.

His dispatch-box stood in the middle of the floor with the lid flung back and the tray tilted sideways, one corner on the floor and its contents spilled.

"Oh, Lor, sir!" panted Mrs Mabb. "You never left it like that, did you? Such a turn as it give me when I opened the door! 'Burglars,' I says to myself, and if I hadn't screamed, I should ha' dropped. I'm all of a shake as it is, what with losing me key, which is a thing that I've never had happen before, all the time that I've obliged—and then to get a turn like this! You never left it that way, sir—did you?"

Jim went past her and knelt down in front of the box. It had been wrenched open; the japan had flaked off and the metal below was dinted. The man who had opened it had been in a hurry. In a hurry for what? Not for the money that he had put away last night; for it was there, tossed out on the carpet together with his cheque-book and the bundle of Laura's letters, which he had not quite steeled himself to destroy.

"Is there much took, sir?" said Mrs Mabb in a flutter of concern.

"No—I don't know. Just get on with your work, will you?"

He had put it under the money. Or had he? He had taken it out and looked at it and put it back again. And it wasn't here. He threw the notes on one side as carelessly as the thief had done.

Behind him Mrs Mabb was picking up her dustpan and brush.

The envelope was gone. He had slept like a hog, and whilst he was asleep some one had come into the flat, forced open his dispatch-case, and taken, not the money, but the envelope which had come to him from Bertram Hallingdon—the envelope which contained a three-cornered piece torn from a bank-note.

A cough sounded in his ear. Quite close to him, on her hands and knees, Mrs Mabb was brushing the carpet.

"Ow! I do hope there's not much took!" she said, and brushed back a strand of hay.

Jim controlled himself with difficulty.

"When did you miss your key?" he said.

"I told you, sir, yesterday—I come back a purpose and told you. Let myself in same as usual yesterday morning, and when I got no more than half-way down the street I wanted me hangkerchief, but it wasn't there."

"What wasn't there?"

"Me hangkerchief, sir—and the key what I always knots in the corner. And I come back as fast as I could and told you, and certain sure I am I never dropped it. It was *took*—and a very good hangkerchief too."

Jim got up and lifted the case on to the table.

"Mrs Mabb, do you mind sweeping somewhere else?"

"Your bedroom, sir?"

"No."

"I can't do the bathroom, sir, if you're going to have a bath."

"Go and do the kitchen—do anything you like to it!"

Mrs Mabb departed sniffing. Jim shut the door on her.

When he had taken everything out of his dispatch-case and then put it back again, the envelope was still missing. And Laura had rung him up last night to tell him to put it in a safe place. Laura had rung him up. Why *Laura*? Because she knew some one was after his piece of the note which Bertram Hallingdon had divided. *Laura*. How did Laura know?

He stared down at the notes which the thief had not taken. Two things stood out with the limelight on them—something that Laura knew—something that Laura did not know. Laura knew that his piece of Bertram Hallingdon's bank-note was in danger. Laura did not know where she herself was. It was like a crazy riddle—a sort of "Why is a bee when it spins?" And the answer was—Basil Stevens. Basil Stevens was keeping Laura in ignorance of her whereabouts. And Basil Stevens had come into his flat with a stolen key and broken open his dispatch-case. He was a fool, or he would have taken the money too and made it look like an ordinary burglary. Or was there method in his folly? Did he count on the torn piece of the Hallingdon note being an awkward thing to go to the police about? If money had been taken, the police would be a possibility; as it was, they were quite starkly impossible. He conjured up an inspector—a notebook—the official manner:

"An envelope missing? Containing what? A torn piece of paper? Nothing else?"

No—it couldn't be done. Why hadn't the swab pinched the notes? That "nothing else" made it impossible to face the police.

Nothing else. By gum, though, there *was* something else missing!

He lifted the case, looked under it, set it down again, flung a cushion out of a chair, turned over newspapers, magazines, books; all with the knowledge that what he was looking for was not there to find. There *was* something else missing.

The thief had not only taken the envelope containing the corner of a bank-note, he had gone off with the typescript of Jim Mackenzie's broadcast talk, "Twenty Years of Invention."

Jim stood stock-still in the middle of the floor. What the something, something, something could any mortal human being want with the typescript of a talk which had just been delivered free gratis and for nothing to the listening ears of everyone who possessed a wireless set? If a passionate desire to read and re-read Jim's carefully thought out sentences was the burglar's motive, he might have indulged it less dangerously by expending threepence on the next copy of *The Listener*.

But he had taken the torn corner of Bertram Hallingdon's bank-note.

Bertram Hallingdon's torn bank-note and the typescript of "Twenty Years of Invention."

The words of Bertram Hallingdon's covering letter sprang into his mind: "This is the torn piece of a five-pound note. Keep it very carefully. If the whole note is assembled, it will give the key to the present whereabouts of the Sanquhar invention. The person who possesses the middle portion of the note will warn you should the need arise." Frankly, he had wondered whether the old man had been quite sane at the last. This talk about the Sanquhar invention.... But the Sanquhar invention had gone up in smoke more than twelve years ago. *Had it?*

He had destroyed Bertram Hallingdon's letter, and he had locked away the torn scrap of paper in the envelope in which it had come to him; and then—yes, *then*—he had blotted out of his neat typescript the paragraph which touched, in passing, on the loss of the Sanquhar invention.

And the burglar had taken the torn scrap of paper, and the burglar had taken the typescript.

The door opened about eight inches. In the opening there appeared a very dirty check duster, Mrs Mabb's bony hand and wrist, Mrs Mabb's long pale nose, and Mrs Mabb's pale inquisitive eyes. The hand held the duster and grasped the edge of the door; the eyes peered round it.

In an agitated whisper Mrs Mabb burst the bonds of silence.

"Your bath's a-running over, and I darsn't touch that there geyser, not after what it done to me last week. That side of me head hasn't bin right since, and I shouldn't wonder if it never was. Banged something crool and went out—and I'm sure I'd barely laid a finger on it, and the smell of gas enough to asphixicate me!"

Chapter Twenty-Three

JIM HAD HIS BATH, dressed, and rang up Agatha Wimborough. Amelia Crofts answered his "Hullo!" with a dismal and almost totally inaudible "Yes?"

"That you, Amelia? I want to speak to Miss Wimborough."

He could hear Amelia sniff, but of what followed the sniff he could make neither head nor tail. That was the exasperating thing about Amelia. Why a person with such a peculiarly penetrating sniff should fade into a mere blur when it came to speech was one of life's insoluble problems.

Jim tried again.

"I'm afraid I didn't get that. Ask Miss Wimborough if she'd mind speaking to me for a minute. It's important."

Amelia sniffed, and repeated the blur. An occasional word emerged from it like the bleating of sheep in a fog.

"Amelia—"

"Yes, sir."

He got that. If she could say, "Yes, sir," she could say all the rest of whatever it was she had been trying to say.

"Look here, Amelia, I can't hear a word you're saying. Put your mouth close to the thingummyjig and put in some lip-work! You're just bleating—and I can't hear you when you bleat. Now carry on! Where's Miss Wimborough?"

"Gone away," said Amelia with a perfectly terrific sniff.

"What!"

"Gone away," repeated Amelia tearfully. She trailed off into a blur again.

"Stop it! Do you hear? *Lip-work*, Amelia! Attention to consonants! And if you sniff, I'll send you a box of poisoned chocolates—I swear I will! That's better! Now—where's Miss Wimborough?"

"F-f-france, sir."

"*France!* Why I *saw* her last night."

"Six o'clock this morning," said Amelia rapidly. "Six o'clock this blessed morning, sir, and in this horful icy cold. And h'anyone may say what they likes about flying, but flying in the face of Providence is what I call it."

There was a pause.

"When will she be back?" said Jim Mackenzie.

"I don't know, sir,"—very lugubriously.

"Oh, *damn*!" said Jim, and jammed the receiver back upon the hook.

What did Agatha Wimborough want to go trapesing off to France for? He had never expected to be desolated by her absence, and yet undoubtedly at this moment a lost and helpless feeling descended upon him. He would have to tackle Rimington himself now. What was it going to look like, his coming and demanding Laura's address? Rimington would have every justification for refusing it.

Mr Rimington refused it so politely and so definitely as to convey the very decided impression that the request was one which should never have been made.

Jim got up and put his hands in his pockets. He wasn't finding this interview easy, and the harder he found it, the grimmer he looked and the more his chin stuck out.

"And that's that!" he said. "I've asked for Mrs Stevens's address, and you've refused to give it to me. You've also informed me that I had no business to ask for it. I'm now going to tell you something."

Mr Rimington was leaning back in his office chair, a very comfortable circular chair with discreet green leather upholstery. He wore an expression of bland and courteous attention. He did not speak; he merely waited. He would let the young man say what he had got to say, and then he would be unable to spare him any more time. Another appointment—yes, another appointment.

Jim clenched his hands and drove on.

"Mrs Stevens—" the name was gall and wormwood—"Mrs Stevens rang up yesterday."

"She rang you up?"

"On a matter of business—a matter connected with Mr Hallingdon's affairs."

"She didn't give you her address?" There was just a pleasant note of inquiry in Mr Rimington's voice.

Jim jerked up his head.

"She didn't give it to me, because she couldn't give it to me. And that's why I'm asking you to give it to me now. She didn't give it to me, because she didn't know it."

"Mr Mackenzie!"

"She didn't know it. You've got to listen! I'm telling you what she said to me. I asked her where she was, and she said she *didn't know.* She said *they hadn't told her.*"

Mr Rimington was looking with interest at his own well blacked shoes. He had one knee crossed comfortably over the other so that he could admire a high state of polish without any undue strain. He had no wish to look up or to meet the furiously earnest gaze of this pertinacious young man; but whether he looked up or down, he could not escape from the feeling that this gaze was both intense and embarrassing.

"Mrs Stevens has been—er—ill," he observed.

"What's that got to do with it?"

"She may not be—er—perfectly recovered."

"What d'you mean by that?"

Mr Rimington had not the slightest intention of explaining what he meant by that. He put the tips of his fingers together and looked at them for a change. Then he said,

"There is no harm in my telling you that I saw Mrs Stevens last week."

"Was she ill then?"

"She was in bed," said Mr Rimington—"but sitting up. I understood that she was convalescent. Perhaps it will relieve your mind if I tell you that I saw her alone. If she had wished to ask me any questions, she could have done so. She asked me nothing. I may add that there was a capable-looking nurse in charge, and that I received the impression that she was well cared for and perfectly satisfied with her surroundings."

"And you saw her alone?"

"I saw her alone. And as I was discharging a somewhat confidential mission, I satisfied myself that there was no one outside the door. If Mrs Stevens had been under any kind of duress, she could have appealed to me. She did nothing of the sort."

Jim stood silent for a moment. He must try and get the address from Stark. But suppose Stark didn't know it? He squared his shoulders and renewed the attack.

"Mr Rimington—will you go and see her again? You've given me to understand that this isn't my affair—but it *is* yours. Is there anything to prevent your going down to see Mrs Stevens this afternoon? You could at least give her her own address."

"I have, at present, no business with Mrs Stevens," said Mr Rimington. "They are, I believe, going abroad very shortly. But—yes—I could go and see her."

"Could you go to-day?"

"No—I think not to-day."

"To-morrow?"

"I am not sure. I am not prepared to give any undertaking on the subject." He glanced at his watch. "And now I am afraid, Mr Mackenzie, that I cannot give you any more time."

Jim came out to a wet street and a drizzle of rain.

Damn the weather! He would have to hang about and catch Stark when he went to lunch. That might mean a couple of hours. Oh, damn everything!

It did not mean a couple of hours. He had walked four times to the end of Dickson Road and back, when Mr Stark, junior clerk in Rimington, Rimington and Greenlees, emerged from the office, turned the corner into Rangeley Street, and began to foot it briskly in the direction of Southam Road.

Jim came up with him fifty yards from the corner and touched him on the shoulder.

"Where are you off to in such a hurry?" he said.

Mr Stark had started nervously. He was carrying an attaché case. He shifted it from his left hand to his right.

"I was just going round to Mallesons' about a lease we're drawing up."

Jim walked along beside him. Rather a slimy business handling Stark. He had several reasons for hating it. Funny that he could never see Stark without simultaneously having a mental picture of old Stark in the potting-shed at home. Why should old Stark, a decent dour old thing if ever there was one, have produced Stark, with his shifty eyes, reedy physique, and general look of having emerged from some underground burrow? He could never help wondering what Stark would have been like if he had stuck to gardening instead of graduating into the black-coated class and embezzling a little money—a very little money—and coming to "Mr Jim", shaking with terror, to be saved from prison for old Stark's sake. Rather disgusting the whole thing. Still he had got to have Laura's address.

All at once the realization of what Stark would think if he asked for it.... Rotten. That's what the whole thing was—*rotten!*

And then Stark speaking, with the shy deprecating note in his voice which was so unlike old Stark's surly gruffness.

"I heard you in the office with the boss just now, Mr Mackenzie."

It had been "Mr Jim" when he wanted some money to save him from prison. The "Mr Mackenzie" was a bid for equality.

"Oh, you did? How much did you hear?"

"We're not supposed to give addresses—you know that, Mr Mackenzie."

"How much did you hear?"

Stark looked sideways under pale lashes and reddened lids. He wasn't like old Stark at all; he was like his mother—like, and unlike. Jim remembered Mrs Stark as a silent, white-faced wisp of a woman who was said to be a dragon in the house and to insist on old Stark taking off his boots before he came indoors. Yes, Stark was like his mother; it was Cissie who took after old Stark.

"For the Lord's sake, Stark, don't squint at me like that! What did you hear?"

"I should get the sack if he was to find out, Mr Mackenzie."

A nasty mess Stark—distinctly a nasty mess.

"What do you want?" said Jim bluntly.

"Would it be worth a fiver to you, Mr Mackenzie?"

Jim stood still.

"Yes, it would." He produced a pocket-book. "Hand it over, and look sharp!"

"The Walled House," said Stark. "Leeming Lane, Putney."

"Putney?" said Jim.

"That's right."

Jim counted out five pound-notes and handed them over. Stark put them away with alacrity. He didn't see why Mr Jim—Mr Mackenzie—should look at him like that. Something for something was the way of the world, and where was the harm?

Jim Mackenzie's voice cut hard across his thoughts.

"Make a good bit on the side one way or another, don't you, Stark?"

Now if that wasn't a dirty, unfair thing to say! Why, he might have stolen the fiver by the way Mr Jim—Mr Mackenzie—was looking at him.

"I don't know what you mean."

"Perhaps you don't—perhaps you do. I'd be sorry to see you in jug, for old Stark's sake. Better watch your step a bit. Well, that's all for to-day."

Chapter Twenty-Four

JIM WENT DOWN to Putney in the early afternoon. He restrained himself till then, because, even to his impatience, it did not seem a good plan to arrive at The Walled House in the middle of lunch. It probably wasn't a good plan to arrive there at all. What he ought to do was to let old Rimington go down. Quite doggedly he admitted this and went.

Leeming Lane was one of those derelict bits of country round London which are being slowly pressed to death. One end of it was already raw and scarred from the erection of a dozen or so little pill-boxes with names like Mon Abri and Locarno. At the other, dark shrubberies and high walls looked down upon the old footpath of the lane.

The Walled House stood alone. Its walls were high and reinforced by evergreens. It had a neglected and forbidding look. Tall stone pillars held between them an oak door with a bell at one side of it.

Jim looked at the bell rather hard. It must have been years since its brass had winked in the sun, so dark and stained and discoloured was it. He rang, and thought that he could hear a faint tinkling that died in the distance. Presently he rang again. No one came; no one answered. The whole place might have been dead and buried for years.

He went back to the other side of the road and took stock of the house. Only the upper windows were visible above the bank of evergreen. Two unkempt laurels made an arch above the gateway. The house stood surprisingly near to the road. Not a large house. The upper windows, which were all that he could see, showed a glimpse of curtain at either side and a few inches of blind at the top. It came to him that he might at any moment see Laura looking out from between the curtains. And then he knew that he would not see her. She had been there last night; she was not there now. The house was a mere empty shell in which the ringing of a bell died with no one to hear it. All the same he meant to get in.

He stopped thinking about Laura and gave his attention to the question of how he was going to get in.

He walked on along the lane. On his left there was a very high wall with bottle-glass on the top of it; on his right, when he had passed The Walled House, a rather battered wooden fence with a hedge inside it. Three or four yards from where the fence began there was a narrow gate that had once been painted green. It bore the remains of lettering which had probably advertised a tradesmen's entrance.

He lifted the latch, walked in, and found himself on a narrow path with a crowding shrubbery on either side of it. The place smelt of damp weeds and sour neglected soil. He pushed his way through the shrubs on his right and came up against the side wall of The Walled House. When he had put a safe distance between himself and the lane, he got over the wall with the help of a convenient cypress. He dropped amongst shrubs. Everyone in the lane seemed keen on the gloomiest type of evergreen. This side of the wall smelt, if possible, worse than the other.

He emerged from the shrubbery, made his way round to the back of the house, and knocked at the kitchen entrance. He was so sure that there was no one in the house that he would have been desperately taken aback if his knocking had produced anything except an echo. The whole place felt deserted. All the same he was going to get in. He wasn't quite sure what happened if you were found breaking into a house in broad daylight. It wasn't burglary before eight o'clock at night—or was it nine?—which seemed a very convenient arrangement. He thought he would have a try at the scullery window. There seemed to be something about a scullery which produced extreme debility of the latch. He had always been able to get in through the scullery window at home, and he had come across several other cases. This scullery window was no exception to the rule. The rickety latch slid back at the merest touch from his pocket-knife. He climbed in over a very dirty sink—tea-leaves, cabbage-leaves, banana skins. Faugh! How beastly!

He came through the untidy kitchen into a passage that ran beside the stairs and opened into the hall. The first door on the left, a study, with curtains drawn; the second, opening from the hall, a dining-room; on the other side of the hall door the drawing-room—all empty and about as cold as the north pole.

He went up the stairs, round the bend, and came to a landing with four doors opening upon it. He tried them all in turn, and every room was empty. In the two rooms which faced each other across the landing, one at the head of the stair up which he had come, and the other at the foot of that which led to an upper floor, the beds were neatly made. In both these rooms a lingering smell of boots conveyed the impression that they had been occupied by men. The other two rooms were in considerable disorder. The bed-clothes had in each case been flung back from an unmade bed. In the right-hand room there was a litter of torn and half burned paper in the grate.

Jim gathered up the paper carefully and spread it out on the dressing-table. There was some part of a bill with the heading burnt through. He read: "Ribbon—three and elevenpence halfpenny", and tossed the charred fragment back into the grate. The other pieces were bits of a letter torn small. After a lot of trouble he fitted some of them together and got what seemed to be a signature—"Your devoted Sasha". He tipped all the bits into his handkerchief, knotted it, and pushed it down into his pocket.

There was a connecting door between these two rooms. He passed through it and stood looking about him. Here everything was neat except the bed, which was half stripped, with a crimson eider-down trailing down on to the carpet. He opened all the drawers, and found them empty. Then he stood at the window and looked out. What he saw was what Laura had seen only yesterday.

As he stood there, the most curious impression came to him— the impression that somewhere in the room behind him Laura was waiting. That this had been her room, he was sure; and he found the thought a moving one. But beyond his certainty that she had been here, and the emotion that this caused him, there was a very strange and definite sense of her presence. She was there behind him, just behind him. And there was something that he must do. Laura wanted him to do something, and he hadn't the very slightest idea what it was. The pressure became like the pressure upon a bruise. He swung round, and there was nothing but the empty room, the trailing bed-clothes, the crimson eider-down.

He went out of the room and up to the attic floor, where he found a box-room, a cistern-room, and two small bedrooms, one of which had been recently occupied. He came down again, and stood for a moment in the doorway of Laura's room.

It was while he was standing there that the telephone bell rang. It rang from somewhere on the ground floor, and as it rang continuously, he had no difficulty in tracing the sound to the study. He clapped the receiver to his ear, the ringing stopped, and a voice said, "Hullo!"

Jim said, "Hullo!" in a guarded muffled voice.

Something in the tone of that "Hullo!" seemed familiar. The voice repeated it, and suspicion became certainty. It was Stark who was ringing up, and the question now arose—to whom did Stark suppose himself to be speaking? The question answered itself immediately.

"Is that you, Mr Stevens?" said the voice of Stark.

Jim tried to remember what Stevens's voice was like. Higher pitched than his own, he thought. Anyhow he must chance it.

"What do you want?" he said.

"You know who it is, Mr Stevens?" Stark was all of a twitter.

"Yes. What is it?"

"I was to let you know if the guvnor thought of coming down again."

"Yes."

"Well, he's thinking about it."

So he had put the wind up old Rimington. That was something. He said,

"When?"

There was a somewhat prolonged pause. Then Stark, all hurried and nervous.

"It's a thing I might lose my job over."

"Well?"

"I can't afford to do that, as you know, Mr Stevens."

So Stark was in the habit of selling information to Basil Stevens. He recognized the formula. He said,

"That will be all right."

"Same as usual, Mr Stevens?"

"I suppose so."

"Well then, he's coming down to-morrow—putting off an appointment to do it. That's all, Mr Stevens—and I'd like notes, not a cheque if it's all the same to you."

Jim hung up the receiver. Master Stark wouldn't get either notes or a cheque this time, the crooked little viper.

He stood for a moment thinking about Stark. He'd have him over the coals for this. Do him good to be caught out on one of his dirty games. Pity old Stark hadn't broken a stick or two over him when he had the chance. Proud of the little worm's brains, and ambitious. Good Lord! For what? To have a son who would be ashamed because his father was a gardener! Poor old Stark!

He broke off to search the study, and found nothing. The drawers of the writing-table had been emptied. He shoved the last one in, and suddenly, standing there with one hand on the table, it came over him that this was where Laura had stood only last night. She had come in through that door and passed round this table. She had stood where he was standing now. Perhaps she had bent to the telephone, leaning upon her hand. Perhaps she had pulled the chair a little nearer and drawn the telephone close. The room all at once was full of Laura. She had a way of pushing back her hair before she picked up the receiver. He could see her leaning forward, pushing back her hair, and watching the door whilst she spoke his name and warned him—warned him.

He shook off the dream, and presently climbed out of the scullery window and over the wall. And so back to town.

Chapter Twenty-Five

JIM WAS WITHIN a hundred yards of his own entrance, when he ran into Kennedy Jackson, who was about the last person on earth he wanted to see. Kennedy Jackson immediately took hold of him, by the arm and began a long apology for his own tactlessness of the night before. His idea of making amends was to go over the whole ground again with the easy grace of a herd of hippopotamuses.

"I hadn't the slightest idea, my dear fellow—not the very slightest idea. But after leaving you I fell in with Brown, and he told me the whole thing from start to finish. I had no idea of course—positively no idea—absolutely not the slightest." And so forth and so on, with a great deal of what Brown had said to him, and still more of what he had said to Brown. A really intolerable performance, with Jackson holding him firmly by the arm and pushing a face like a crumpet to within six inches of his.

"Look here, Jackson, I'm sorry, but I'm in a hurry."

"I know, I know—but I really had to explain. I said to Brown, 'Why, I wouldn't have done it for the world.' And all he'd got to say was, 'Well, it's not the sort of thing you can explain away.' And I said, 'Explain be damned! Of course I'm going to explain! I don't want Mackenzie to go about thinking I'm the sort of fellow who comes crashing into your private affairs without so much as a by your leave.' Well, that shook him, and I came charging round here after you, and up all those damned stairs because the lift was out of action, only to find that you weren't there. I wasn't the only fellow to draw a blank either."

"What d'you mean?" said Jim sharply.

He stepped back a pace, and Jackson followed him up.

"Oh, that fellow Stevens," he said with casual indifference.

Jim twisted himself free.

"What d'you mean?"

"Stevens—that fellow Stevens, you know. Met him coming down as I went up. Nasty stand-offish sort of manner he's got too—thought he was going to cut me till I got in front of him and asked him what he was playing at."

Jim did some rapid thinking.

"When was this?"

"Oh, last night. And as I was telling you—"

"What time?"

"Well, let me see…. It would have been about ten o'clock when I met you—and then I went along and ran into Brown, and we forgathered a bit, and had some stout and oysters, and passed the time of day, and so on—and then he had to meet a party at a night club—can't remember the name; it wasn't going a year ago—so I said I'd go with him—"

"Look here, Jackson—do you know what time it was, or don't you?"

"Well, I do, because I know I couldn't get another drink at the club, and it was after that I thought I'd come along and look you up. And I walked, so it must have taken me the best part of half an hour, and what with one thing and another I should think it must have been getting on for one o'clock."

"You came up to my flat at one in the morning—and you met Stevens? What was he doing?"

"Well, he came out of your flat."

"*What?*"

"He came out of your flat and said you weren't there, so we walked down the street together, and then I buzzed along home."

"*Basil Stevens came out of my flat?*"

Jackson's round light eyes became rounder.

"The fellow's name isn't Basil."

"What is it?"

"Alec," said Jackson. "Basil's another sort of bird altogether. Basil's an engineer—and—oh, Lord—yes, of course—it was Basil Stevens who butted in and did the dirty on you with Miss Cameron! Sorry, old fellow—I wasn't going to mention it, but it just cropped up! The fellow who came out of your flat wasn't Basil—it was Alec."

"And who is Alec?" said Jim rather grimly.

"Well, I believe he's some sort of cousin of Basil's."

"And he was coming out of my flat at one in the morning?"

"Well, I won't swear to the time, because now I come to think of it, I went home with Brown, or Brown came home with me. Funny thing, you know, but I can't remember which of us went home with the other—but as a matter of fact we did ourselves pretty well, and then I went home with Brown, or Brown went home with me, and we had one or two more—and after that it seemed quite a good idea to blow in on you, so I did—but it may have been later than one—in fact, now I come to think of it, I should say it might have been as much as two, or even three."

"Look here, Jackson—will you swear you saw Stevens?"

"Of course I saw Stevens! I may have been doing myself a bit well, but I wasn't blind. And I didn't see Basil Stevens—I saw Alec."

"And he let himself out of my flat?"

"And put the key in his pocket and came to the end of the street with me."

When he had got rid of Kennedy Jackson, Jim walked upstairs to his flat, the lift being still out of action.

Alec Stevens, who was a cousin of Basil Stevens, had come into his flat last night and lifted the torn piece of Bertram Hallingdon's bank-note. He had probably used the key which Mrs Mabb had lost a couple of days before. Well, what did one do? Send for the police? He didn't think so—no, he didn't think so. Laura had told him to put the note in a safe place, and he hadn't taken her warning. How did Laura come to know anything about the torn note? It looked to him as if she might have another of the pieces, in which case the Stevens family were obviously out for a full hand.

The piece that had come to him from Bertram Hallingdon was an irregular bit torn from the left-hand corner diagonally downwards across the note. It was about three inches wide at the lower edge. From the general size and shape of his bit he thought it likely that the note had been torn into three pieces. Of course there might be more pieces. He could only guess, but he guessed that there were three.

Well, what to do next? Find Stevens—this new Stevens—Alec. Find Laura. To find Stevens was probably the best way to find Laura. Rimington had said they were going abroad—taking Laura abroad. That made the whole thing much more difficult—and of course it was just what the Stevenses would do if they were on the doubtful side of the English law. You've got to have a damned good case for extradition— everything cut and dried. Well, at any rate he could find out whether Laura had been taken abroad. The passport nuisance had its points after all.

He rang up Peter Severn. Then he looked at his watch. Master Stark would be coming out of office in about half an hour, and he thought of having a word with him. Peter would deliver the goods all right, but it would take a little time. Meanwhile, Jim had an idea that a straight talk with Stark was what the situation called for.

Stark was anything but pleased to see him. He was smiling as he came round the corner, and the smile came off when he saw Jim Mackenzie waiting for him. He had the sensation, the very unpleasant sensation, of having missed a rather deep step. The soles of his feet tingled, and his eyelids twitched.

"Glad to see me, Stark?"

"Oh, Mr Mackenzie!"

"Of course you are—damned glad—you look it."

"Oh, Mr Mackenzie!"

"I want to talk to you." Jim's voice was rough. "Don't say 'Oh, Mr Mackenzie!' again, because I'm on the edge of losing my temper now, and if I go over the edge you won't like it. I'd better come along to your rooms—we can't talk in the street."

Stark turned a sort of yellowish pink. He stood still and fidgeted with his umbrella.

"I don't think that would be at all suitable, Mr Mackenzie."

Whatever it was that he kept in the place of a conscience had run up a danger signal.

"Oh, you don't? And why not?"

"It wouldn't be at all suitable, Mr Mackenzie."

After all, whatever he had found out, Mr Jim couldn't very well assault him in the street. He looked up and met an intimidating frown.

"You can come to my flat if you like," said Jim.

Stark didn't like at all, and opened his mouth to say so, but before he could get an objection into words Mr Jim was speaking again.

"That's not suitable either, I suppose! Now look here, Stark—you're for it, and you'd better get it over. If you don't talk to me to-night, you'll find yourself talking to Mr Rimington to-morrow. I suppose with twelve hours notice you'll be able to think up some sort of reason for giving office secrets away to Mr Stevens, but I very much doubt whether it will be satisfying to Mr Rimington. So I think on the whole you'd better have a talk with me."

Stark felt himself going at the knees.

"I'm sure I don't know what you mean, Mr Mackenzie," he said. But he got into the taxi which Jim hailed, and sat biting his lips and looking nervously at his own feet until they arrived at the flat.

Jim left a heavy silence to do its work. Not one word did he say until his sitting-room door had shut upon them. Then he leaned against it with his hands in his pockets and looked Stark up and down.

"Well, you crooked little cur?" he said.

Stark had backed against the table. He held his umbrella as if he might have to use it to defend himself. Jim caught his nervous glance at the telephone.

"I'm sure I don't know what you mean, Mr Mackenzie."

"No—of course you don't! Look here, Stark, you can cut all that out! I'm not guessing this time—I've got you cold. You can either come across and make a clean breast of the whole thing, or I'll thrash you first and smash you afterwards."

The umbrella fell with a clatter.

"Mr Mackenzie—"

"Cut it out, Stark!"

Stark put a damp hand behind him and clutched at the edge of the table. Why had he been such a fool as to come here?.... Mr Jim would have got him sacked if he hadn't.... He'd get him sacked anyhow.... What did he know?.... What had he found out?....

He fumbled for a handkerchief and dabbed at a forehead that had suddenly grown wet.

"Well?" said Jim.

"I—I don't know what you're talking about."

"All right, I'll explain. You're trying to run with the hare and hunt with the hounds, and it won't do. No—wait a minute! You needn't bother to think up a lie—I tell you I *know*. You sold me a piece of information this morning. This afternoon you supplied Mr Stevens with another piece of information. Mine was a cash transaction, but you probably run an account with him. Does he pay you a fiver a time, or do you give him quantity rates?"

Stark leaned against the table. He wanted something to lean against badly.

"I don't know what you mean," he quavered.

"It's no good, Stark—I answered the telephone."

Stark had begun to mop his brow again, but as the last words penetrated the confusion of his mind, his hand dropped. He stood there clutching the clammy handkerchief, his mouth a little open and his breath coming audibly.

"Mr Stevens has gone abroad," said Jim. "I happened to be in the house when the telephone rang, and I answered it."

Stark made a superhuman effort.

"There wasn't anything in what I did—not really, Mr Mackenzie. Mr Stevens just asked me to let him know if the guvnor was coming down, and I couldn't see what harm there was."

"No," said Jim. Then he looked very directly at Stark and smiled. It was not the sort of smile that was calculated to raise a sinking courage. "Mr Stevens has gone abroad," he repeated.

Stark said nothing. He was wiping the palms of his hands.

"He has," said Jim. "And I—*I*, Stark—have not gone abroad. I am here—I am very much here. If you've got to choose between the devil abroad and the devil at home, which is it going to be? I'm afraid you've got to the point when you can't serve two masters any longer—it should perhaps be three, but poor old Rimington doesn't seem to count."

If Stark's hands were wet, his lips were dry. He ran a shuddering tongue over them.

Jim stood away from the door and began quite slowly to take off his coat. When he had thrown it across a chair, he had another look at Stark.

"Well—which is it to be?"

"Mr Jim—"

"Stand up to it, man! You've got your choice."

Stark backed away from him, one hand on the table. When he came to a chair, he fell on to it all of a heap.

"Mr Jim—don't! Don't hit me! They'll kill me if I tell you. I'd sooner tell you—gospel truth I would—but they'd kill me!"

"Perhaps I shall kill you," said Jim pleasantly.

"You wouldn't, Mr Jim—I'm no match for you."

"No, I won't kill you," said Jim—"I'll only thrash you."

He came a step nearer, and Stark flung up a hand.

"If I tell you—will you let me off?"

"I'll see about it."

Stark moistened his lips again.

"They'll kill me!"

"Have it your own way—but I'm here, and they're not." He paused, and then said, *"Well?"* with a good deal of emphasis.

"All—all right."

Jim reached behind him for a chair and straddled across it with his arms over the back.

"Fire away," he said.

"What do you want to know, Mr Jim?"

"Everything. Who *they* are, to start with."

Stark looked sideways, a glance of pure panic with a sort of question in it.

"Basil Stevens, I suppose." Jim spoke slowly, watching him. "And Alec Stevens—he's in the cast, isn't he? And—let me see—who else?"

Stark made no denial, but he produced no other name.

"You're not getting along very fast," said Jim.

Stark threw him a hunted glance.

"I wish I'd never gone into it. I wouldn't if I'd known what they were, but all he wanted at first was just to know silly little things like when Mr Hallingdon rang the guvnor up, and if any appointment was made."

"With Mr Hallingdon?"

Stark nodded.

"And then he wanted to know about letters, and whether there was anything of Mr Hallingdon's in the safe. And I was short of cash—I'd dropped a packet on Mossy Face."

"I see. And after the letters and the telephone calls—what next?"

Stark fingered his collar. It seemed as if he found it tight.

"There wasn't much—gospel truth, there wasn't, Mr Jim. Copies of letters, when I could get them—but I got scared."

"You're not very hard to scare. But what scared you?"

Stark crumpled his handkerchief.

"You don't know where you are with foreigners," he said.

"Foreigners?"

"They're Russians, Mr Jim—both of them. Name of Stefanoff—only they call themselves Stevens to be taken for English. Why, when they're alone they call each other Vassili and Sasha. That's Russian for Basil and Alec, and—"

"Who told you that?"

"No one."

"Oh, I think some one. Out with it!"

"A girl," said Stark. "She's not anyone for you to worry about. She told me, and that got me scared."

There was more, a lot more, behind all this. It appeared from under Stark's twitching eyelids; it hid behind his stumbling words. Jim's mind followed a line that led from Bertram Hallingdon, through the Sanquhar invention, to Vassili and Sasha Stefanoff, who presented a British front to the world as Basil and Alec Stevens.

The thought of Laura struck him a sharp stabbing blow.

"Get on!" he said harshly.

It took time, but in the end he managed to extract details—such and such a telephone message repeated; such and such a letter copied; such and such a conversation overheard and passed on. Stark appeared to have been a remarkably efficient spy. It seemed certain that Basil Stevens had known all the terms of Bertram Hallingdon's will.

Jim wrote everything down in his neat, careful hand. He came, towards the end, to an item that fixed his attention.

"When was this?" he said sharply.

"Last week, Mr Jim."

"Basil Stevens was abroad then?"

Stark nodded.

"He had to go to France on business; but he didn't want to be away in case the guvnor went down to see Mrs Stevens—Miss Cameron that was." Stark was talking quite freely now. "The fact is he'd got it into his head that the guvnor had got some sort of confidential papers of Mr Hallingdon's that he was to hand over to Mrs Stevens, and he wanted to be there when they were handed over, so I was to send him a wire when the guvnor settled to go. You see, he knew by this time that there's never anything done in a hurry, not in our office—so I was to wire him, and he'd come over, by air if necessary."

"I see. The address, please?" (This was a bit of luck.)

"What address?"

"The one you wired to."

"I've forgotten it."

"No, you haven't!"

Stark gulped and produced the address.

"Villa Jaureguy, Sarrance, France."

When he had written the address, Jim brought a frowning gaze to rest on Stark, who was engaged in smoothing his hair, straightening his tie, and giving other indications of a care-free mind. Relieved—that was what Stark was. He had been genuinely frightened of the Stefanoff pair, and was beginning to have a feeling that he had handed his worries over to Mr Jim.

Jim remembered suddenly Stark breaking a window when their united ages fell several years short of twenty. Stark had whimpered and lied, and Jim had had his pocket-money stopped, and had had to put up with a jawbation of a most tiresome length. He had kicked Stark behind the potting-shed afterwards, and his father had thrashed him for bullying. He frowned portentously as he remembered old Stark glowering through a cobwebby window with a geranium cutting in one hand and a sharp little knife in the other. And little Cissie Stark had stood and watched them, with her dark eyes as round and wet as little black pools, and the knuckles of one brown hand pressed up against her lips in the way she had when anything frightened her. He wondered what had happened to Cissie; he hadn't heard of her for ages.

"Look here, Stark," he said, "why don't you run straight?"

Stark had revived sufficiently to look offended. Jim put out a hand and brushed away his protest.

"You took scholarships, so I suppose you've got brains of a sort. Why don't you use them? All this rotten sort of game you've been playing—where's it going to put you? I can tell you—anyone can tell you—in jug. You'll get a short sentence, and you'll come out and you won't be able to get a job, and you'll do something crooked and get a longer sentence and start all over again. You're the stuff that habitual criminals are made of. Seems to me if you've got a brain, you might get it to work on whether that's your life ambition. It hardly seems worth while to take scholarships and do four years of London University if you're going to spend most of the rest of your life in jail. Think it over!"

He got up and threw the door open.

"All right, that'll do. Better be getting along."

As Stark went by him, Jim had a curious impulse.

"Where's your sister Cissie now? Is she married?"

What a nervous little rat the fellow was. He started as if some one had tripped him. Then with a jerk he righted himself and stood there twitching.

"What did you say?"

"I asked about Cissie—your sister Cissie. Nothing's happened to her, has it?"

"Oh no, Mr Jim."

"Is she married?"

"Oh no, Mr Jim."

"What's she doing?"

He didn't know why he was asking all these questions about Cissie Stark. He hadn't seen her since she was ten years old—a pretty, cheeky kid, just beginning to make eyes at anything in trousers. Perhaps she had come to grief. That might account for Stark's manner; but he was a little surprised to find him so sensitive on a point of honour. He began to feel sorry he had asked after her. But Stark was answering quite glibly.

"She's on the stage, Mr Jim—in the chorus of *As You Were*."

Poor old Stark! What would he have said to a daughter in the chorus, a strict, old-fashioned Church-and-State conservative with views on young women "dressing quiet and keeping 'emselves to 'emselves"? Poor old Stark!

Stark was now producing quite a flow of words.

"I don't see much of her, Mr Jim—not once in a twelvemonth."

Jim cut him short. He really wasn't interested in Cissie Stark. The old people were dead, and she'd gone her own way. He wasn't surprised that she'd cut loose from her brother; he wasn't exactly an asset— probably tried to borrow money from her.

He shut the door on Stark with relief.

Peter Severn rang up ten minutes later. Mr and Mrs Basil Stevens had crossed from Dover to Calais that morning. Their passports were for France.

Jim picked up his notes and looked at the address to which Stark had sent a telegram the week before—Villa Jaureguy, Sarrance.

Chapter Twenty-Six

JIM STOOD ON the edge of the road and looked at the iron gates which defended the Villa Jaureguy. Vassili Stefanoff seemed to specialize in houses with good high walls. He had no doubt excellent reasons for this.

The walls of the Villa Jaureguy were, he judged, some six inches higher than those of The Walled House at Putney. The gates, which were locked, had a fine seventeenth century air, and were certainly not climbable. There were, as far as he could observe, no friendly evergreens. The lodge had an unlit, empty look.

The hour was between half-past four and five in the afternoon, and a miserable cold daylight was dying gloomily. The wind—a very considerable wind—blew straight from the north pole. It seemed to intimate that at any moment it might become a blizzard; once or twice already a little burning point of ice had struck Jim on the cheek.

He walked on up the road slowly.

In Sarrance, which was about a mile and a half away, they had told him that the Villa Jaureguy was for sale. It had been the extravagance of a financier who had come to grief. Until it was sold, the executors were letting it furnished. The people of Sarrance evidently considered that only a person deprived of his wits would wish to inhabit a lonely house in the country at this time of year. The present tenant had arrived the day before—a Mr Stevens—English like m'sieu. Oh yes, there was a Madame Stevens—but certainly. They had arrived yesterday. There were servants in the house, a man and wife who acted as caretakers, and their son. No—no one in Sarrance had seen Madame Stevens. It was said that she had been ill—"and for an invalid, *mon dieu*, what a desolate spot!"

Jim walked a hundred yards and saw the wall take a right-angle turn and run back from the road. He walked on, wasting time. It had better be a little darker before he tried to get over that wall. The road, which was hardly more than a lane, began to run up hill. He walked for ten minutes and then came back. The dusk had deepened, and the stinging points of ice were more frequent. He left the road and followed the wall.

The place appeared to be stuck down in the middle of fields. The grounds might have been four or five acres in extent. Sarrance spoke with bated breath of the money that had been spent on them. There was a green marble swimming-bath, an orangery of huge dimensions, a maze, fountains, and so forth and so on. Meanwhile Jim could see no more than the looming blackness of a wall which he could not climb.

He went on following the wall. Since Laura was on the other side of it, he meant somehow to reach that other side; but at the moment he hadn't the slightest idea how he was going to do it. He continued to walk, and after a while came out upon the road again. It was now quite definitely snowing. He wondered what would happen if he were to ring the bell and ask for Laura by name. He stood back from the gates and put his hands in his pockets. He couldn't ring, and he couldn't ask for Laura, because by every possible canon of behaviour he had no business to be here. Instead of coming to the Villa Jaureguy he ought, obviously, to have tracked down Miss Wimborough, escorted her to Sarrance, and then stood aside whilst she paid an orthodox call. Miss Wimborough could have rung that bell as loudly as she pleased. An aunt may visit her niece in the face of the most secretive of husbands. In fact Miss Wimborough should have been standing in his shoes. He knew all this perfectly well. He continued to disregard it.

What exactly would have happened if Pierre Clement, the seventeen year old son of the caretaking couple, had not been in the first flush of his first love affair, it is impossible to say. It was not an affair which had the approval of his parents, and he had therefore to resort to subterfuge in order to leave the Villa Jaureguy and put in an hour with his Solange. He had an appointment with her at six o'clock, an hour when his mother was particularly busy. He had, by an exercise of sleight of hand, possessed himself of the key of the gates, and at the moment in which Jim was engaged in bludgeoning his conscience he inserted the key in a well oiled lock, turned it, and swung the gate wide enough to allow him to pass through.

Jim had ears like a cat. He heard the key go into the lock, and at the first sound he was over the road. If anyone was coming out, he was going in. As Master Pierre slipped through the gap, a hand fell hard upon his shoulder. Conscience is fairly active at seventeen. Pierre conceived the hand to be his father's, dropped the key, and then stood shaking.

With the first quiver of the shoulder under his hand, Jim knew that his luck was in. It was a law-breaking shoulder, a guilty and terrified shoulder. He shook it sharply.

"What are you doing?"

Pierre still trembled, but since it was not his father who had caught him, he began to recover. After all, what he was chiefly afraid of was that he might be late for his tryst; and Solange wouldn't wait—not she, not a minute.

"Well? Who are you?" said the voice that belonged to the hand.

"Pierre, m'sieu."

So it was a boy—a boy sneaking out on his own probably nefarious business. Luck was certainly in.

"Pierre, are you? Well, Pierre, have you any objection to a tip?"

"No, m'sieu. What does m'sieu want?"

"I want to go up to the house. I think I want that key, Pierre."

"But, m'sieu—"

"Is there anyone in the lodge?"

"No, m'sieu. The gardener left last week."

"All right then, just leave the gate open for a bit—say an hour. How's that?"

"But, m'sieu—"

"I'm not a burglar. I only want to speak to Madame."

A glow of fellow-feeling warmed Pierre. He became talkative and full of helpful suggestions. Madame, it appeared, was alone. Monsieur had taken the auto an hour, two hours, ago, and it was not known when he would be back. Madame was in the little salon. If m'sieu would turn to the right when he came to the portico and keep right on round the house until he saw a light behind the curtains, that was the little salon. It opened into the orangery, and the door of the orangery was unlocked, because that was the way that Pierre had used himself. His parents, in fact, believed him to be chopping wood and stoking the furnace. In fact the orangery door was open, and—

"Oh, thank you, m'sieu! *Merci bien*, m'sieu!"

Jim walked up a straight, formal drive. He could distinguish none of the things upon which the late financier had squandered so much money. The gardens of the Villa Jaureguy might be an earthly paradise or a sandy desolation. For him they were filled with dense strange shadows of a hundred different shapes, some tall and spreading, others low and massed, but all submerged in a soft darkness that was like water because it moved continuously, and when it moved all the shadows moved too, like seaweed when the current is running strong. It was the wind which blew the shadows to and fro and gave this illusion of a vast flowing tide of darkness. And all the time the snow kept falling, very hard, and small, and stinging.

He almost ran into the portico; but when he had turned and come round the house he was out of the wind, and in a moment he could see the windows of the little salon marked out with lines of light where the drawn curtains left a crack and the rosy shine came through—rose-coloured curtains and a warm rosy light. He went past the windows and came on the orangery. There seemed to be masses and masses of it, all glass. It showed like a spectral tent faintly outlined by lines of frozen snow which melted on the glass but clung to the iron tracery.

The path led straight to a door, and the door opened easily to his hand.

Chapter Twenty-Seven

JIM STEPPED INSIDE the orangery and closed the door behind him. That one step took him eight hundred miles or so south. He stood in a warm dense darkness heavy with the smell of wet earth and the scent of flowers. Hyacinth? Tuberose? Freesia? There was something very sudden about it. One moment there had been the wind—and even under the lee of the house it had an edge like a saw—the wind, and the pelting ice-pointed snow. And the next this heavily scented warmth. For the moment, of course, it had its points; but for any length of time he thought he would prefer the blizzard.

He advanced carefully, feeling his way. His outstretched hand touched a rough-leafed plant, and at once the faint smell of lemon was added to the blend. They had had lemon-scented verbena in the conservatory at home. He picked off a bit and stuck it in his button-hole. Old Stark used to be down on him like a knife if he pinched a bit. It was a good smell—a clean, decent sort of smell.

The place was dead dark, but away on the left there were lines of light like thin gold wire, and the oblong they framed was dusk not dark, and the dusk was shot with a pinkish glow. He made his way very cautiously to what was evidently a glass door leading to the little salon. He turned the handle, and the door opened towards him, leaving only a curtain between him and the room where Laura was.

He stood there, and could not make out what had happened to him. If he had been made of wood, he would have had as much feeling. The thought of meeting Laura had been a goad stabbing on a raw place, but now the place was numb. He had not known what he would do or what he would say when he and Laura met, whether he would rage or be dumb; but that he should feel nothing at all—this had never come into his thoughts.

The curtain was really two curtains. He put up a steady hand and parted them by the merest fraction, of an inch. Everything beyond swam in a pink glow. He could see the light, but not much else, because a yard from the door a brocaded screen blocked his view. He parted the curtains a little more and stepped into the room. The screen hid him completely. It stood on a pale flowered carpet. He took a step to the right and looked round it.

The little salon was furnished in an ornate style with a good deal of gilding. It was lit by wall brackets in the shape of pink shells supported by golden cupids. The curtains were of rose-coloured velvet. The chairs and the two couches were covered with a delicate pink and blue brocade.

Jim's eyes went to the nearest couch. It stood at an angle which gave him a view of one high end, some piled-up cushions, and the top of a woman's head. Her dark hair rested on a golden pouffe. He straightened himself to see more, and caught a glimpse of pale silken draperies. He still felt nothing at all. It was no longer in him to feel anything for Laura.

He walked from behind the screen and came out in front of the couch. The dark head lifted itself from the cushion; its owner gave a faint scream and sat up. She was a very handsome young woman with fine dark eyes and an elaborately artificial complexion. She was not Laura.

She looked at Jim, and Jim looked at her. This was why he had felt nothing. She wasn't Laura. Laura wasn't here. He had a most complete conviction that Laura wasn't here. He said quickly,

"I beg your pardon—I'm afraid I startled you. I wanted to see—Mrs Stevens." And there he stopped at the impact of a most surprising idea.

The girl was staring at him with her eyes as round and dark as two dark pools. She had one hand against her lips with the knuckles pressing hard against the soft curves. There was fright in her eyes; but there was something else—something that it was quite impossible to mistake—recognition. Quite suddenly she threw out both hands in a wide graceful gesture and said in a laughing voice,

"Oh, you *did* frighten me!"

Her eyes sparkled at him. She showed some very pretty white teeth.

Cissie Stark! Was it possible? He thought so—but—Cissie Stark—*here*....

She was dressed in a diaphanous négligé. It was composed of a great many yards of material and a quantity of expensive fur, and it hid very little of Cissie Stark. It *was* Cissie Stark.

Jim said his piece all over again.

"I'm so sorry I startled you. I wanted to see Mrs Stevens."

There was still that recognition in her eyes.

"Well—who do you think I am?" she said, laughing.

She really had marvellous teeth.

"Cissie Stark?" said Jim.

A curious flashing look went over her face. It took the laughter with it. All at once she was as grave as a judge.

"How did you recognize me?" She paused, and added, "Mr Jim."

"It was when you put your hand up to your mouth—you always did that when you were frightened. And besides, I saw that you recognized me—I don't know how."

She made a slight impatient movement.

"Oh, that's easy! You haven't changed. Besides I saw you with Ernie the other day. I was coming to meet him, and I saw you talking. I thought it was you, and I got it out of him, though he wasn't particularly anxious for me to know. Poor old Ernie, he's funny like that."

Stark *would* have a name like Ernie. And what a liar he was! But why should he have lied? Why should he have gone out of his way to pretend that he practically never saw Cissie? Was Cissie the girl who had told him that Basil and Alec Stevens were Russians and dangerous? And what was Cissie doing *here*? He asked her, quite directly.

"I was told that I should find Madame in this room."

"Well—and so you did," said Cissie Stark.

"You are Madame?"

"Well, for the present. My stage name is Cecile St Arc. Rather good—isn't it?"

"Very, I came to see Mrs Stevens. Are you Mrs Stevens?"

"What do you think?" said Miss Cecile St Arc.

She flung herself back into the sofa corner, rummaged under the cushions, and produced an ornate cigarette case. It was, or appeared to be, of gold with a large C in brilliants. Old Stark and the potting-shed were a long way off.

She offered the case to Jim and lit a cigarette herself.

Jim sat down at the other end of the couch.

"Well," he said, "that is where you have me. I don't know what to think. I come here to see Mrs Stevens—I'm told she's in this room—I find you here—and—you ask me what I think. We're old friends. Can't you help me out a bit?"

She laughed.

"It's not against the law to call yourself anything you fancy."

"And you fancy calling yourself Stevens—is that it?"

"Perhaps I do. It's not going to hurt anyone, is it?"

"I don't know."

"What are you getting at? You can't kid me, so I shouldn't advise you to try. You didn't come here to see *me*—now did you?"

"I came to see—Mrs Stevens."

"Miss Laura Cameron,"

"Yes."

"Why?"

He ought to have had an answer ready. He had none. He had come because he couldn't keep away, because Laura had cried out to him. He could not say these things to Cissie Stark, so he said nothing.

She was watching him through a light haze of smoke.

"Well, Mr Jim—what about it?"

She had turned the tables on him. He had asked her something and she had not answered, and before he knew where he was it was she who was asking the embarrassing questions. All right, let her ask—she wasn't going to get an answer from him that way.

He took a good look at her, and wondered what he was up against. An odd recollection of little Cissie Stark's prim starched pinafores mingled with his wonder. Cecile St Arc didn't look as if she had ever worn a pinafore in her life—a handsome, heady creature with a frank physical appeal. But there was something else too; and it was the something else that he wanted to be sure about. He thought of a soft cushion with a needle in it—you might miss it, or you might get stuck to the bone. He went on wondering.

"Miss Laura Cameron—that's who you came to see, didn't you?"

He said, "Yes. I want to see her. Is she here?"

"Here? What do you think?" She laughed and shook the ash from her cigarette.

"No, she's not here," said Jim. He was quite sure about this. "But Mrs Stevens *is* here."

Something just came and went at the back of the dark eyes. Impossible to say just what it was. She leaned a little farther into the cushions and blew out a cloud of smoke.

"Stevens does me as well as any other name when I'm on a holiday. I don't see that it's your business what I call myself—but there, I dare say you know best about that." She paused, and added in a mocking voice, *"Mr Jim!"*

Jim felt the angry blood come to his face. He spoke more roughly than he had meant to.

"Are you here with Basil Stevens?"

"Why should I be?"

"Are you?"

"Why *shouldn't* I be?" She smiled warmly, teasingly, invitingly. But she was watching him. He had a sense of something alert and wary.

He got up.

"What you do isn't my affair," he said.

"And what Miss Laura Cameron does?"

"Why do you call her that?"

She burst out laughing.

"To get a rise out of you, of course! I bet you don't think about her as Laura Stevens! Hit you pretty hard, didn't it, when she married Basil?"

She was trying to throw him off his balance. All right, let her try. The mere fact that she was trying steadied him. He stood looking down at her quite coolly.

"Will you tell me where she is?"

She shook her head.

"Not me! I don't go shoving myself into other people's affairs."

"Well, I do—when it suits me." He continued to look at her. "You're not by any chance married to Basil Stevens?"

She blew out a puff of smoke and turned her left hand for him to see that it wore a wedding ring.

"Looks nice there, Mr Jim—doesn't it?"

"*Very.* Are you married to Stevens?"

"What d'you think?"

How many more times was she going to say that?

"I don't want to think—I want to know. Are you married to Basil Stevens?"

She sat up a little at that. The hot ash fell on her knee, and she brushed it off with an extraordinary violence.

"What makes you go on asking me that? Isn't he married to your Miss Laura Cameron? Well then, how can he be married to me?"

"I asked you a question, and you haven't answered it."

She flung her cigarette away and jumped up.

"I suppose you think you're funny, coming here and insulting anyone like that!"

"You haven't answered me."

She looked remarkably handsome; but he wondered whether she was going to scratch his face. And then on the top of that, like a sharp prick, came the thought, "*Is* she really angry?"

"Oh, I haven't, haven't I? All right then, Mr Funny Jim, you can have it straight from the shoulder! You men are good enough to play about with, and I've no objection to your paying the bills! But *marry* one of you—well, I don't think! A wedding ring will give me all the respectability I want! Marry? No thanks! What am I going to get out of marrying? Why, you've no sooner got back from signing your name in a registry office than the man begins to treat you like something he's bought and paid for! Regular parcel—done up in brown paper and handed over the counter!" She laughed angrily. "No *thanks*! I know when I'm better off than that!"

"You talk as if you'd tried it," said Jim.

She gave him a dark look.

"Perhaps I have," she said, her voice sullen. She pulled her soft pale draperies about her. "Anyone can be had for a mug once. But I'm damned if anyone's going to have me on a second time."

There was something real there. He felt compunction—he'd been rough with her.

He said quickly,

"I'm sorry, Cissie," and all at once she was laughing again.

"You needn't be."

She kissed her fingers to him, and as she did so, a door banged and Basil Stevens called from the room beyond,

"Cis!"

Chapter Twenty-Eight

IF THE BANGED DOOR had been a pistol shot, it could hardly have brought Cissie's laughter to a more sudden end. Her hands dropped, her mouth formed a soundless "Oh," and as Basil Stevens called her name, she went running to the door. As she ran, she looked over her shoulder and made a gesture towards the orangery.

Jim was already behind the screen. The glass door was ajar. He slipped noiselessly into the heavy scented dusk, and behind him, in the room he had just left, he heard Basil Stevens say in a loud accusing voice,

"The gate was open!"

"Was it?"

Jim could admire her cool indifference. He stayed a moment with the door ajar and the screen shielding it.

"I tell you it was open!"

"Well, what about it?"

"I had my key, and when I went to put it in the lock the gate was open."

"You keep on saying that."

"Yes, I keep on saying it, because I mean to know why it happened!"

Jim thought that possibly Miss Cecile St Arc here shrugged her shoulders. She spoke in the voice of a young person who is bored to tears.

"Better ask old Guy Fawkes Clement, or Mrs Guy, or the boy! I don't look as if I'd been out opening gates, do I?"

Jim knew very well that he ought to be gone; yet he did not go.

"Do I?" said Cissie in a soft, warm voice.

Basil Stevens answered her impatiently.

"I don't know. Some one opened it."

"Bit of a bear with a sore head, aren't you?"

The man's voice changed to a ferocious rasp. He flung out a Russian oath and followed it with a,

"Take care, or I shall think you know something! And if I think that—if I think that—"

"Why, what is there to know?" said Cissie Stark.

Jim guessed at a wide, half sulky stare. She had twice her brother's pluck.

Inside the room Basil Stevens caught the girl by the shoulder.

"Have you been meddling with my pocket-book?"

She threw back her head and looked angrily at him.

"I tell you I never touched your blooming old key! Why should I?"

"It is not the key!" His voice had a raw, savage note. "It is not the key. The key is nothing by itself, and the gate is nothing. But some one has been tampering with my pocket-book—and if it is you, Cecile—if it is you—"

She wrenched herself free with a movement that showed how strong she was.

"Well, it wasn't me—and you can put that in your pipe and smoke it! Do you think I'm a dirty thief? And who do you think you are anyway? Bluebeard? Or Ali Baba or something?"

She picked up her pale draperies, did a dance step or two, and landed a high kick just short of his ear.

"Blooming pantomime king—that's what you are! And look here, my lad—when I do play in panto, I want an audience!"

She had one behind the glass door. Jim wondered whether she knew it.

"Be quiet!" said Basil Stevens not at all loudly.

Cissie shivered.

"Oh, come off it, can't you!" she said. "You give me the pip when you talk like that! What have you gone and lost out of your old pocket-book then?"

"Not lost," he said. "Not lost. It has been taken. And I am sorry if anyone has taken it—for them. And they will be sorry for themselves— very sorry."

"Drop it!" said Cissie. "I've not been near your pocket-book. What's gone? Money?"

"No."

"All right, don't tell me if you don't want to, only don't say afterwards I wouldn't help you—that's all."

"It is a piece of torn paper," he said.

Jim knew now why he had waited.

"A piece of torn paper—a piece of a bank-note if you like—but it is of no value without the other pieces."

"I don't know what you're talking about. It sounds tripe to me. What does anyone want with a bit of a bank-note—unless they'd got the rest of it?"

"Ah!" said Basil Stevens. It was not an English sound at all; there was a half obliterated guttural in it—the Tartar showing where the Russian surface was scratched.

Cissie had her hand at her mouth, her teeth pressed against the pink knuckles. With a sudden exclamation she threw out her hand.

"I'll tell you who had your pocket-book!"

"You'll tell me?"

"Yes, my lad—I—Cissie the sleuth! You aren't half impatient—are you? All right, if you want to know, it was your cousin Alec."

Jim's hands tingled on the door.

"Sasha?"

Cissie laughed.

"Of all the silly ways of saying Alec! Sasha—*Sasha!*" She mimicked him. "Oh, Lord! What a name!"

He took her by the wrist.

"Cissie, you ask for trouble! What is this about Sasha and my pocket-book?"

"Let me go then! All right—well, I saw him with it."

"You saw Sasha with my pocket-book?"

"Yes, ducky."

"When?"

"Just before we started. He came into the room with it in his hand, and when he saw me he went back into the bedroom."

"You are sure?"

"Of course I'm sure! No bats in my belfry, old dear!"

"I was changing." His voice dropped to a running mutter. "Changing—he talked—I wondered why he talked—he went on talking—I was stooping—down on my knees to pack—my coat was off—he could have got it then—" All at once his voice came out full strength again. He swept an arm round Cissie and held her close. "You're sure? You're *sure*?"

"Cross my heart!"

"With a knife—" said Basil Stevens.

Her laugh had a shudder in it.

"Let me go! Basil—*Basil*—let me go!"

Quite suddenly he let her go.

"What's that door open for?" he said, and stared at the hand's-breadth that showed above the screen.

Cissie backed away from him.

"What door?" she said, and eyed him.

He went across the room at a run, pushed the glass with the flat of one hand, and with the other jabbed at the switch. An orange light sprang into brilliance. It flooded the glass house from end to end.

There was nobody there.

Chapter Twenty-Nine

SOMETHING HAD WARNED Jim Mackenzie. As Cissie laughed and called out to Basil Stevens to let her go, Jim had begun a noiseless retreat. He was at the outer door when he heard the rush of feet. He had time to open and close it behind him, but no time to get away. As the switch clicked down, he fell on his hands and knees hard up against the wall and at once began to crawl towards the house.

The yellow light made the orangery look as if it was on fire. The glass shone with a hot glow. The palms and the orange trees in their green tubs looked black against it, as if they had been burned. A little of the light came through the glass and made the path look as if it were paved with gold for a yard or two; then it lost colour and was swallowed up by the dark.

Jim had got beyond its radius, when the orangery door swung open. He had risen to his feet and stood pressed against the wall of the house beyond the windows of the little salon. He saw Basil Stevens stand looking out and heard him call over his shoulder,

"Another door unlocked!"

Cissie must have suggested Pierre as the offender, because Basil Stevens said, "Then his father had better take a stick to him!" and with that, shivered, cursed the cold, and went in. A moment later the orange light went out and left the baffling darkness unbroken.

Jim pushed on to the gate. The snow was not lying or it would have been lighter. Perhaps it would lie later on when the earth had lost the warmth drawn from a few mild days. The cold was in the wind. It froze the rain and flung it freezing against the earth, the trees, the grass. Jim thought that it was cold enough for Russia—very appropriate weather in fact.

He ran the last twenty yards, came to the gate, and found it locked. A nasty blow; but of course he should have expected it. Basil Stevens wouldn't ramp into the house and raise Cain about the gate being open and just leave it at that. Of course he had locked it with his own key. And the lodge was empty, and Master Pierre off the map. The gate was no more climbable from this side than it had been from the other. He would just have to wait for Pierre. He had a pious hope that the young rip wasn't going to make a night of it. There was a little patch of turf beside the lodge. He paced up and down upon it, glad to be able to stamp his feet without making a noise; he had had to walk like a cat on the gravel.

Well, he had come where he had no business to come, and the event had justified him. He had acquired two valuable pieces of information. Laura wasn't here; he didn't believe she had ever left England, and she certainly was not with Basil Stevens. That was the first thing. And the second was the news that Alec Stevens had robbed his cousin. That meant that Alec Stevens now held two of the three pieces of Bertram Hallingdon's five-pound note. If he could lay hands on the third piece, there would be very little between him and the Sanquhar invention. Perhaps he had the third piece already. Laura had had it. Jim felt sure that Laura had had one of the pieces; she had been so urgent, so insistent that he should hide his piece. He hadn't hidden it, and Sasha had got away with it. He wondered now whether Sasha had got away with all three pieces.

For a moment a hard laughter shook him. Bertram Hallingdon and his torn five-pound note! He wondered how much more trouble they were all going to buy with it before they were through. And then his mood darkened. Laura had bought her trouble and his already, full measure, pressed down and running over. Why had she done it? And again why—and again. *Laura*—to break everything—and for a swab like Stevens who couldn't be faithful to her for a month! He thought of Cissie Stark, and then again of Laura. Why in God's name had she done it, and plunged them both into this immeasurable misery?

He jerked his thoughts away from the contemplation of what Laura had done. It was done, and if he went on thinking about it he would go mad. What he had got to think about now was some way of getting out of this place. He supposed he would have to make a circuit of the grounds and see if there was anything climbable on this side of the wall. Only if there wasn't and Pierre slipped in whilst he was away, he would be absolutely dished. Hang the boy—why couldn't he come home?

He stepped up to the gates and looked through them. The wind blew and the snow fell. If it hadn't been for the snow, he would hardly have been able to see his hand before his face. As it was, he could just distinguish a faint movement in the darkness, as if it was a black curtain shaken by the wind. And then all of a sudden he saw a far-off flash of light and heard the faint sound of an approaching car. The flash came as the headlights swung round the sharp bend where the lane left the high road from Sarrance. As the sound of the engine grew louder, Jim wondered very much whether the Villa Jaureguy was to have another visitor, and who that visitor might be. He stood on one side as the full blaze of powerful headlights cut a lane through the night. Then the engine slowed, the car stopped, a door was flung open, and some one sprang out a few yards short of the gate and hurried towards him. As she came into the light, Jim saw that it was a woman in a dark fur coat. She came right up to the gates and pushed at them. When they did not move, she called out in a voice of assured authority,

"*Ouvrez!*" And then again, "*Ouvrez! Ouvrez vite!*"

For a moment Jim Mackenzie stood rigid with surprise. Then he walked forward and faced the lady through the bars.

"How do you do, Miss Wimborough?" he said.

It must be conceded that Agatha Wimborough possessed a really remarkable degree of self-control. There was a scarcely noticeable pause before she said in an accusing voice,

"What are you doing here, Jim Mackenzie?"

"I might ask the same thing—in fact I will. What are you doing here, Miss Wimborough?"

Agatha Wimborough was under his guard in a flash.

"I have come to see Laura," she said. "Have you?"

"She is not here," said Jim Mackenzie.

"That I propose to ascertain for myself. Will you kindly open this gate!"

"I should be delighted—if I had the key."

"Will you call the porter then!"

"There is no porter."

"Rubbish!" said Agatha Wimborough. "There's the lodge staring me in the face."

"The lodge is empty."

"Oh," said Agatha Wimborough. "I suppose you're sure of that?"

"Quite sure."

"Oh. Then will you go up to the house and tell them to send some one down with the key!"

"I'm afraid I can't do that."

"And why not?"

"Well—officially, I'm not here."

"You mean that this is a clandestine visit to Laura?"

"Laura is not here," said Jim Mackenzie in a hard angry voice.

Agatha Wimborough took her hand off the gate and stepped back a pace.

"I know the man who had the letting of this house. He told me that he had let it to Mr Basil Stevens of London. He told me that Mr and Mrs Basil Stevens were arriving at the Villa yesterday. Are you telling me that they haven't arrived?"

"Oh no," said Jim—"they've arrived all right."

"And you say that Laura isn't here?"

"The woman who is here is not Laura."

"What!" said Agatha Wimborough. *"Already?"* And then, in a voice of angry suspicion, "How do you *know*?"

"I've been up to the house, and I've seen the lady. She is not Laura."

Agatha Wimborough threw up her head.

"Where is she? Where's Laura? She hasn't been married a month, and you tell me her husband is here with another woman!"

Jim said nothing. He found the scene intolerable and did not know of any way to end it.

Agatha Wimborough took hold of the gate and made a futile attempt to shake it.

"I've got to come in and see for myself!" she said.

Jim's temper broke.

"My dear Miss Wimborough, do you suppose I should stay here if I could get away? I can't, and you can't get in, till Pierre turns up with the key. If he chooses to stay out all night, you're better off than I am, because you can get away and I can't."

She turned her back on him, went over to the car, and got in. He thought she was going to drive away, but instead she leaned back into the corner and stayed there motionless. Jim could not see her, but he felt her as an angry, resentful presence. Curiously enough, he had never come so near to liking her.

It was perhaps ten minutes later that he saw something move in the darkness behind the car. He could not see what it was, but he chanced it and called out, "Pierre!"

There was a moment of hesitation before the moving something disclosed itself as an obviously terrified boy. The way of transgressors was hard. Couldn't one slip out for a moment without finding a strange auto at the gate on one's return?

"Open this gate and look sharp!" said Jim.

Pierre fumbled with the key and nearly dropped it as the door of the car banged behind him—and there was not only the gentleman inside the gate, but a most angry and impatient lady on the same side as himself; and whilst the gentleman wanted to get out, the lady was in no end of a hurry to get in. Between the two of them Pierre was fairly flustered. He dropped the key, picked it up again, tried to put it into the lock upside down, and finally had it snatched from him by the seething Miss Wimborough. The gates flew back, and whilst Pierre was retrieving the key Agatha Wimborough had begun to walk up the drive.

She found Jim Mackenzie at her side.

"Miss Wimborough—"

"Are you coming too? I don't want you!"

"Miss Wimborough—"

"What is it?"

"Why are you going up to the house?"

"That's my business!"

"I'm not so sure that it is."

"And what d'you mean by that, Jim Mackenzie?"

"I mean—" No, he couldn't tell her what he meant. She would go her own way whatever he said—and after all what was there to tell? "It doesn't matter," he muttered.

"You meant something," said Miss Wimborough sharply.

All right, he would warn her. He stood still between her and the house, on the black edge of the drive.

"Stevens isn't English," he said. "His real name is Vassili Stefanoff. I think he's a dangerous man. I don't think you ought to see him alone."

Miss Wimborough said, *"Laura,"* under her breath, quickly. Then, with a sudden violence, "Why did she do it?"

Neither of them had the answer to that.

She spoke again almost immediately in her usual loud, firm voice.

"I shall certainly see him. I shall go up to the house and I shall see for myself who is there. You say there is another woman there. Do you know who she is?"

"Yes."

"Who is she?"

"Her stage name is Cecile St Arc."

Miss Wimborough gave a sort of groan. Then she said,

"Laura can divorce him for this—that's one thing. She can have my evidence, but you must keep out of it. I shall go on up to the house, and you will go back to wherever you came from. Do you hear?"

"But—Miss Wimborough—"

"I'm not going to have any scandal on Laura's side!" said Agatha Wimborough sharply. "If this Stevens is here with another woman, she shall divorce him. But I should think even a man could see that *you*'ve got to keep out of the way. Go away and keep away, and go on keeping away! And please believe that I'm perfectly capable of managing my own affairs. Good night!" She walked past him towards the house, stepping briskly.

Jim felt the blood rush into his head. What that woman wanted was the rough side of a man's tongue. Words banged and jostled one another in his mind—satisfying, meaty words that would have done

Agatha Wimborough a power of good. Oh, damn being civilized! He flung about, passed Pierre without seeing him, and went striding through the gates and down the lane towards Sarrance.

He came back to his flat in the dusk of the following day—a very cold and discouraging home-coming. The place had a deserted smell about it, a kind of chilly fog. He threw up his sitting-room window, put a match to the gas fire, and turning, saw the sheet of paper. It lay on the empty table, a sheet of hard blue paper, boldly written on. He went over to it, picked it up, and read:

"The right address is, Hermitage, Lynn Cliff, Devon."

He stood staring at it.

The writing was quite strange.

He went on staring.

Chapter Thirty

LAURA OPENED her eyes upon a strange room. A puzzled frown came and went. She shut her eyes again. She was lying in bed, but she felt as if some one were rocking her. She had been dreaming that she was in a train—or was it a boat? She couldn't remember. The dream was gone. Only this curious rocking feeling persisted. She wondered what time it was, and opened her eyes again.

This was not the room in which she had gone to sleep. It had a low ceiling with a large rough beam running right across it, and the walls were white and ran into strange shapes, with a bulge here and a curious angle there. She raised herself on her elbow and her head swam.

When the giddiness passed, she sat up. This was certainly not any room in the house where she had gone to sleep. This was an old room, in an old house. The polished floor was bare, and dark and uneven with age. The windows were deeply embrasured. There were two windows, both facing her, and they framed a curious heaving greyness.

Laura sat bolt upright and looked with all her eyes. Then she got out of bed and crossed the floor on her bare feet. The walls of the room were so thick that it was almost like leaning into a tunnel to reach the window. It was a casement set with little panes of uneven glass. She pulled down the latch and opened it.

At once the wind came clapping into the room, blowing her hair, filling her lungs, bringing a salt taste to her lips—a cold wind; a strong wind; a salt wind. It blew away the last of her doziness, and though it was so cold, it did not chill her. She looked through her blowing hair and saw grey water and a grey lowering sky. For a moment she saw nothing else. The clouds moved in the wind, and the water moved with a curious restless motion of its own.

She shook back her hair and leaned out as far as she could. The wall of the house went down to a wall of grey rock, and the wall of grey rock went down to the grey lapping water. When she looked to the left, she could just see the line of rock curving back as if it had been built like that to guard the house, and, a little way off, a rough cliff that began with rock and sloped away into brown grass. When she looked to the right, there was another cliff, much nearer, so near in fact that she had to crane her neck to see the top of it. It seemed to lean right over the house.

She drew back from the window and began to shiver. Where was Catherine? Catherine had promised that she would not leave her. Where was she?

She went over to the door, and as she touched the handle, she felt a scream rise in her throat. If the door was locked, she would not be able to hold back the scream. Her hand closed and turned. The door moved inwards, and the relief was so great that a warm weakness came over her and she stood there, not pulling at the handle, for very nearly a whole minute. Then at the sound of a step in the passage she stood back, bringing the door with her, and in a moment there was Catherine with a tray.

"Well?" she said. "You have slept. You should be hungry. You were still asleep half an hour ago, but I thought you had had enough of it, so I was bringing you some coffee. Are you hungry?"

"I don't know," said Laura.

"Get back into bed before you freeze. There—drink your coffee, and then you may tell me whether you like being in France."

"Is this—France?" said Laura.

The coffee was very hot and very good. English people couldn't make coffee. She took another sip and looked up, to see Catherine regarding her curiously.

"Where are we?" said Laura. "I want to know."

"Did not Vassili tell you?"

"No."

"Officially," said Catherine, "you are in France." She laughed a little. "I also."

"And *really*?"

"Laura, you shock me! Is it possible that you do not believe everything you are told?"

Laura laughed.

"It is very disillusioning for me," said Catherine. "You are the sweet, pure heroine, and it is your rôle to have no brains at all and to believe everything that is said. As a consolation you are permitted to be beautiful, and in the end you will live happy ever after."

The colour came into Laura's face. Catherine put out a hand and steadied the trembling cup.

"Laura, you are a fool!" she said. "You are like this cup—you are fine china, and you have gone into the stream with the iron pots. Did you think that it would be possible that you should not get broken?"

Laura had nothing to say. Her hand was steady again. She lifted the cup and drank from it. Its fineness gave her pleasure. It had a worn gilt edge, and it was flowered lightly with little bunches of cottage blooms.

Presently Catherine went out of the room and down the stairs. In the room that was under Laura's she found Alec Stevens.

"Well?" he said, and stopped in his pacing to and fro.

"Oh, she's awake."

He nodded.

"All right?"

"Yes."

"What did I tell you? You are never happy unless you are fussing over something."

"All the same she slept too long."

"Nonsense! Were we to risk her waking on the way?"

"Why should it have mattered?"

He laughed suddenly.

"Ask Vassili! It was not I who drugged her. Now that she is awake again, I don't mind telling you that I should not have given her so much. But since she is all right, why are you making a fuss? Now I want to talk business with you. Last night you were too tired, and this morning too fussed up. Perhaps now I can have your attention."

Catherine set down Laura's empty cup.

"What is it?" she said.

"You can really attend?"

"Yes."

"Well then, look here—"

He took a letter case from an inner pocket, opened it, and took out a couple of envelopes. From each envelope he extracted a torn piece of paper, which he laid on the old polished table, leaving a space between them. The paper was white, with black letters and flourishes upon it. On the left-hand piece was a medallion which displayed Britannia with a trident.

"Well," said Alec Stevens—"you see what this is."

"The five-pound note—you have two pieces of it. How did you get them?"

There was elation in his laugh.

"This—" he touched the right-hand piece—"this was our dear Vassili's fragment. And this—" he flicked the other lightly—"this was Mackenzie's. As you see, the whereabouts of the middle piece is now most vitally important."

Catherine shrugged her shoulders.

"Well, I have not got it," she said.

"I didn't suppose that you had."

She spoke quickly.

"Did Vassili give you his piece?"

He laughed again.

"What do you think?"

"That you are running a great risk," said Catherine gravely.

"Yes—a great risk—for a great prize. Listen! Vassili is making a mess of this. He's a fool really. He'd never have got the job if it hadn't been for his engineer's degree—and after all what does that matter? I'd have made old Hallingdon a better secretary than he did—yes, and got more of his confidence—but they wouldn't give me the chance— they *would* have Vassili. And you know, and I know, the mess he's got himself into. And when Moscow knows—" he snapped his finger and thumb—"exit Vassili!"

She said, "I suppose so," in an absent voice.

"He might save himself if he could hand over the Sanquhar invention. Well, he can't. And if I can—if—I—can—"

"Can you?" said Catherine in a cool, dispassionate voice.

"I believe so—if you will help me." He picked up the pieces of the torn five-pound note and put them carefully away. "Help me to pull it off, and—"

"And what?" said Catherine.

"Wait and see, *liebchen*. Now come round here—I don't want to shout." He put an arm about her and drew her close, so that she stood at his knee looking down on him with a curious twist of the lips.

"Well?" she said.

"The middle of the five-pound note is missing. I believe it was torn in three, and I'm sure—I say I'm sure—that the third piece came to Laura the day I was fool enough to let her see old Rimington alone. If I had known.... Well, Vassili kept us in the dark, and he'll deserve whatever he gets, for that alone. Laura had her bit of the torn note, and she managed to hide it. And we haven't managed to find it—and we've *got* to find it."

His arm dropped from Catherine's waist, but she did not move.

"How did you get the other pieces?"

He threw back his head and laughed up at her.

"Good work, *liebchen*! I listened in to Mackenzie's talk about Twenty Years of Invention. Well, when he came to the place where he might have said something interesting about the loss of the Sanquhar invention, he just checked for a moment, like you do when you come to a place where there's a mistake or an alteration in the paper you're reading from. It gave me the feeling that I'd like to have a look at that paper. So off I went to his flat—and there I had a first class piece of luck, for I picked up a key on the stair, and it fitted his lock."

"Picked it up?"

She saw a look of admiration come into his face.

"*Liebchen*, you have a brain! Perhaps you are right—perhaps I had already provided myself with the key. Anyhow, I walked in—and there was his talk, all neatly typed. And when I came to the place I was looking for, there was a good fat paragraph crossed out, but not so much crossed out that I couldn't read most of it."

"And?" said Catherine.

He nodded.

"It was about the Sanquhar invention. Well, that made me think. He'd written it, and he'd crossed it out. Why? Something had happened to make him cross it out. I began to look for the something, and presently I found a torn piece of a five-pound note put away very carefully. Then I remembered that Vassili also had a piece of a five-pound note, and that you had heard him talk in his sleep of the Sanquhar invention—also he looked as if he would murder you when you spoke to him about it. I thought that I would collect his piece and add it to mine. It was quite easy. So here I have two pieces—and when I have Laura's piece, I shall have the note complete."

"When," said Catherine.

"Laura shall tell us where it is," said Alec Stevens.

Catherine's faint scornful smile deepened.

"You are very foolish if you think that."

"I am sure of it."

"Laura will not tell you anything. You don't know her. She has the air of being fragile, but there is something in her that will not break. She is vulnerable because she *feels*. But you will not be able to make her do what she thinks wrong. If she suffers too much, she may die, but she will not tell you what you want to know."

"She will tell me," said Alec Stevens. There was a cheerful note of certainty in his voice.

Catherine looked at him.

"What do you mean?"

"I mean that she shall tell Jim Mackenzie, and I mean that I shall listen while she tells him."

Chapter Thirty-One

LAURA CAME OUT of her room on the following day and passed down the shallow steps which led into a square hall. The steps were of bare dark oak polished by the feet of many generations. The hall was narrow and low, with a huge fireplace on one side of it.

She opened the door which faced the stairs and came out into a little square garden. It had a path edged with scallop-shells, and on either side a heart-shaped bed where rose bushes were sprouting. The path ended at a low wicket gate, and beyond the gate a steep flight of steps climbed the cliff. The house was set on a rocky ledge not more than a dozen feet above high water mark.

Laura went round the house and saw bare sand and shell-drift where yesterday morning she had seen only a stretch of grey water. It was three o'clock in the afternoon, and the tide was out. The cliffs enclosed a little bay, with a rocky pool here and there and a shelving bank of pebbles that had dried in the wind and the sun.

On the left a wooden ladder led down to the beach. Laura climbed down it, skirted a pool, and picked her way to the far side of the ridge. Here the sun shone and the wind did not come. The cliff rose steeply at first then shelved, and rose again by easier degrees. She looked up, and thought that a man might climb it if he had a good head. Then she sat down on the rug that Catherine had spread, set a cushion between her and the rock, and leaned against it savouring the sun. It was so warm here that the month might have been June instead of January—or had they slipped into February while she was ill? She reflected that she knew neither the date, nor where she was. Officially she was in France, but actually she felt fairly certain that these were English cliffs, and this an English sea. It was grey no longer. The sun shone down on it and showed it as blue as a drift of bluebells. It reflected a cloudless sky.

She watched the clear, soft colour, and felt comforted. She had a sense of respite, even of release. To be alone, to watch the sun upon the water, to see the gulls flash and turn and take the light with their shining wings, gave her a feeling of freedom. She had left an empty house behind her—empty, that is, of Sasha and Catherine. The tow-headed girl was probably in the kitchen, but she didn't count. Sasha had been gone since twelve o'clock, and half an hour ago Catherine had asked her whether she would mind being left alone for an hour—"You can sit in the sun and dream any dream you like. Are we not clever to provide you with a sun to sit in? Only you had better not dream about running away, because you would certainly lose yourself on the moor, and then I should have to nurse you again."

Laura had laughed a little sadly.

"Where should I run to?"

"That is what I call practical," said Catherine. "English people are very practical. I can leave you without the slightest uneasiness, because there really is nowhere for you to run to. I am taking the car, and this house is about seven miles from anywhere at all. I am sure you are too practical to try and walk seven miles.

"Why should I?" said Laura.

Her words came back to her as she sat and looked at the sea. Where the blue of the water met the blue of the sky there was a faint haze. Why should she run away? Even if there were no seven miles, where would she go and what would she do? She had no money. Besides, she had set her hand to a bargain, and she meant to stick to it. Only the Sanquhar invention was not in the bargain. She had to try and save the Sanquhar invention.

Suddenly it came over her that she had left her third of Bertram Hallingdon's torn five-pound note in the house from which she had come two days ago, and that she had not the slightest idea of where this house might be. She had been brought to it unconscious, and she had left it in a drugged sleep. A feeling of panic swept over her. She had already betrayed Bertram Hallingdon's trust if she had lost her precious fragment. She ought to have been able to think of a better hiding place. She ought to have contrived to bring it with her. She ought—

She heard a sound, and turned her head. Jim Mackenzie was coming towards her across the wet sand.

Her heart knocked hard against her side just once, and joy came in. Laura had never felt such joy in all her life before. It was a purely irrational, purely instinctive joy. It was like warmth after the dead cold which freezes to the bone. It was like water after desert drought. It was like the sun and the moon and the stars after an eternity of formless night. You do not think of joy like that, you feel it. It broke upon Laura and took her off her feet. She did not make any physical movement, but the colour came up into her face and the light into her eyes.

She saw Jim come nearer and then stop. She heard him say, "Laura!" And then the enchanted moment was past. The joy ebbed so quickly that it was gone before she could speak his name. It left her cold and bewildered. She leaned against the rock at her back and looked up at him with wide, piteous eyes.

Jim Mackenzie did not come any nearer. He would have had to take two steps to touch her hand. He stayed where he was and looked past her at a trickle of water that darkened the face of the cliff and fell drop by drop to a little pool of clear sea water. He had come here to see her, and now that he was here he did not know what to say. That gave the knife a twist—he did not know what to say to her. The days hadn't ever been long enough for all that they had to say, and when they did not speak the silence brought them closer; but now they had not anything to say, and the silence was like a chain that dragged between them. He laid desperate hands on it and broke it.

"You will wonder why I have come."

Laura said, "No." It had not been a thing to wonder about; it was the only natural thing that had happened to her for a long, long time. It was all the other things that were strange—the wedding ring on her finger; the bargain she had made with Vassili Stefanoff; the fact that she wasn't Laura Cameron any more. These were the unnatural things—not Jim. It could never be anything except natural that Jim should come to her. Warmth, and light, and water for one's thirst—these were natural things. She felt as if she had waked up from a dream.

He spoke again with an effort.

"Laura—I've come because of what you said when you telephoned. I had to know—that you were all right."

Laura said, "Yes," in a gentle absent voice. It seemed a long time since she had crept down in the night to try and warn him. Then she remembered why she had tried to warn him; and with that she remembered the Sanquhar invention. She got up and stood against the cliff, her colour coming and going, her hair lifted by the wind.

"Jim—I tried to warn you. Did you understand? Did you put it away safely?" Then, as he stood silent, she went on, "Won't you tell me—won't you please tell me? You see, I *know* that you are one of the trustees of the Sanquhar invention. Mr Hallingdon told me."

Jim Mackenzie stared at her.

"How?" he said almost roughly.

"He wrote. I got it after I was ill."

"Why were you ill?"

"It doesn't matter—I am all right now." She oughtn't to have said that about being ill. She went on quickly. "Mr Hallingdon told me who had the three pieces of the five-pound note which he had torn. You had one—and I had one—and Vassili—"

"*Vassili?*"

"Basil Stevens is Vassili Stefanoff."

"Did you know that when you married him?"

"Yes, I knew," said Laura.

"You knew—*Laura*—"

She put out her hand to stop him.

"Don't—Jim—*please!* I've got to tell you about the Sanquhar invention. It's got to be saved, and I can't do anything. Will you just listen?"

He nodded without speaking. Yes, he would listen. But he would do something more than listen before he left her. Now that they were face to face, she was going to tell him why she had smashed their lives. The blood drummed in his ears so that he could hardly hear what she was saying. He mustn't look at her. He must watch the drops that raced one another down the overhanging point of rock, to fall into the pool below. They were like beads sliding from a broken string—like bright, clear beads—glass beads....

Laura was speaking.

"I destroyed his letter. He told me to. I wetted it and made it into a ball and threw it out of the window. I don't think any of it could be read. My piece of the five-pound note was in the letter. They don't know whether I've had it or not. At first they thought I had, but when they had looked for it everywhere they began to think that I'd never had it. I hid it, and they couldn't find it."

"They haven't found it?"

"No. But I don't know where it is."

"*You don't know?*"

"I hid it in the house we have just come from. But they took me there when I was ill, and I don't know where it is, or the address, or anything."

He came a step nearer.

"Well, I know that. It's The Walled House, Leeming Lane, Putney. I went there to look for you, but you were gone."

A cold lonely feeling touched Laura's heart, not for herself but for him. The empty house—and Jim looking for her.... And then all of a sudden the cold and the loneliness were unbearable. She saw the whole world as an empty house in which he must look for her in vain. She turned very pale.

He spoke quickly.

"Where did you hide your piece of the note? I had better get it—it can't stay there."

Laura pressed her right hand against a sharp ridge of rock.

"It's in the room I had—not at first, but afterwards. When I was ill I had the room just at the top of the stairs, and when I had to find a hiding-place I managed to get as far as the next room but one. It was empty, and I pinned my piece of the note on to the under side of the mattress. And afterwards they moved me into that very room."

"One of the two front rooms?"

"Yes."

"Right or left as you come up the stairs?"

"Left."

"You'd better tell me the whole thing while you're about it. What happens when the three pieces are put together?"

Laura lowered her voice.

"All the papers about the Sanquhar invention are in a safe—somewhere. Only one person knows where or in what name. That person has the key, and she will give it up to whoever brings her the whole five-pound note. It's her authority to hand over the key and to say where the safe is,"

"Who is she?" said Jim Mackenzie.

"His old housemaid, Eliza Huggins. She doesn't know anything at all about the Sanquhar invention. She only knows that she's to give up the key to the person who brings her that five-pound note."

"And Stefanoff has two pieces—"

He hardly knew that he had spoken aloud. The words went through his mind like a bitter taste.

"Two?" said Laura.

"I'm afraid so. I went for a tramp after you telephoned that night, and whilst I was away some one walked into my flat and pinched my piece. Has Stefanoff got a cousin called Alec Stevens?"

"Yes."

"Well, a man who came to see me met him on the stairs. He'd a cock-and-bull story of having tried to find me—and, I suppose, my piece of the note in his pocket."

Laura put her hand to her breast.

"They've got your piece?"

"Yes."

"They've got two pieces?"

"I'm afraid they have."

She drew in her breath quickly.

"There's only my piece left—"

"I'll get it—don't worry."

Her hand dropped. She leaned back against the rock. The sun had entered the grey haze that lay like a scarf along the horizon. It could be seen through it, a rayless crimson disk; and suddenly the water was grey, and the air cold.

Laura closed her eyes. She must tell him to go. At any moment Catherine might return, or Sasha. In less than an hour it would be dark. The sun had made it seem like spring, but when the sun was gone it would be cold. When Jim was gone, it would be very cold and dark. She must tell him to go now. She heard her own voice saying very faintly,

"You must go."

"Not just yet," said Jim.

Laura repeated the same words again.

"You must go."

Then she opened her eyes and found him close to her, with a look on his face which troubled her to the depths.

"I'll go when you've told me why you did it." Then, as she looked at him dumbly, "Why did you do it—why did you do it?" He saw all the colour leave her face. "You've got to tell me! I've got a right to know! There's something damnable about it! You're not happy. If you were I'd take my toss and make the best of it. But you're not. He's not even with you. He's—"

He pulled himself up, his hands clenched, the blood rushing to his face. He couldn't tell her in so many words about the Villa Jaureguy. Agatha Wimborough could do that—she'd enjoy it, and he had no manner of doubt that she'd do it with a will.

"You've got to tell me why you did it!" he said.

Laura looked at him, her hands pressed against cold ridges of rock. What was she to say? She made a great effort and found trembling words.

"Please—go—Jim—"

"No—I won't go. You've got to tell me. You don't care for him."

Laura shook her head.

"Then he threatened you—he made you do it. But how—*how?*"

Laura could not find any other words. She said them again.

"Please go."

Something broke in Jim Mackenzie. With a smashing certainty he knew what threat had brought Laura to this place. The knowledge broke his anger, his pride, and his self-control. He took a stumbling step towards her, pitched upon his knees, and caught at her with a desperate clutch.

"Was it for me? Laura—was it for me? Did you do it for me? My darling—*my darling!*"

For a moment Laura did not know which of them was shaking so. She felt the hard clasp of his arms and heard his breath come, heavy and choked with sobs, and suddenly his need gave her words. She bent over him, touching his hair, his cheek, holding him and murmuring the soft unconsidered words she would have used to a hurt child.

"Don't, darling—*don't!* It's all right. Tell Laura. Oh, my darling—don't cry! I'm here—I'm holding you."

They clung together, and presently he lifted a convulsed face.

"*Laura*—it was for me!"

"I had to."

"*For me!*"

"They would have shot you."

"What did that matter?"

"I couldn't, *couldn't* bear it."

"Isn't this—worse?" His voice went on the last word. She felt him shudder.

"Darling—don't! Let me tell you—I want to tell you."

He said, "What is there to tell?" in a despairing voice.

"I want to tell you—it's not a real marriage."

"*Not?*" His arms tightened.

"He didn't want me—he's not in love with me—it's nothing like that."

He lifted his head a little.

"The damned swab!"

In the middle of it all Laura laughed.

"But, darling, you don't want him to be in love with me, do you?" Then the laugh slipped into a sob. "He didn't want me—he wanted the control of the Hallingdon combine."

"He married you for that?"

"Yes, for that."

He got to his feet, still holding her.

"What did you promise?"

"A seat on the boards of the different companies—and—and—to marry him."

"And in return I was to go free. Is that it?"

She leaned against him without speaking.

He held her for a moment. Then he said,

"I would rather have died—you know that."

"Yes—I *couldn't* bear it."

After a little while he said in a different voice,

"Did you promise anything about the Sanquhar invention?"

"No."

"They mustn't get that. He's only an agent of course. They mustn't get the Sanquhar invention."

Laura steadied herself.

"You must go."

He went on as if he had not heard.

"You must divorce him. He has given you cause. Your aunt will tell you, and—" he gave a short hard laugh—"for once in a way you can believe everything she says!"

"*Jim!*" It was her old half laughing, wholly tender reproof.

"Well, she does lay it on a bit thick."

"But how does she come into this?"

"She'll tell you. I don't want to go into it, but you can divorce him."

"Can I?" said Laura. Something cold touched her heart. "I don't know.... I made a bargain—"

"He's given you cause," said Jim roughly.

She leaned away from him to the hard rock.

"It's not like—a real marriage. I made a bargain. They did their part—they set you free."

"*Laura—*"

She spoke with pale, steady lips.

"I think—I must keep my bargain."

"*Laura—*"

She put out her hands as if she were warding something off.

"Don't talk about it. Not now. You must go. Some one might come. They mustn't see you."

"Who are *they*?"

"Catherine and Sasha."

"Sasha?"

"Alec Stevens."

"The fellow who took my piece of the note? Are they good, to you?"

"Oh yes. I love Catherine."

"Well, don't love Sasha. And remember I'm coming back. Now kiss me!"

"*Jim!*"

"Kiss me!"

"*Jim—please—*"

She was at the end of her strength. So easy to let his arms take her—to slip down into his love and forget everything. If she were once in his arms, would he leave her? Or could she—*could* she let him go? She felt as if everything were failing and flowing away from her—will, strength, honour. A verse she had learned as a child came into her mind, "He that sweareth to his neighbour and disappointeth him not, though it were to his own hindrance...."

She looked at Jim, and did not know what a desperate appeal was in her eyes.

She saw his brows draw together and his chin stick out in its most obstinate way. Then all of a sudden his face changed. He picked up her hands and kissed them gently. Then without another word he turned and went away across the sand.

Laura watched him go. There were tears in her eyes, but they were not unhappy tears. Just for the moment it was enough to have seen him.

When he was out of sight, she picked up the cushion and the rug and went back to the house, and Alec Stevens, rather cramped, got to his feet on the ledge a dozen feet up and proceeded to climb to the top of the cliff. After which he walked rapidly as far as the road, where he got into the car that was waiting for him and drove away.

Chapter Thirty-Two

JIM MACKENZIE had a half-mile walk across a stretch of rough moorland to where he had left his car. He walked with a kind of furious energy. If he had slackened his pace, he would have gone back. The impulse that had taken him from Laura was caught by half a dozen wild cross-currents of passion, jealousy, and fear. To leave her when he had found her again! What a fool's game! He didn't deserve his luck if he could throw it away like that. He should have made her come with him. Made her? You couldn't *make* Laura do what she thought wrong. The currents beat themselves against something that he knew was rock.

Anyhow he was coming back. They'd got to have the whole thing out. At the moment it was his business to get to Putney and make sure of Laura's piece of the five-pound note; but as soon as that was safe he was going to come back and have the whole thing out with her. An angry triumph lifted itself in him as he thought of the arguments that were to demolish her scruples. Stevens would have to be bought off. There was one point about dealing with a blackguard—he would have his price. Well, if it took the whole Hallingdon fortune, he could have it, if he would stand out of the game and let Laura go.

He reached the road and got into the car. The grey of the dusk was closing in; a half light made everything colourless. He switched on his lights, started up, and got away, revving the engine all out on the lower gears. The flat, dark headland fell away, the road came rushing to meet him, a long straight road that ran for miles within sound and sight of the sea.

He had gone perhaps a couple of miles, when the honk of a horn sent him over to the left and a car shot by like a black streak. The tail-light dwindled to a red pin-point and was gone. The roar died to a hum and faded out.

Jim took the middle of the road again. His speedometer showed a steady fifty-three. The car that had passed him must have been doing something like sixty-five.

He drove on, and had his thoughts for company.

Laura.... No, it didn't do to think of Laura—not of the way she looked, or of her sweetness—not now, when he'd got a job on hand—better think of other things—plenty to think about, and better get it all straightened out. He could think very well while he was driving like this. He wondered who had given him Laura's address.... Damned odd, to come back from France and find it lying on his table.

"The right address is Hermitage, Lynn Cliff, Devon,"

Who had sent him that? No, not sent—*brought*. It was an open sheet of paper lying on his table. How did it get there? Who had brought it? Who wanted him to have Laura's address? He hadn't stopped to ask any of those questions at the time, but he asked them now. If he had kept his head, he would have asked them of Laura. But he hadn't kept his head; he had most surprisingly and suddenly lost his self-control. On a dangerous wave of emotion came the memory of Laura holding him, comforting him. He *must not* think about Laura—at least not like that. He must think about the business in hand.

Some one had walked into his flat and put that address on his table—some one who had a key. Mrs Mabb's key had never been found. If that fellow Stevens—what was his name? Alec—Laura called him Sasha—Alec Stevens—Sasha Stefanoff—he had pinched the piece of the five-pound note. Kennedy Jackson had seen him letting himself out of the flat. If he could let himself out, he could let himself in. If he let himself in, he had the key. He could walk in and out and put a sheet of paper down on the table any damned time he liked—a sheet of paper with Laura's address. But why in the name of all that was inexplicable should Sasha Stefanoff want him to have Laura's address? He felt as if he were walking in the pitch dark through unknown country, and the dark full of faint sly whispers—sounds that were not quite sounds—words that you couldn't catch, and footsteps that you couldn't hear. You guessed, you listened, you strained, and there was nothing there; but as soon as you stopped listening, the faint sly whispers came crowding back.

He put his foot down hard on the accelerator and hoped for a clear road.

It was getting on for nine o'clock when he turned into Leeming Lane, slowed to a crawl, and stopped some thirty or forty yards short of where he guessed the house should be. He took the torch which he always kept in the cubby-hole and began to walk along the right-hand side of the lane. Pretty soon he came to where the wall began. He didn't want to show a light if he could help it, so he felt his way with a hand on the rough stone till he came to the oak door, and so past it to the continuing wall. It was most extraordinarily dark. The fine day had gone down in fog. Leeming Lane was full of it, thick to breathe and like a bandage over one's eyes. If he hadn't had the wall to guide him, he could hardly have found his way.

When he came to the corner, he had to feel for the tradesmen's entrance which had served him before. He passed through it, dived into the evergreens on the right, and made contact with the wall once more. It wasn't so easy to get over the wall in the dark. In the daylight he had only had to pick his tree and the rest was simple enough; now he had to feel for a limb that would bear his weight, and with fantastic perversity the shrubbery teemed with thin saplings and bristling mounds of holly. In the end he found a rough-barked, tree, and could only guess at the condition in which it would leave his clothes.

Once on the other side, he had to risk a cast of his torch. The faint questing beam struck the fog and showed him nothing else. He switched it off and began to grope his way towards where he thought the house must be. After a while his foot struck brick. He stopped to think, and remembered some sort of paved yard at the back of the house.

Another dozen yards ran him up against a window ledge. Well, what he had got to find was the scullery window. But this wasn't it; the latch felt too strong. What he wanted was a latch in the last stages of decline.

He found the scullery window after five minutes careful groping, and once found it was soon opened. He climbed over the sink, objurgating all females who leave refuse to rot, and emerged cautiously through the kitchen upon the passage which led into the hall. At the baize door he stopped, then pushed it gently for a couple of inches and stopped again. The passage and the kitchen and the scullery were all black—no light, no gleam, no anything; just a dead, even blackness. But the hall on the other side of the green baize door was not quite black;

it wore its dark with a difference; it had shadows, and an uneven ebb and flow of gloom.

Jim opened the door a little wider, took a step forward, and there halted. Somewhere on the upper landing there was a light. He couldn't see it, of course, but the fact that he could see at all told him that it was there. What he actually saw was the faint, very faint, outline of the rail that guarded the landing. Some one was in one of the rooms with a light. And all at once there rushed into his mind the sound and the shape of a black car passing him at getting on for seventy miles an hour. It came to him with bleak certainty that some one had heard what Laura had said to him, and he thought that whoever it was had been in a hurry to get here first.

After a moment of indecision he moved forward again. There would be plenty of time to retreat if the light approached the stair. It was in his mind to see who carried it. Whoever it was, he was in one of those two front rooms, and Laura's third of the five-pound note was pinned to the under-side of the mattress in the left-hand room. He wondered if it was still there, or whether the gentleman with the candle was putting it away in a pocket-book with the piece he had pinched from the flat and the piece he had pinched from Vassili. The business fairly reeked to him of Alec Stevens.

His thoughts had reached this point, and his left hand, groping, had just touched the study door, which gave a little as he pressed it, when something happened. There was the faint unmistakable click of a latch-key, and immediately upon that the sound of the front door swinging in. A complete rigidity halted Jim with a step half taken. The study door slid away from his fingers, leaving him with the strangest sensation of giddiness. It was as if the house had tilted. In the second that followed he heard the front door close. Now, if the light came on, he was caught.

But no light came. Instead, his straining ears picked up the only just audible movements of some one crossing the hall. At the foot of the stair the sound stopped. Jim could distinguish a dark something which remained immobile for the space of perhaps a minute and a half. It had the appearance of a black shadow. There was still that faint greyness from above, but not a sound, not a single sound of any sort.

Very slowly Jim let his left hand fall to his side. As if it had been a signal, there broke upon the stillness a noise of footsteps overhead, and the stair-rail on the landing sprang sharply into view against a background of candle-light. Some one with a candle had come out of the left-hand bedroom and was making for the head of the stair. The shadow that stood at the foot at once receded. The light advanced, and on an impulse Jim stepped sideways into the study and closed the door within half an inch of the jamb. He might have retreated by way of the baize door and the scullery window. But he had no intention of retreating. He wanted to have a look at the man who was coming down the stair, and he wanted to have a look at his pocket-book. He wanted to know who had just entered the house, and he wasn't going away until he did know.

The light had almost reached the foot of the stair. He took a look, and saw a man with a candle in one hand and a pocket-book in the other. The man's back was towards him. He appeared to be of medium height. He wore a light tweed cap and a heavy leather coat. All his movements were brisk, and it came home to Jim that his next movement would take him round the corner of the stair in the direction of the study. He stood away from the door and, turning, made the quickest going he could for the shelter of the drawn curtains. He remembered from his first visit heavy stuff curtains of an ugly shade of green drawn close before the window. He had drawn them back to get the light and closed them again before he left.

He skirted the table, grazed a chair, and plunged into safety just about ten seconds before the door was pushed open and there came in a youngish man with lively hazel eyes, a small brown moustache, and an alert and confident expression. The first thing he did was to switch on the light in the ceiling and blow out the candle. Then he shut the door, set the candlestick down on a chair, and came over to the writing-table. As he came, he threw up the pocket-book and caught it again. Then with a sound that resembled a suppressed laugh he opened the case, laying it flat on the blotting-pad.

Jim watched him with a curious misgiving. It was almost too easy. Alec Stevens would take out the piece of the five-pound note and look at it, and he, Jim, would take it from him. It was as easy as falling downstairs. *It was a great deal too easy.*

Alec Stevens spread out the pocket-book and took from it three pieces of thin white paper printed with black. He pushed the blotting-pad on one side and arranged the three pieces in order—the right-hand piece, which had been Vassili's; the left-hand piece, which had been Jim's; and the middle piece, which had been Laura's. Each piece stood for an adventure achieved, and the whole stood for the Sanquhar invention. Alec Stevens had the right to feel pleased with himself. At that moment he saw visions and dreamed dreams. For the Sanquhar invention he could ask what he liked. If he wanted money, he could have money; if he wanted power, he could have power. Meanwhile Mackenzie would be here at any moment. His hand rested on his hip pocket and then came down to the table level again. He had better put the note away before the poor fool came blundering in.

Behind the curtains, Jim noted the movement and guessed its significance. He carried a gun, did he? Well, he wasn't going to get a chance to use it. He measured his distance, gathered himself together for the rush that would take the fellow off his balance—and stopped short.

The door was opening.

Chapter Thirty-Three

JIM MACKENZIE had the opportunity of admiring a lightning draw. He had a passing wonder as to where Alec Stevens had acquired this accomplishment. One moment his hand was on the table lightly taking his forward stoop as he bent above the spread out note, and the next, almost without visible movement, it had sprung to his hip and back again with a lift. It happened whilst the door swung in. Vassili Stefanoff, halting on the threshold, looked straight into the muzzle of an automatic. The next instant Alec Stevens fell back into the writing-chair laughing.

"My dear Vassili—how melodramatic!"

Vassili did not laugh. His face was set in a heavy, sullen frown. He came in and pushed the door to roughly with his foot.

"Is it I who am melodramatic, or you? What are you doing with that gun? What are you doing here at all?"

Jim looked through the chink in the curtain. Alec Stevens was an adversary to be respected. Quick as lightning, that's what he was. Even as he laughed and threw himself back, he had pulled the open pocket-book across the five-pound note. It was very neatly done; no more than a corner stuck out, and that on the side away from Vassili. The hand that held the automatic lay along the arm of the chair. There might be shooting yet, for all that careless laughter.

Vassili came to the edge of the table and stood there lowering, and under his eyes Alec Stevens leaned forward, opened the middle drawer, and with his left hand very coolly slid the pocket-book and what it covered into it. He shut the drawer and leaned back as Vassili spoke.

"I asked you what that gun was for, and what you were doing here?"

Alec Stevens laughed again.

"I came back for something I had left behind."

"And the gun?"

"Don't be alarmed—it wasn't for you."

"Then why don't you put it away?"

Alec Stevens allowed a smiling glance to rest for a moment upon the automatic.

"I wonder!" he said, and under the edged mockery of his voice Vassili broke bounds. He brought both fists down with a ringing blow upon the table. The heavy mask was gone; a face of primitive fury was there instead.

"What did you come here for? You won't tell me? You think you can make a jest of me? Do you think you can double-cross me and get away with it? I will tell you what you came here for! I will tell you—" He broke off and, leaning on the table, stretched across it, shaking with rage. "What did you push into that drawer just now? Tell me that!"

Alec Stevens tapped on the arm of the chair with his pistol.

"If you touch that drawer, I shall break your wrist!" he said. "Don't say I didn't warn you."

There was a moment when nothing happened. Then Vassili lifted himself slowly, his hands splayed out upon the table. His body drew back. He straightened himself. Last of all he took his hands from the table and thrust them deep into his trouser pockets. With each movement a violent control imposed itself upon him. It was rather horrible to watch, but Alec Stevens appeared pleasantly unmoved.

Vassili spoke at last in a perfectly calm voice.

"You took my piece of the five-pound note."

"I did."

"How did you know anything about it?"

Alec Stevens smiled.

Vassili spoke again.

"I suppose Catherine told you. There are too many women mixed up in this affair—it is always a mistake."

"That, my dear Vassili, depends on the point of view."

The mask had closed down over Vassili's features; they betrayed nothing. He went on asking his questions in a cold, formal voice.

"How many pieces have you got?"

Alec smiled again.

"You know, Vassili, you weren't the right man for this job—one of their mistakes. Now I'm proposing—out of family feeling, shall we say—to relieve you of the consequences of failure."

The mask quivered.

"Be careful, Sasha!"

"I'm being very careful, I am a careful person—I don't leave anything to chance. And when I say I'm taking this job over from you, I mean what I say. Do you get that?"

"How many pieces have you?"

"I've got a full hand—and I don't mind telling you that I mean to play it for every cent it's worth."

From where Jim stood he could see the half of the writing-table, and Alec Stevens thrown back in his chair, alert and wary beneath a manner of careless ease. Vassili did not come into his field of vision. He had seen him only when that furious forward thrust had brought his head and shoulders into view. It was difficult to connect the controlled formality of his voice now with the spectacle of animal rage which he had then afforded.

He said, "*You* mean to play it?"

"Oh certainly. You had your chance and you simply chucked it away. I may have been lucky—but after all one makes one's luck. Anyhow I have succeeded where you failed—and I don't suppose it's necessary for me to point out that failures are not exactly regarded with enthusiasm in Moscow."

"You have the impudence—"

"Oh, any amount of it. Look here, Vassili, the game's up. Throw in your hand, and I'll do my best for you. Give trouble, and I'll smash you. I can."

The controlled, formal voice said,

"You are talking like a fool."

Alec Stevens laughed lightly.

"Am I? I don't think so. I think the shoe's on the other foot. I think you're in a pretty tight place, and I think you know it. I think you've been fool enough to imagine you can play a double game with Moscow."

A horrible raucous voice shouted furiously,

"That is a lie—a lie—a lie—*a lie!*"

The hand that held the automatic lifted a little. There was a pause. Then Vassili said, quite low and tonelessly,

"It is a lie—but what did you mean?"

Jim saw Alec Stevens straighten himself in his chair.

"What were you doing in Birmingham last July?" he said.

Instantly there was dead silence—no answer, no sound of any kind—dead, frozen silence. Jim could see Alec Stevens leaning a little forward now and smiling that faint amused smile of his, but he could not see Vassili. He could not hear him either. But though he could neither hear him nor see him, he was nevertheless intensely conscious of him. In some horrible way Vassili filled the room—Vassili, with brute rage, beating against brute fear behind a dead sound-proof silence.

Jim clenched his hands and tried to think of what he was going to do. He ought to be thinking, he ought to be making a plan, and for the life of him he couldn't get his thoughts off Vassili. Then quite suddenly the strain gave; Vassili more or less ceased to exist. At a sound—no, something that couldn't really be called a sound—Jim's head turned and he saw pressed up against the glass within an inch of his shoulder a face and part of a hand.

The hand pressed on the glass—the palm of it and three finger tips. The face did not touch the pane, but appeared to float in the thick air like a pale shadow. Jim stared down at it and saw the eyes gazing and the lips parted. They looked dark; the rest pale and very nearly formless. The hair on the nape of his neck stood up and a cold finger touched his spine. Then, as the silence in the room behind him broke in a torrent of Russian oaths, the hand left the glass and went with a quick movement to the dark lips, pressing them—pressing.

With a jerk of the pulses, Jim became aware that it was Cissie Stark who stood there with nothing but the thickness of a sheet of glass between them. Then, even as he recognized her, she was gone, swallowed up by the fog.

Had she seen him? Impossible to say. He had seen her. Why was she there, and what did she want? There was an easy answer to this—she didn't trust Vassili, and wanted to know what he was up to.

He dismissed Cissie Stark and her affairs. He had got to make up his mind what he was going to do. The odds were hopelessly against him here. Suppose he were to wait for Alec Stevens by his car.... He would have a good chance of catching him off his guard. Well, now was the time to get away, with Vassili making the father and mother of a row in the room behind. He blessed the inventor of casement windows, and took hold of the catch. And on that there came a lull, and Alec Stevens speaking in a tone of pleasant mockery.

"Well, well—what an exhibition! It must really be very uncomfortable to have a temper like yours. I expect you find it quite a relief to let it go for once."

"What are you going to do?" said Vassili in a voice of rage.

Alec Stevens laughed.

"I am going to collect on the Sanquhar invention. I told you that before."

At the curse that followed he laughed again, and as he did so, a loud and prolonged knocking resounded through the house.

Jim stood rigid behind the curtain, one hand on the latch.

Vassili stopped short in the midst of a pungent phrase and said sharply,

"What's that?"

Alec Stevens said in a careless voice,

"Quite possibly the police." He spoke in English as he had done throughout.

"The police!"

"What it is to have a guilty conscience! Why should you be afraid of the police? You're in your own house, aren't you?"

The knocker fell again insistently.

"You think it is the police?" said Vassili. The wild beast anger was gone; he used a hesitating tone.

"You'd better go and see."

"I?"

"Certainly. You are the tenant, are you not? Come on, man, pull yourself together! They won't eat you."

Whilst they were speaking, Jim's hand moved with the moving latch. As a final burst of knocking made Vassili exclaim, the catch came clear. He had only to push the window and his way was before him. He heard Vassili go out, leaving the door open. And on that the sound of Alec Stevens crossing the floor and the noise of the slammed door. Back in the room something clicked as he swung the window wide. The smell of the fog came into his nose and throat. He put one knee on the window-ledge, and was drawing up the other, when the curtain rings clattered overhead and in a glare of light something cold pressed hard upon his neck, A hand with an iron grip took his shoulder. Alec Stevens said pleasantly,

"Hands up, Mackenzie! I've got you cold."

If the window had been a wider one, he would have risked the forward plunge, but with the narrow casement there wasn't a chance. He stuck up his hands.

"Now step back!" said Alec Stevens—"three paces! No—keep away from the window!" He drew the curtain close and stood before it, pistol in hand, frowning a little.

"You're damned inconvenient, you know," he said, and then stopped to listen to the wrangle of voices in the hall. "What am I going to do with you?" he went on after a moment. "Of course, there are the police. You could probably be run in for burglary, or at any-rate breaking and entering—I suppose you did break and enter. No—you'd better go on keeping your hands up."

"It would be a very interesting job for the police," said Jim. Then he laughed. "There's the telephone. Why don't you get a move on? You can charge me with burglary—and Vassili can charge you with pinching his pocket-book—and I can get in a piece about some one who pinched my charwoman's latch-key and broke open my dispatch-box. Unfortunate for you, meeting Kennedy Jackson like that on the stair—he'll be a valuable witness."

The handle of the door turned, but the door did not open.

Alec Stevens did not look round. He kept his pistol hand steady and his eyes on Jim. Only the contraction of the pupils gave away the fact that he was under a strain. He raised his voice and said easily enough,

"That door is locked, Vassili."

It was most violently shaken.

"Open it! Open it! Do you hear me?"

"Presently."

"At once! Do you hear me? I say at once, or I break in!"

Alec Stevens's predicament was plain. He had robbed Vassili, and he had robbed Jim. If they made common cause against him, he could scarcely hope to get away. He might, of course, shoot Jim; in which case Vassili would be equally interested with himself in hushing the matter up. He might.... Jim saw the thought in his eyes as Vassili beat again upon the door. Should he rush him and chance a miss?

As he drew himself together for a desperate spring, the danger was past. Alec Stevens reached for the writing-table drawer and, jerking it open, caught up the pocket-book containing the five-pound note and slipped it into his breast pocket. As he took a long step backwards, the door splintered under a furious kick. One panel gave, but the lock held. Vassili shouted, and a woman screamed. Alec Stevens took another backward step, looking only at Jim and keeping that steady aim. Then, as the door gave with a rending crash, he threw up his hand and shot out the light. The violence of the report, the splintering of glass, a smell of powder and Cissie's piercing scream exploded together, and immediately there was a confused darkness, with the hall light showing through the doorway. The smashed door swung drunkenly. Cissie screamed again, and Vassili came into the room with a rush.

Jim had not waited for him. As the light went out, he sprang for the window and, with his knee on the sill, heard Alec Stevens's laugh and the sound of running feet. He dropped on to the earth of a flower bed, blundered into what must have been the kitchen wall, and had to feel his way along it with the noise of angry voices following him through the open window. The wall turned, and he with it. His feet were on the brick pavement. Suddenly he remembered that there would be no need for him to climb the wall; he could skirt the house and go out by the front gate. Vassili would scarcely have stayed to lock it.

The fog was thicker than ever. He kept by the wall of the house, and when he could feel gravel under his feet he turned and went groping down to the gate. The solid oak door was ajar. He pulled it open, took a forward step, and ran into a woman in the dark. Her hands closed on his arm. She pressed against him, breathing in a quick sobbing way, whilst a scent of violets came warmly up from her soft furs.

"Mr Jim—" said Cissie's voice, tripping over a caught breath.

"What is it?"

"Oh, Mr Jim!"

He said, "Let me go;" but she pressed closer, throwing her weight on his shoulder.

"Take me with you! I'm afraid."

He began to hurry her along towards the car.

"Where do you want to go?"

"I don't know. I'm afraid he'll kill me."

Jim frowned in the darkness. What a damned nuisance women were.

"I could take you to Stark. What's his address? He's moved, hasn't he?"

"26 Rolling's Court, Mornington Road," she said. Then as they reached the car, she added quickly, "But I can't come."

"I can't wait," said Jim bluntly.

She held on to his arm.

"What's it all about? I came because I wanted to know what Vassili was up to. And he's mad—right down mad. But all the same I'd better get back. It's Sasha he's mad with really, not me—at least—"

"Come along to Stark."

"No—I can't. I'm all right really. I didn't bargain for the shooting— that's all." She giggled suddenly. "I thought we'd have the neighbours in, but it don't seem to run to any. Cheery sort of spot, I don't think I Well, so long!"

She came nearer, kissed him on the cheek, laughed rather unsteadily, and was gone.

Leeming Lane was full of fog from end to end. Jim started the car, and crawled. The open windscreen let the raw thick air into his eyes and his throat. Somewhere ahead of him Alec Stevens must be crawling too. He wondered whether he would finish the evening by bumping into him. And then he wondered how on earth either of them were going to get anywhere unless the fog lifted. He remembered that the lane took an S-shaped curve about fifty yards beyond. The Walled House, but he had almost touched the paling on the left before he realized that the curve had begun. Another crawl, another near shave, a violent bump over something that felt like a paving stone; and then after twenty or thirty yards a sudden and most welcome rift in the fog. Five minutes later he was on the main road, and the fog no more than a light mist. It was a most tremendous relief to be able to move again.

He had no idea which way Alec Stevens had gone, and didn't intend to waste any time looking for him; he felt perfectly clear about that. What he had to do was to find Eliza Huggins and tell her straight out what had happened—and to find Eliza Huggins he must get hold of Stark. It was tolerably certain that Bertram Hallingdon would have provided for his old servants, and in that case Stark would be able to lay hands on the address. He might even remember it off hand—he had that sort of memory.

Mornington Road is N.W.—a long road, full of dingy shops. Rolling's Court is the third turning on the left. Jim pulled up in front of No. 26 and rang the bell. There was a considerable delay before a depressed-looking middle-aged woman opened the door. She had a long face and thin hair scratched together with aggressive black hairpins. She wore an overall of faded chintz with a magenta pattern. She said that Stark was out, and that she didn't know when he would be back, and with that made to close the door.

"You can't give me any idea where he's likely to be?"

"No, I couldn't really." She paused, rubbed her nose, and added, "Unless he's down, at the club."

"What club?" said Jim quickly.

"There's a good many of them goes there, and I don't say there's any harm in it—"

"If you would kindly give me the address—" said Jim.

"And of course there's no saying whether he'll be there or no, and so I told the other gentleman."

"What other gentleman?"

"Come to the door and asked for Mr Stark same as you did, and I'd no more than got down the stairs—scarcely turned round, as you might say—when I heard the bell go again."

Jim got the address in the end—the address, and the knowledge that Alec Stevens was also looking for Stark.

He found the club easily enough, inquired for Stark, and was presently asked to "step this way." He followed his guide into a room thick with smoke, where a game of billiards was in progress and about twice as many men as the room was meant to hold were looking on and betting on the play. It took him a minute or two to discover Stark, and more than that to make his way to him. When he touched him on the arm, Stark turned round with a kind of nervous impatience, but when he saw who had touched him, his jaw fell and he went green.

"Evening, Stark. Did you think I was Stevens?" said Jim, a little grimly.

Stark's jaw stayed dropped.

"Mr J-Jim!" he said at last.

"Yes—not Alec Stevens. I suppose you thought he'd come back."

"Comeback?"

"Yes, come back. You needn't bother to lie, because I know he's been here, I also know what he wanted—Eliza Huggins's address. I want it too."

As soon as Stark turned, he lost his place by the table. By the time he and Jim had exchanged a couple of sentences he had been squeezed out to the edge of the crowd. Jim took him by the arm and walked him into the passage.

"I want Eliza Huggins's address. You've just given it to Alec Stevens, haven't you? Well, now you can give it to me—and I'm in a hurry."

The perspiration shone on Stark's pale forehead.

"I—Mr Jim—we're not allowed to give addresses—I'd get the sack."

"Cut the cackle, Stark! I want that address. It's worth a tenner to me, and I haven't got time to talk about it." He put his hand into his pocket and pulled out a thin crackling note. "Here's the tenner. Now, what's the address?"

Stark looked at the note, looked at Jim, ran his tongue over his lips, and said,

"3 Laburnum Cottages, Smayle, near Exeter."

Jim laughed out loud.

"What—all the way back again?" Then he gave Stark the note, clapped him on the shoulder, and said, "Buck up! You're not dead yet, but you'd better be, if there's any hanky-panky about that address."

Chapter Thirty-Four

ELIZA HUGGINS had been trained for service in the days when early rising was early rising. She had her own opinion about girls who lay in bed till seven or even later—"Reading novels when they did ought to be sleeping, and sleeping when they did ought to be doing their work!" In her honourable retirement Eliza breakfasted at eight sharp; and she did not breakfast until her stove had been blackleaded, and her kitchen brought to the highest possible pitch of shining cleanliness and order.

As her clock struck the hour, she sat down to a table spread with a spotless cloth and partook of two rashers of bacon, two rounds from the loaf, a large pat of fresh butter, and two cups of very strong tea. She ate slowly, savouring her food and enjoying it. Her bulky old-fashioned figure was encased in a tight dress of lilac print made after the manner of her youth with innumerable gussets and a long full skirt. Her very abundant dark hair, which scarcely showed a thread of grey, was parted in the middle and done in a large knob at the back of her head. She had so much of it that it stood out on either side of her broad fleshy face and made her head look very big. But if her head was big, her shoulders were immense. She had been heard to thank God that she was not as other women were—"They haven't got no busts, and they haven't got no hips, and they haven't got no waists, and what the world's coming to, I don't know and I shouldn't like to say."

She was finishing her last mouthful of bread and butter, when there came a knock on the front door. A mild surprise showed in her face, but she finished her mouthful very calmly and deliberately, and then rose and took her unhurried way into the parlour. The front door opened directly into this room from a little porch. There was a neat brown linoleum on the floor, and a black woolly mat in front of the large old fireplace. There was no fire on the hearth. Eliza would have considered it waste. She didn't sit in her parlour, she kept it for company. It boasted two easy chairs and a sofa covered with bright green plush. Each chair had an antimacassar over the back, and the sofa had two. Eliza had made them herself, and they were a faithful copy of those which had defended her grandmother's chairs from the well oiled heads of three generations. In the middle of the room stood a round table with a single twisted leg and a walnut top polished to a most extraordinary degree of brilliance. On this shining surface there reposed, each on its own woolly mat, a heavy Bible with gilt clasps, a photograph album with an embossed cover and gold edges, and one of the primmer ferns in a bright pink china pot. The walls were covered with an indigo paper very gloomily patterned in brown. Eliza considered it serviceable, and expected it to last her time.

She went to the door and opened it. The knocking had become very loud, but she did not hurry herself. She lifted the latch, opened the door about half way, and beheld a young man with brows drawn together in a frown above restless hazel eyes. There was something so bright and quick about his glance that she began to think about shutting the door in his face, but before she had got any further than that his hat was off and he was speaking very politely.

"Miss Huggins? Miss Eliza Huggins?"

Eliza gave the slow nod which brought her third chin into evidence. Her rather prominent dark eyes dwelt upon the young man with a ruminative expression. He thought she was exactly like a cow, and spoke with a touch of impatience.

"May I come in, Miss Huggins? I've come on a matter of business."

Eliza Huggins pursed up her lips. She didn't like people who were in a hurry. Slow and sure was her motto, and if anyone tried to hustle her, she became a great deal slower. After a maddening pause, she said without moving her hand from the door,

"Mr Rimington does my business."

"I've not come about your business, Miss Huggins, I've come about Mr Hallingdon's."

Eliza's eyes dwelt upon him. Presently she said,

"Mr Hallingdon's business?"

"Mr Bertram Hallingdon's business. And if you'll forgive me, Miss Huggins, I would like to come in. It's not a matter I can discuss on the doorstep, so if you don't mind—"

After a moment she took her hand off the door and stepped back. Alec Stevens came in and shut it behind him.

Eliza Huggins resumed the conversation.

"What's your business?" She paused for a moment before she added "Sir."

"A five-pound note," said Alec Stevens.

There were Nottingham lace curtains at the parlour windows, very white, very stiff, very heavily starched. They were looped back with wide pink ribbon. Eliza walked to the window and pulled the curtains together until they overlapped by a couple of inches. Then she came slowly back to the table and stood there.

"What were you saying about a five-pound note?"

Alec Stevens smiled like a man who is pleased with himself. He had been driving most of the night. He was stiff, and sore, and cold, and hungry, and the Sanquhar invention was his for the asking. He might well be pleased.

Eliza repeated what she had already said.

"What were you saying about a five-pound note?"

"I was saying I'd got one. I want to show it to you."

Eliza sat down on a hard chair.

"And what might your name be?" she asked.

"My name is Stevens."

The third chin again came into evidence as she nodded. She said, "Mr Stevens...." not addressing him, but just saying the name over to herself.

As she said it, he had his pocket-book out and, opening it, put down one by one three irregular fragments of thin white paper. He smoothed them out and set them in order; they lay on the polished table between Eliza and the pink flower-pot. They were not three pieces of paper any more, but a five-pound note.

"Now do you know what my business is?" he said.

Eliza looked at the five-pound note. She looked at it until Alec Stevens could hardly restrain himself from swearing at her. Then she got up and walked round the table and opened the Bible with the gilt clasps. She opened it in the middle, and the leaves parted over a faded sprig of lavender and a lock of straight black hair tied with what had once been a piece of bright blue ribbon. She turned two or three pages more, scanning each page deliberately, until she came on a half sheet of note-paper. She picked it up and came back with it in her hand. It took her about five minutes to compare what was written on the paper with the number of the five-pound note. Slow and sure was her motto, and if gentlemen liked to be impatient, it was no affair of hers.

When she had quite satisfied herself, she walked ponderously round the table again, put the half sheet of note-paper back in its place, and closed the book upon it. Then she sat down and folded her hands in her lap.

Alec Stevens controlled himself as well as he could.

"Well?" he said.

"That's the note," said Eliza Huggins.

"Very well. Then will you kindly give me the key of the safe."

Eliza nodded slowly. Her hands lay in her lap.

"The key of the safe—" she said.

"And tell me where it is, and in what name." He let himself go for a moment. "I'm in a hurry."

"Hurry brought the mare down," said Eliza.

"I understand that Mr Hallingdon left you the key—"

Eliza nodded again.

"And instructions to hand it over to the person who brought you this five-pound note—"

Eliza leaned back in her chair, she looked straight into his impatient face and said,

"The note's all right."

"Then will you give me the key."

"The note's all right," said Eliza in her slow, heavy voice.

"Of course it's all right! Will you give me the key."

"Not without Miss Laura Cameron."

Alec Stevens had the horrid sensation of having missed a step in the dark.

"Miss Cameron?"

"Miss Laura Cameron."

"What do you mean? Miss Cameron's piece of the note is here." He tapped it with an angry finger. "The key was to be given to the person who brought you this note."

"Not without Miss Laura Cameron, it wasn't," said Eliza.

At the moment when Eliza Huggins was opening the heavy Bible with the gilt clasps a car passed the door and drew up a little way beyond it. Jim Mackenzie got out of the car and walked back along the row of cottages until he came to No. 3.

Alec Stevens's car was on the other side of the road, but he did not glance at it. He walked stiffly, and his eyes had a hard, fixed look. He was almost at the end of his tether, but he meant to see Eliza Huggins. He held on to that—he had got to see Eliza Huggins and stop her handing over the Sanquhar invention.

He stood in the little porch and heard voices within. With his hand on the latch, he hesitated for a moment, then lifted it and pushed the door ajar. He heard Alec Stevens speaking in a controlled, reasonable voice:

"But, my dear Miss Huggins, Miss Cameron has been ill. And, by the way, she is not Miss Cameron any more; she is married. You know that?"

Jim stood where he was. He could not see Eliza's nod, but he heard her say,

"Mr Rimington told me as much."

"Then he told you that she was Mrs Stevens."

He was going to play the part of Laura's husband, was he? The damned impudent swab! Jim leaned on the doorpost and waited. Give the fellow rope and he'd trip himself up.

"That makes no difference," said Eliza Huggins.

"What doesn't?" Alec Stevens's tone sharpened.

"Not who she's married—whether it's you, or whoever it is, it don't make any difference. I've got to see her, and she's got to say she's willing. Mr Hallingdon was very particular about it."

"Have you ever seen her?" said Alec Stevens. "Do you know her?"

"I've seen her," said Eliza. "Mr Hallingdon, he sent me where I could see her, and when I come back he arst me would I know her again, and I told him I would for certain. 'She's not one that's easy forgot,' I told him."

The words did something to Jim Mackenzie. He was near the edge of sleep, hearing what passed as if through layers of cotton wool. And then Eliza Huggins said, "She's not one that's easy forgot," and he came awake with a jerk. Laura—she was speaking about Laura, It wasn't easy to forget Laura—he hadn't tried—it wouldn't be any use trying. For a moment she was there, vivid and tender as a dream, invading his every sense with sweetness and pain. He straightened himself up. If he leaned against anything, he would go to sleep.

Alec Stevens was talking about Laura being ill—about Laura not being able to come—about how urgently necessary it was that Eliza should give him the key of the safe. He had a pressing manner and a persuasive tongue. If Eliza moved to get the key, Jim would push open the door and go in. But he mustn't go to sleep—it was all up if he went to sleep.

The persuasive voice ceased on a most persuasive note. Eliza Huggins was speaking again.

Jim kept his hand on the door.

"Well, sir—"

What was she going to say? His hand closed. The deliberate voice went on.

"Well, sir, seeing Miss Laura Cameron has been ill and can't be expected to take a journey, and seeing you've got the five-pound note and you want me to give you the key and let you know where the safe is and what name it's under—"

"Yes?" said Alec Stevens.

Eliza paused weightily.

"Seeing as such is the case," she said very deliberately—"to my mind there's nothing to be done until Miss Laura's got her health again."

Jim let go of the door and stepped back. The immovability of Eliza came home to him. Even with his head packed with cotton wool he understood that if Alec Stevens were to talk all day, Eliza would not budge. Bertram Hallingdon had picked well.

He turned and walked through the little gate and along the grass-bordered path to where he had left his car. A new idea possessed him to the exclusion of everything else. He must get to Laura before Alec Stevens did. She'd got to be warned. She'd got to be told about Eliza and warned.

He started the car and began to drive in an automatic manner, his thoughts set firmly on reaching Lynn Cliff.

Chapter Thirty-Five

JIM DROVE ON. He had about twenty miles to go. The thought of them was like a rushing noise in his head. He would have given everything in the world except Laura to let go of the wheel, slump down where he was, and sleep; but because of Laura he had got to go on.

When he had been driving for half an hour, a car passed him, going very fast. The noise that it made increased the noise in his head to an almost unbearable degree. The man in the car, who was Alec Stevens, turned round and looked back, but Jim did not see him. His field of consciousness had narrowed to the road and the things which he had to do to keep on the road and to reach Laura. He went on doing these things with the mechanical efficiency of a robot.

Alec Stevens pressed his foot on the accelerator and went away. The needle of his speedometer slipped over to sixty and stayed there. The speed exhilarated him and stimulated thought. He was not conscious of undue fatigue. To drive up to town the night before and down again in the small hours of the morning was nothing very much out of the way. He had not, like Jim Mackenzie, had the down run twice, nor had he come on the road within a few hours of a hurried journey over to France and back.

He kept at sixty, and thought of what he was going to do. He wasn't going to be beaten on the post by Jim Mackenzie; that might be taken as a stone-cold certainty. He was going to have the Sanquhar invention, and if Laura's consent was necessary, he was going to have Laura's consent.... What would force that out of her? There was no time to persuade, to bring pressure to bear; consent must be wrenched from her now, within the limits of this day, before Vassili could butt in. Laura's consent.... What lever to use? What lever had Vassili used to force her into marriage? Jim Mackenzie's safety—Jim Mackenzie's life—the only lever that would have moved her then, and the only lever that would move her now. Jim Mackenzie's life, and—perhaps—her freedom. Good levers—powerful levers.

His mind began to work upon a plan. It might come off, or it might not. When he stopped taking risks he would be dead. It was in his temperament to be stirred by danger. All the same he would take his risks cautiously and plan every possible detail. The small combe would be the place. He had the rope, and the chance of any other traffic on the road was remote. Even in summer it was a lonely place, and at this hour of a January morning.... Added to everything else, it was beginning to rain heavily, and by the look of the sky there was worse to come.

As he came over the last ridge, the road ran close above the grey and stormy sea and the rain fell in sheets. The combe lay below him, with the road dipping to cross it within a stone's throw of high water mark. It was a short, steep ravine going down to a little inlet not large enough to be called a bay. Where the road crossed it by an old stone bridge the sides were thickly wooded, but immediately below the bridge the trees stopped. The sea was in sight and the tide coming up.

Alec Stevens crossed the bridge, left his car by the side of the road, and ran back. In his left hand he swung a heavy coil of rope. Here, just short of the bridge, was the place for his turn. The trees were oaks, stunted with the buffeting of the sea winds. He made fast his rope to one that grew below the bridge, and then carried the other end across the road. Here he had to climb, the ground falling away so sharply that he must hitch the rope about the trunk some ten or twelve feet up. He tied his knots skilfully, leaving the rope taut some two and a half feet above the road. Without any appearance of haste, he had been very quick, but even so, he had no more than reached the ground before he heard the first sound of the following car, and for a moment through all his violent stubborn purpose there pricked the thought, "Suppose it's some one else."

There was no time to do more than jerk an impatient shoulder. The car slowed on the slope, shining grey in the rain—and Jim Mackenzie's car it was, rushing down to the combe, and the bridge, and the rope. Alec Stevens had seen Jim Mackenzie's face when he passed him. His second look had confirmed what the first had told him, that here was a man drunk with fatigue. Too drunk to see a rope across his path? That was part of the gamble. But, with a streaming windscreen, who was going to see a rope until it was too late?

He stood under the bridge and heard the car come on. The arch echoed. And then with a sickening crash the thing had happened.

Alec Stevens scrambled up the bank, avoided some broken glass, and surveyed the wreckage. The rope had broken, but it had served its turn. The car had smashed into the end of the parapet and lay on its side with the windscreen shattered and the bonnet crumpled. He threw just the one glance at the mess, and then proceeded very coolly to unfasten and roll up the two straggling ends of rope. He walked to his car and put them away under the seat, and then came back to look for Jim Mackenzie.

He was frowning as he came. The smash was worse than he had intended. He didn't want Jim Mackenzie dead; he wanted him as a hostage, as a means of bringing pressure to bear on Laura.

The car lay on its left side. He looked through the smashed window by the driver's seat and saw Jim Mackenzie lying in a heap where he had fallen, clear of the wheel, fortunately the door had not jammed. He got it open, took Jim under the armpits, and after something of a struggle pulled him out and let him down on the wet road. He was bleeding from two or three cuts on the hands, but his face was not touched.

Alec slipped a hand under his coat, and felt a steady heart. A wave of relief flowed over him. If there were no bones broken, his luck was in. He made a rapid and not unskilful examination, and laughed out loud. He had taken his risk, and fortune had favoured him. The man had no more than a bang on the head, and a thick enough head to survive a dozen worse knocks. His luck was in all right. But the next step—the next was the very devil; for if he couldn't get Jim Mackenzie down to the cave, his whole plan went for nothing. He hadn't really reckoned on his being knocked out like this. A badly shaken man who could be made to walk down the path with a pistol held to his head was what he had been counting on. Well, he'd got to have a shot at it, and at once; for if another car came along, he would be done.

He propped Jim Mackenzie into a sitting position and, kneeling, got him by the arms and pulled the weight on to his back. Then he had to get up; and it wasn't very easily done, for Jim Mackenzie was strongly built and a dead weight. Once up, he made use of the parapet of the bridge to take some of the weight until he got it balanced. He had not far to go. The path ran down from the far side of the bridge to the rocks and shingle of the inlet. For the first yard or two the slope was an easy one, then it sharpened, and fell by half a dozen steps to a level stretch. The first two steps were the worst, for after that there was hand-hold. He came past the level to more steps, very shallow and running wet with the rain. When he set foot on the shingle below he was as hot as he had ever been in his life. Well, he had done it, and if he had been asked in cold blood to say whether he could do it, he would certainly have said no.

He went grinding across the shingle, bowed forward by the weight on his back, and before he expected it the water was over his shoes. He had not thought that the sea would be so far in, with another two hours to high tide. He had it in his mind to reach the cave, but from where he stood he could see that he wasn't going to be able to do it. What then? Cart this heavy carcass up that damned slippery path again and be caught by a passing car? Not much! Well, he'd got to do something, and he'd got to do it quickly.... If he could get round the next point, there might or might not be a place where he could dump Jim Mackenzie.... He went forward, feeling his foothold.

The point was only a few yards away, but the water deepened alarmingly, and a fair sized wave nearly knocked him off his feet before he reached it. Another ten minutes, and he might have got by himself, but he couldn't have carried Jim Mackenzie.

When he was round the point, another and a heavier wave took him in the small of the back. Under its impact he broke into a staggering run and fell sprawling on the dark slimy mass of seaweed left by the last tide. He was up again in a moment, and dragging Jim Mackenzie past the weed up on to the small triangle of dry shingle above high water mark.

A glance told him that the place would do. The cliff hung over, its face fretted away to form a beach no more than a couple of yards wide and three in length. His hostage should be safe enough here until the tide went down. That gave him four hours. If he couldn't talk Laura round in four hours, he couldn't talk her round at all. Meanwhile, if he didn't hurry, he'd be here for four hours himself.

He watched the next wave break—cold grey water, laced with foam. Then as it receded with the sound of shingle dragging over rock, he ran for it, slipping and stumbling in the backwash, and as he ran, he saw another wave come pounding on with the wind behind it and a heavy spray flying. If it caught him at the point, he wouldn't have a chance. He had a moment of cold fear, and then he was round the point. He came panting up the beach and flung himself down on the dry shingle. It had been touch and go, but he had pulled it off.

When he had got his breath back, he climbed out of the combe. He had almost reached the road, when something caught at his nerve and shook it.

Suppose his luck had failed him at the eleventh hour. Suppose some one had come on the wreckage whilst he had been away. A tramp, a cyclist, another car, and he would be in it up to his neck. He took the last rise with the coldest feet in the world.

The road was empty. The wreckage lay untouched. The rain poured down on it out of an even leaden sky. His own car stood not fifty yards away. In five minutes he could reach the Hermitage.

Chapter Thirty-Six

THE HERMITAGE had two sitting-rooms, and both of them faced the sea. In the room on the right of the hall Laura was sewing. Every now and then her needle stopped moving and she looked out of the window. It was like looking out of one of the windows of the ark when the flood was out. The window was a square bay. She sat on a wide seat that filled it, and she looked straight out at the grey water, and the grey sky, and the grey curtain of the rain. The water heaved and fell with a curious giddy rhythm, and the sky looked as if it was falling too, so heavy was the rain.

Laura's ears were so full of the sound of water that she did not hear the door open. Catherine came into the room in a bright green dress.

She said, "Sasha wants to speak to you," and then turned her shoulder to the room.

Laura laid her sewing in her lap, and saw Alec Stevens. He had changed into dry clothes, but he looked blue with the cold. He held a steaming glass of hot whisky and water, and when he had gone over to the fire he began to sip from it, warming his hands on the glass.

"You must have got very wet," said Laura rather timidly.

What did Sasha want to say to her? And why was Catherine staring out of the window? A little tremor of apprehension troubled her, and she spoke because it was easier to speak than to be silent.

Alec Stevens smiled.

"I got very wet," he said, and sipped from his steaming glass.

There was a momentary pause. Then he sat down on the fender-stool with his back to the fire and leaned forward, tumbler in hand.

"I'm going to ask you a rude question. I'm going to ask you whether you think of yourself as intelligent."

Laura smiled her charming smile.

"Moderately," she said.

"Because I want to drive a bargain with you, and a little intelligence would be helpful."

"What sort of bargain?" said Laura in a grave voice. The word troubled her.

"A perfectly simple one. You will benefit—I shall benefit—Catherine will benefit—Mackenzie will benefit."

Laura's hand moved quickly. The needle in her fine white work pricked her and a bright spot of blood spread on the cambric. She tossed the work aside and put her finger to her lips.

"Vassili, I am afraid, will not benefit," said Alec Stevens—"but I have an idea that you will be able to bear that."

Laura drew herself up a little.

"I think you had better say what you mean."

"I'm going to," said Alec Stevens, and took a good long drink. "I'm just getting up my courage, you see." And then, "One can't do oneself justice when one is so damnably cold. As soon as I am thawed I'll explain myself."

Catherine looked over her shoulder.

"You'd much better go and have a hot bath."

"I can't spare the time. Besides, I'm really quite hot now—my back is singeing pleasantly. Well, let's get down to brass tacks. I want the Sanquhar invention, and I'm prepared to do a deal with you."

Laura's eyebrows went up. Her lips relaxed into a smile.

"I'm afraid there's nothing doing." Then, with a shade more gravity, "Is it really worth talking about?"

He raised his glass and set it down.

"Oh, *quite*. Now I'll give you a piece of good advice. Never turn an offer down until you've heard what it is. We've all got our price, you know."

Catherine looked round again.

"You are being stupid, Sasha."

"Never mind, *liebchen*—I shall improve as I go on. *Now*, Laura—just listen to me. I have the five-pound note, and I have the address of Miss Eliza Huggins—no, don't turn pale—I have not got the Sanquhar invention—*not yet*. I'm going to be perfectly frank with you—all the cards on the table and no aces up my sleeve. Eliza is a most formidably virtuous and trustworthy female. Mr Hallingdon told her that she was only to hand over the key of the safe in your presence. No—you didn't know that, and nor did I. When I came along with my five-pound note, thinking I'd got the ace of trumps, she produced the joker and swiped the trick. You've got to be there, or Eliza doesn't part. And if it was only the key, I'd have had a shot at tying her up and looking for it, but as she's the only person who knows where the safe is and in what name, I had to think of something else. I thought of you."

"Then I think Catherine is right and you are very stupid."

He said, "No," with a smiling face.

"You do not really think that I will give you the Sanquhar invention?"

He nodded.

"Yes, I think so—in exchange for Mackenzie's life."

Since she had tossed her work away Laura's hands had rested idly on the edge of the window-sill. She leaned on them now as if she were about to rise, whilst the colour rushed into her face. But the impulse failed. The colour ebbed.

She said, "What do you mean?" and all at once she felt giddy, as if time had turned upon itself and taken her back to the moment when Vassili had offered her Jim's life at a price.

She steadied herself with an effort. That dreadful moment was gone, and no one could make her live it again. Jim was not in Russia now, and this was not Vassili, but Alec.

He was speaking.

"I'll tell you what I mean. I'm not asking you to do anything in the dark. Mackenzie has had an accident. No, he's not hurt. He was driving too fast, and he ran off the road and smashed up his car. I give you my word that he's not hurt in the least. If you will go with me to see Eliza Huggins, I can undertake to hand him over to you in perfectly good repair."

"Where is he?" said Laura in a low, steady voice.

"He was foolish enough to get cut off by the tide. But as soon as we have done our business with Eliza we can see about releasing him. Perhaps a rope let down over the cliff would be the best way—unless we just wait till the tide goes down."

Laura sat quite still for a moment. Then she said,

"I don't believe you."

"My dear Laura"—he shrugged his shoulders—"what can I do to convince you?"

Catherine looked over her shoulder again.

"It is true, Laura," she said.

Laura felt as if the ground had been shaken under her. Her own words came back upon her with no substance in them. She had said, "I don't believe you." But it wasn't true. She believed everything, and she was helpless.

"Look here," said Alec Stevens, "I'm trying to do you a good turn. Mackenzie's all right, and as far as I'm concerned you can have him back safe and sound. But I've got to have the Sanquhar invention—just make up your mind to that. I've got to have it, and I'll stick at nothing to get it. If you're obstinate, I'm afraid Mackenzie's accident will turn out to have been a fatal one. Do you see?"

Laura turned desperately to Catherine. But Catherine was watching the grey lift and fall of the stormy water, her door so plainly shut and barred that Laura's hope died.

"Come, Laura!" said Alec Stevens.

Laura threw up her head.

"You are trying to frighten me. But this isn't Russia. If you touched Jim, I should go straight to the police."

"Would you? Trina, do you hear that—she would go straight to the police. One of us would drive her to the nearest police-station, and then she would tell them that I had murdered Mackenzie, and when they asked her for a spot of proof, she would say, 'He *told* me he was going to murder him.' No—I'm afraid they would think you were crazy. At the inquest it would come out that Mackenzie had been on the road for the best part of twenty-four hours. It would be quite obvious that he had had a smash, and that afterwards he had fallen over the cliff in a dazed condition. I should deny what you say, and Catherine would deny what you say. Catherine will wear her nurse's uniform and explain that you have had a nervous breakdown." He rose from the fender-stool and stood with his back to the fire. "Come, Laura—be sensible. What is the Sanquhar invention to you? You bought his life from Vassili, and paid dearer for it than that. What are you boggling at?"

Laura looked up at him. She was perfectly white, but her eyes and her lips were steady.

"I can't do it," she said.

"You did it before."

"I ought to have let him die—he said so—I knew it really—but—you won't understand—I was expecting to be so happy—I couldn't do it."

Alec Stevens stared at her curiously.

"And now?"

"That's all gone," said Laura. "I don't know what good it will do you to kill him, but I can't give you the Sanquhar invention."

He looked at her with some admiration. Her beauty and the simplicity of her manner affected him as music or a fine play might have done. They did not deflect his purpose in the least.

He came nearer.

"You talk like that because you are unhappy. You don't see any future. Now here are all my cards on the table. I can give you back everything that you have lost—I can give you back your future—I can turn you into Laura Cameron again—I can give you the proof that your marriage with Vassili was not legal. Now, Laura—*now*."

Laura was on her feet, one hand on his wrist and one on the sleeve of his coat, her eyes dark fire, her cheeks aflame.

"Sasha!" she said. *"Sasha!"* and did not know that she used the name that Catherine used for him.

He nodded, smiling.

Catherine turned round and watched them, her lips close, her eyes wary.

"It's true, my dear," he said. "But you'll never prove it without my help—and if you can't prove it, you can't marry Mackenzie. *Think*, Laura—you can marry him—you can be free, and you can marry him—you can have his life, and you can share it. What's the Sanquhar invention?"

Laura let go of him and went back a step, and then another, and after that another, until the wall brought her up short and she stood against it.

"I can't," she said, and heard Alec Stevens laugh.

Immediately after that Catherine called out. A door had banged, and with no more time than it took to draw a breath Vassili was in the room, his face scowling and his hands clenched.

"Oh, you are here!" he said, and stopped a yard inside the door, lowering.

"My dear Vassili, how sudden!" said Alec Stevens.

With a kind of roar Vassili ran at him. Laura saw the other man step aside, and as the blundering rush carried Vassili on, she saw Alec's hand go to his hip. When Vassili turned he looked along the barrel of an automatic pistol. He stood where he was.

"Vassili, I am tired of you," said Alec Stevens. "I would rather shoot you than not. Perhaps if you can get that into your head you will behave reasonably."

Vassili stood, his shoulders forward, his hands hanging, a dangerous look of fury on his face.

Catherine put herself between the two men.

"Are you both mad? Sasha, give me that pistol! I am as good a shot as you, and I have some common sense. Vassili, behave yourself! If you attack Sasha, I shall break your ankle—and you will not find that at all amusing. Now, Sasha—the pistol!"

He let her take it. Perhaps he was afraid to take the chance of what might happen in a moment of rage.

Catherine went over to the door and stood beside it just clear of the jamb.

Alec Stevens fell back into his old place before the fire.

"If you are wise, you will get out of the country," he said. He spoke in Russian, and in Russian Vassili answered him.

"Why do you say that?"

"I told you why last night."

"And if I will not go?"

Chapter Thirty-Seven

JIM MACKENZIE threw up his arm and turned over. It was the most confoundedly lumpy bed, and he had lost his pillow. Between sleeping and waking, he rested his head on his arm, and became aware of cold daylight. He opened his eyes and blinked, and a handful of ice-cold water took him in the face. He gasped, rolled over again, and sat up.

It is safe to say that he was very much astonished at what he saw. He was sitting on a small triangular patch of shingle. On either side of him was an ugly, dirty, uneasy sea coming up in choppy waves with the wind behind it—a perfectly beastly wind that was drenching him with spray.

The rain had stopped.

It was the thought of the rain that jogged his memory. The last thing he remembered was the rain coming down and his windscreen streaming with it. But he had been driving the car, and how in the world had he got here? He put his hands to his head, and became aware of an out-size in bumps. He must have had a smash and gone over the cliff.

He got on to his feet rather stiffly, and was relieved to find himself sound. His hands were cut and he was soaked to the skin. Had he fallen into the sea and been washed up? It didn't seem likely—but then he couldn't think of any likely way of getting here. And then all of a sudden he remembered that he was going to Laura, and that he had got to beat Alec Stevens and get to her before he did. He turned his wrist quickly to see what time it was. The watch had stopped at a quarter past nine. Now had it stopped when he crashed, or had it run down? No—the water would have stopped it. But now that he was moving, he wasn't so sure about having been in the sea. His things were wet through, but not with the heavy, drenching wet of clothes which have been under water. Well, it didn't matter. All that mattered was to get out of this.

He turned and surveyed the cliff. A more unpromising sight could hardly have confronted him. The smooth slippery rock, undercut by the sea, offered no possible hold for foot or hand. He gave it but the one glance, and switched his thought back to that picture of pouring rain and a wet windscreen. What was the last thing that he could remember seeing through that windscreen? He could remember feeling dog tired.... He broke off, frowning. He didn't feel like that now. Did that mean he had been here for hours? Never mind—get back to what you remember. He remembered his hands feeling like lead on the wheel, and the streaming windscreen, and the sea—yes, the sea, below him on his left. That was it—the road ran along the cliff. Good Lord—he must have gone over! His frown deepened. Odd—because he remembered swinging away from the sea and running downhill to a ravine with a stone bridge across it. He remembered it distinctly. But he couldn't remember crossing the bridge. The last thing he could see was the bridge, and the way the trees grew round it, and the little scooped out bay that ran to meet it from the sea.

His face changed suddenly. He couldn't get up this beastly cliff, but he must be quite near that bay. All he had to do was to swim out far enough to get his bearings and make for the bay or any other likely landing-place. He was so strong a swimmer that, barring an exceptional current, the risk was negligible. He could hardly be colder or wetter than he was. The rain had to some extent stilled the sea. The waves were nothing out of the way now.

He took off his shoes and tied them round his neck, shed his jacket, and, wading into the water, struck out. Almost at once he saw the inlet, and made it easily. He was not to know till afterwards that if the tide had been past the turn, he would have been caught by the race. From the cliff above it shows like a pale green ribbon in the dull water and runs like a dozen millstreams. Had he lain between sleep and unconsciousness for another hour, he would never have seen Laura again.

He wrung the worst of the wet from his clothes, got into his soaked shoes, and climbed out of the combe.

As he came on to the road, he saw the car. So he had remembered right. It was the bridge that had smashed him, and he hadn't gone over the cliff. He wondered about that smash and put it away to be dealt with later. For the moment what he wanted was a coat to cover him. His overcoat was in the back of the car, and he was glad enough to get into it.

He wondered how far it was to the Hermitage.

It was not quite a mile. Just before the footpath turned off, a car ran past him and, wheeling, made off in the direction of the house, lurching and bumping with one wheel in the heather. It was not the only car that had taken that road. When Jim Mackenzie came in sight of the wicket gate above the steep steps, there was a car on either side. He began to wish that he had a weapon, but he wouldn't stop for that. There was a spanner in his overcoat pocket, and if the worst came to the worst, it might be handy.

He went down the steps and through the door into the square dark hall. And there he stopped, because he could hear the sound of voices. He stood still, and dripped upon the floor whilst he listened. There was a door on his right and a door on his left, and the stair going up from the middle of the hall. The voices came from the right. He went close to the door and listened again. He heard Vassili Stefanoff say, speaking Russian, "And if I will not go?"

So the second car was Vassili's. And it was Vassili who had passed him just now. He could not mistake the voice. It had the same accent of barely controlled fury which he had heard in the Villa Jaureguy, and again outside the locked door in The Walled House.

He stood where he was. He wanted to know what was happening before he broke in on them.

Alec Stevens was speaking, also in Russian.

"Oh, I think you will go."

And then a woman's voice, startlingly close at hand.

"Vassili, if you will not control yourself, I shall shoot and break your leg. I mean it."

That must be Catherine.

Jim had drawn back involuntarily as she spoke. Was she standing against the door? No, the voice was a little more to the left. She might be standing against the jamb. And she was armed. If he could get her weapon.... The thought rose in his mind even as Vassili said hoarsely,

"Why should I go?"

"You might make yourself useful in America and retrieve your position. In another continent I should have no grudge against you."

"I will not go!"

Alec Stevens answered him coolly.

"Then you have a choice between Moscow and Dartmoor. I believe long term prisoners go to Dartmoor. If you choose Moscow—but no, really, Vassili—I have quite a family affection for you, and I do not recommend Moscow—they are not merciful to failures. No, no—you've made a mess of things, and if you won't take my advice and go to

America, you will have to make the best of a sentence for bigamy. I believe that English prisons are not too bad."

There was a silence—a strangled sound—another silence.

Catherine said, "Take care!"

After a moment Vassili muttered, "What do you mean?"

Jim Mackenzie's heart was beating thickly. *Bigamy....* Was it possible? *Laura free!* He strained his ears, and heard Alec Stevens say with perfect distinctness,

"You surely haven't forgotten that you married Cissie Stark on the sixth of July last in front of the registrar of the Solihull division of Birmingham?"

This time there was no sound at all, not for a long time. But behind the silence there were forces that strained, one against the other. At the last of it Alec Stevens laughed. He spoke, and this time spoke in English.

"Don't be more of a fool than you can help, Vassili! Go whilst the going's good, and keep out of the way until things have blown over."

Jim stepped quickly back from the door. He had no more than time to get into the angle of the staircase before Vassili came violently out of the room and banged the door behind him. He neither paused nor looked about him, but went out of the front door, banging that too.

Well, that made the odds more even.

As soon as the sound had died away, Jim went straight to the sitting-room door and opened it. What he was afraid of was that Catherine might have moved away from the door. In another moment she would have done so; but she would not move for Vassili, and she had stayed where she was to listen for the sound of his going.

She had opened her lips to speak and straightened herself to take the first step towards Sasha, when the door opened and a wet, strong hand twisted the pistol from her grasp. Jim Mackenzie's left hand took her by the shoulder and held her out of the way. With his right he covered Alec Stevens lounging by the fire. At Laura, who filled his consciousness, he did not look at all. All through the scene that had just taken place she had not moved. She stood against the panelling, her eyes dark and wide, her lips a little parted, her face dreadfully white. She had not understood a single word of what had passed, but the angry voices, the half choked pauses, and the pistol in Catherine's hand had spoken a language which chilled the blood at her heart. And then all at once the door was open, and Jim on the threshold, and the pistol in his hand.

He said, "Hands up!" to Sasha and held Catherine away, and the water ran down out of his clothes and made a dark wet patch upon the floor, and he was as pale as a drowned man.

"Keep them up!" said Jim sharply. "Miss Catherine, I'm dreadfully sorry, but I must ask you to go and stand over there beside him."

Catherine looked at him coolly. His grip on her shoulder was amazingly strong.

"And if I don't?" she said.

Jim continued to look at Alec Stevens.

"Oh, I hope you will—because if you don't—"

"Well, Mr Jim Mackenzie—if I don't?"

Rather a grim smile showed for a moment about his mouth.

"I heard you tell Vassili what you would be obliged to do if he played the fool."

He felt her twist, and his grip tightened.

"You'll break my leg? You've very nearly broken my shoulder!"

"Not *your* leg," said Jim—"his. I'd much rather not, so if you'll just go over there—"

Catherine went over to the hearth and dropped down on the fender-stool.

"*Now*, Stevens," said Jim—"I want that five-pound note."

"Do you really? Then come and take it!"

"Don't be a fool, Stevens! You can put your left hand down. Now take out your pocket-book and throw it on the floor between us! I'll give you whilst I count ten, and if you haven't done it by then, I shall smash your right hand."

He began to count immediately. When he reached eight, Alec Stevens snatched out the pocket-book and flung it on the floor.

Catherine turned round and warmed her hands at the fire.

"Laura—" said Jim. "Will you pick up that pocket-book and see if the five-pound note is there?"

For the first time Laura moved. She crossed the floor, picked up the case, and looked through it until she came on an envelope containing the torn pieces of the note.

"Now put it into my pocket. Yes, it's wet, but that can't be helped. And now you've got half a minute to get your hat and coat."

Where was he going to take her, and how could she go with him? How could she stay here? Jim didn't look at her. She saw a grim and angry profile.

"Do as you're told and hurry!"

The words were fairly flung at her, and she went.

When she came back, Jim was saying,

"I'm taking your car, Stevens. You smashed mine, didn't you? I'll leave yours in a garage and let you know where it is, so you needn't bother the police. I expect we're two minds with a single thought where the police are concerned. Laura—the car is at the top of the steps. Go and get in!"

"Will you shoot me if I say good-bye to her?" said Catherine.

"From where you are, please."

But Laura slipped behind him and put her arms round her.

"Catherine—*dear!*"

Catherine allowed herself to be kissed. Then she pushed Laura away.

"Oh, run along and be happy!" she said. "He'll probably beat you, but I suppose you won't mind that."

"*Laura!*"

Laura went out of the room with a strange happiness at her heart. Nothing had changed, and yet she felt as if everything had changed. It was as if she had been in a nightmare and was beginning to wake up. It didn't feel real any more.

When she had reached the top of the steps, she saw Jim come out of the house. He kept his face towards it, and the pistol in his hand, and so came up the steps.

He said, "Get in," when they came to the car, but when she had got in, he leaned heavily against the door.

"You'll have to drive. I'm all in."

And when she had moved into the driver's seat he heaved himself in and slumped down in a heap, the pistol falling from his hand.

She started the car, and when they reached the road she said,

"Where?"

He roused himself to tell her, and did not speak again until they drew up at Eliza Huggins's door.

Chapter Thirty-Eight

ELIZA HUGGINS had not been too well pleased with her visitor. She thought about him a good deal as she peeled potatoes at her scullery sink. In the end she summed him up as ferrety-eyed. Her mental processes might be slow, but when she had once arrived at a conclusion nothing moved her from it, and having set Alec Stevens down as ferrety-eyed, ferrety-eyed he would remain as far as she was concerned. The term stood for complete untrustworthiness. A ferrety-eyed person was capable of anything from murder to what Eliza called pick-pocketing.

When the knocking came on her front door, she first turned her head and looked in that direction, and then said, "Drat!" When the knocking was repeated, she took her hands out of the cold water in which she was rinsing the potatoes, dried them slowly and methodically upon a roller towel, and went without haste to the door.

Two people stood on the doorstep, and after a moment's sheer surprise Eliza recognized them both. The lady was Miss Laura Cameron, and the gentleman whose arm she was holding was Mr Jim Mackenzie that she did ought to have married. "And oh, my gracious mercy me!" said Eliza to herself. "Whatever has he been a-doing of?"

Jim Mackenzie leaned against the doorpost. In spite of the overcoat which he had put on it was apparent that his clothes were drenched. His shirt was open at the neck. His rough fair hair stood on end above a face grey-white with fatigue.

"Miss Eliza Huggins?" said Laura in a quick, anxious voice.

Eliza stood back from the door. Her manner conveyed a respectful welcome.

"Come in, Miss Laura," she said.

Jim walked stiffly to a chair and sat down. He leaned his elbows on the table and put his head in his hands. He could hear Laura talking and Eliza talking. Their voices were a very long way off, and he himself was slipping quite slowly down a smooth inclined plane that went on and on and on for ever. He had no power to stop this sliding process. It took him farther and farther down into a white deadening mist.

"It's a good thing I'd got the kettle on the boil," said Eliza. "A good cup of tea with an egg beat up in it and his bed—that's what he wants.

Sopped to the skin, and goodness knows what else! Now, sir—you drink this up!"

Jim didn't want to drink anything. But Eliza was very firm with him. For all her bulk she was strong. When he had drunk the tea, she got him up the narrow stair and put him to bed, very much as if he had been ten years old.

"*Now*, Miss Laura—he's got my best night-gown on and sleeping beautiful, so don't you trouble."

Laura took both Eliza's hands in hers.

"You're frightfully good to us," she said. And then, "Suppose he comes after us."

Eliza looked her straight in the face.

"Your husband, miss?"

The colour flew to Laura's cheeks.

"Oh no! Oh *no*!"

Eliza continued to look at her.

Laura dropped her hands.

"It's Mr Alec Stevens, his cousin—he came to see you this morning. He wanted me to come back with him and ask you to give him the key of Mr Hallingdon's safe."

Eliza nodded.

"I wouldn't give it to no one without you was willing. Very particular, Mr Hallingdon was, and I gave him, my word."

"Mr Stevens may come back," said Laura.

"It wouldn't be any manner of use if he did."

"The pieces of the note are in Mr Mackenzie's pocket."

"It don't matter where they are now," said Eliza with strong common sense. "There—Miss Laura, don't you trouble. If he comes back, he'll get no for an answer, same as he did before."

"He might make trouble," said Laura.

Eliza turned to the kitchen with her arms full of wet clothes.

"What? With the police just over the way?" she said with a fine scorn in her voice.

Jim Mackenzie wakened in the late afternoon. He did not wake because he wanted to, but because of an insistent something which called on him to wake. He opened his eyes and looked into darkness. He sat up, threw back the bed-clothes, and was aware of most unfamiliar entanglements. Where in the world had he got to, and what in the world had he got on? Some voluminous, flowing garment enveloped him. There were frills on it, round the neck, and down the front, and round the wrists, all edged with some beastly prickly kind of lace. He felt about him and discovered a table, and upon it candle and matches. The light showed him a room with a sloping roof, and himself attired in a long white night-gown.

Where was he? For a moment he had to think; and then, like the rolling up of a curtain, the fog was gone from his brain and he remembered. Everything came back with such a rush that it fairly swept him off his feet. He flung out his arms and could have shouted aloud. Laura was free! Laura wasn't married to Stevens after all! Laura was free, and he had got her away! Laura was his again!

But where was he?

He looked round the room. There was a Bible on the table. He opened it to look at the fly-leaf, and saw in a solemn, laboured writing, "Eliza Huggins, from her godmother, Hannah Huggins." Well, he was in Eliza's house, and this dreadful female garment was Eliza's. Of his own clothes there was not a single vestige.

He opened the door and saw a tiny landing and a steep stair going down. From its foot came a glimmer of light and the sound of voices. Oh, hang it all, he couldn't go down and find Laura in this ghastly kit....

He drew back into the room. Behind the door hung Eliza's dressing-gown, a huge red flannel shapelessness. He flung it on and pushed the white frills out of sight. Eliza's comb reduced his hair to something like order. He was tingling with excitement as he blew out the candle and, picking up his skirts, made his way warily down the dark stair.

In the parlour Eliza was holding forth on the proper way to wash woollens.

"Combinations or blankets, Miss Laura, it's all one. Wash them in suds and rinse them in suds, and you'll never have no bother with them at all. Mr Hallingdon never had a blanket go to a laundry, not the whole time I was with him, and they kep' as good as new—and let me fill your cup up, Miss Laura, for it don't keep hot long this weather."

"It's lovely tea," said Laura. And with that the inner door opened and there came in Jim Mackenzie in flowing red flannel with a half embarrassed grin on his face.

"Don't I get any tea?" he said.

Eliza heaved herself out of her chair.

"A fresh brew—and I hope you've slep'—and some bacon and eggs—and I've got your clothes a-drying in the kitchen, sir."

"I've borrowed your dressing-gown, I'm afraid."

"And welcome," said Eliza.

She went out and shut the door.

Laura looked into the fire. Why had Eliza gone away and left them? It was too hard, too bitterly hard, to remember that Vassili and her pledged word still stood between them. Her body was free, but her conscience and her will were bound—unless.... Was it possible that Alec Stevens had been speaking the truth when he said that she was not bound after all? The room seemed full of Jim, and she could not look at him, because if she looked, she might not be able to keep herself from running to him. She had such a longing to feel his arms round her again—such a terrible longing.

Jim came across the floor with a couple of strides and caught her up.

"Laura! My Laura!"

She could not help it; she clung to him.

"Laura—you do love me still—you *do!"*

She began to weep bitterly, helplessly.

"I can't bear it, Jim—I can't bear it!"

He was tilting up her wet face and kissing her.

"You haven't got to bear anything. Laura—*darling*—it's all right—you're not married to him—you never were—the swine! Alec let it out when they were talking Russian together before I came into the room. He was threatening him with it. That's what made Vassili go off like he did. You know he was in France with a girl. Well, she was his *wife*. He married her in Birmingham last July."

Laura looked up at him wildly.

"He said—Sasha said—I wasn't married to Vassili—but he said I couldn't prove it—he said he'd help me to prove it if I gave him the Sanquhar invention—and I couldn't—"

"We shall be able to prove it all right if Alec was speaking the truth—and he must have been, or Vassili wouldn't have thrown up the sponge like that. Laura—kiss me! You haven't kissed me properly yet."

Laura kissed him properly.

Chapter Thirty-Nine

ALEC STEVENS might have been dead, for all the signs of life he gave. They ran his car into an Exeter garage and sent a telegram announcing its whereabouts. Then Jim's own car had to be arranged for. He telephoned instructions to a different garage. Then sleep—hours of dead, blank sleep from which he awoke a new man.

They took a morning train to London, and found Miss Wimborough at the flat. When she had heard what they had to say she flung up her hands.

"Are you mad?" she said to Laura. "Or do you expect a succession of miracles? Providence has no sooner delivered you from one man than you propose to deliver yourself over, bound hand and foot, to another! If you won't help yourself, how do you expect heaven to help you?"

Jim had the audacity to laugh.

"She shall come to you the very first time I beat her," he said.

They interviewed Mr Rimington, who was duly shocked. Yes, he would have the Birmingham marriage verified immediately, and if the facts were as stated, the steps necessary to establish Miss Cameron's freedom could be taken without delay.

As they went out, Jim caught sight of Stark, assiduous over a typewriter. He wondered how much Stark knew. And then they were in a taxi on their way to transfer the papers relating to the Sanquhar invention from the safe rented by Bertram Hallingdon under the name of Bernard Jaffray to the vaults of the Bank of England. Eliza had produced from the middle of her Bible a letter introducing Miss Cameron, and, from the bottom of a flower-pot in which a fine geranium was wintering, the key of the safe.

They met with no difficulties of any kind. The letter and the key were an Open Sesame, but when the key had turned in the lock and the steel door swung open, a shiver passed over Laura. From the moment they had entered the offices of the company they had not been alone. But they were to all intents and purposes alone now. The official who accompanied them had remained by the door.

Laura put her hand on Jim's arm and said in a low voice,

"Jim—"

"What is it?"

"When we got out of the taxi, I thought I saw Sasha."

"You thought you saw Alec Stevens?"

"Yes."

"Where?"

"There was another car behind ours."

"You're sure you saw him?"

"No, I'm not sure—but I'm afraid."

Jim caught her hand.

"You needn't be afraid. I can get a police escort if necessary. Let's get on with it."

He thrust the key into the lock and turned it.

Laura drew back a little. The place was brightly lighted and rather hot, but she shivered. She had suffered so much because of the Sanquhar invention. And yet her suffering and her agony of loss were as an infinitesimal point to the agony and suffering that would be loosed if the Sanquhar invention were given to the world. It was as if they were opening the cage of some terrible wild beast. The beast might be chained, but who could say how long the chain would hold?

The steel door fell back with a clang, and there appeared a most innocent looking manila envelope, large and official. Jim picked it up, and at once she saw his face change.

"What is it?" she said, whispering.

"It's so light." He turned it over. "It's not sealed."

"Oh—"

Jim Mackenzie pushed back the flap of the envelope. A folded white paper showed, its edge doubled over to keep it in place. He drew it out with a puzzled frown. There were black smears on it, and amongst the smears Laura's name scrawled in pencil.

"What is it?" she said, trembling a little.

"Open it."

Her hands felt stiff as they unfolded the paper. She leaned against Jim's shoulder, and they both read Bertram Hallingdon's pencilled words: "After all, I couldn't risk it."

"What did he mean, Jim—what did he mean?"

Jim Mackenzie pressed on the edges of the envelope and tipped it up. A soft black mass fell out upon the shelf of the safe, and as Laura leaned forward her breath stirred the insubstantial ash so that the charred flakes rose a little and then settled again.

She said, "What is it?" again.

Jim pulled her hand through his arm and held it in a comforting grip.

"That's all that's left of the Sanquhar invention," he said.

Laura's heart sang and shouted for joy. All her terrors, and all those other terrors which had whispered to her of blood, and tears, and women crying for their dead—all these were just a little ash that she could blow away. A verse from the Bible went through her mind: "The wind bloweth over it and it is gone, and the place thereof shall know it no more." The red shadow was gone.

Suddenly Jim began to gather up the soft loose ashes and put them back into the envelope. He was laughing to himself. He shut the safe door with a bang, looked over her shoulder at the official's back, and gave her a schoolboy hug.

"Let's give Sasha a run for his money!" he said.

Laura had not been mistaken. Alec Stevens was making his last desperate throw. Since he couldn't get the key and the name from Eliza Huggins, his one chance was to shadow Jim and Laura. He guessed that they would not leave the papers where they were. His plan was bold and simple—Catherine at the wheel of a fast car, and then snatch and run. And the plan succeeded—amazingly, triumphantly it succeeded.

He was on the steps as they came out, and the car at the kerb with the engine running. He could trust Catherine's nerve through anything. And then, by a miracle of imprudence, there was Mackenzie with the envelope in his hand. Why, the game was given away. It was mere child's play. A shove, a snatch, and the thing was done. The car was already moving as he sprang in, and they were away.

Jim Mackenzie hailed a taxi and put Laura into it. He flung himself down beside her, still laughing.

"I want to see his face when he opens it! *Laura*—what's the matter? What is it, darling? The whole damned nightmare's over, and you've got to be happy. Do you hear? You've got to be happy."

"I am happy."

"Then why are there tears in your blessed eyes? You've no business to cry when I can't kiss you."

"I was thinking about Catherine."

"You're not to think of anyone but me," said Jim.

THE END

Printed in Great Britain
by Amazon